Acclaim for the authors of

BROKEN VOWS, MENDED HEARTS

LYN STONE

"Lyn Stone masterfully blends excitement,
humor and emotion."
—*Romantic Times BOOKclub*

"Stone has done herself proud with this story…a cast
of endearing characters and a fresh, innovative plot."
—*Publishers Weekly* on THE KNIGHT'S BRIDE

GAIL RANSTROM

"Gail Ranstrom certainly has both writing
talent and original ideas."
—*The Romance Reader*

"…a unique story…Ranstrom comes of age."
—*The Romance Reader* on SAVING SARAH

"Ranstrom draws us into this suspenseful tale right up
to the very end…"
—*Romantic Times BOOKclub* on THE MISSING HEIR

ANNE O'BRIEN

"O'Brien…does an excellent job of inserting historical
detail into the story without overwhelming readers…the
book feel[s] like a compact, complete world in itself."
—*All About Romance* on PURITAN BRIDE

"Delightful characters light up the pages of this
poignant, emotionally moving love story."
—*Romantic Times BOOKclub* on
THE OUTRAGEOUS DEBUTANTE

LYN STONE

a painter of historical events, decided to write about them. A canvas, however detailed, limits characters to only one moment in time. "If a picture's worth a thousand words, the other ninety thousand have to show up somewhere!"

An avid readers, she admits, "At thirteen, I fell in love with Brontë's Heathcliff and became Catherine. Next year I fell for Rhett and became Scarlett. Then I fell for the hero I'd known most of my life and finally became myself."

After living for four years in Europe, Lyn and her husband, Allen, settled into a log house in north Alabama that is crammed to the rafters with antiques, artifacts and the stuff of future tales.

GAIL RANSTROM

was born and raised in Missoula, Montana, and grew up spending the long winters lost in the pages of books that took her to exotic locales and interesting times. That love of the "inner voyage" eventually led to her writing.

She has three children, Natalie, Jay and Katie, who are her proudest accomplishments. Part of a truly bicoastal family, she resides in Southern California with her two terriers, Piper and Ally, and has family spread from Alaska to Florida.

ANNE O'BRIEN

was born and lived for most of her life in Yorkshire, England. Here she taught history, before deciding to fulfill a lifetime ambition to write romantic historical fiction. She won a number of short story competitions until published for the first time by Harlequin®.

As well as writing, she finds time to enjoy gardening, cooking and watercolor painting. She now lives with her husband in an eighteenth-century cottage in the depths of the Welsh Marches.

Broken Vows, Mended Hearts

Lyn Stone
Gail Ranstrom
Anne O'Brien

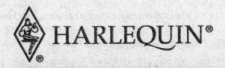

HARLEQUIN®

TORONTO • NEW YORK • LONDON
AMSTERDAM • PARIS • SYDNEY • HAMBURG
STOCKHOLM • ATHENS • TOKYO • MILAN • MADRID
PRAGUE • WARSAW • BUDAPEST • AUCKLAND

ISBN 0-373-29403-4

BROKEN VOWS, MENDED HEARTS
Copyright © 2006 by Harlequin Books S.A.

The publisher acknowledges the copyright holders
of the individual works as follows:

A BOUQUET OF THISTLES
Copyright © 2006 by Lynda Stone

PAYING THE PIPER
Copyright © 2006 by Gail Ranstrom

BATTLE-TORN BRIDE
Copyright © 2006 by Anne O'Brien

Printed in U.S.A.

CONTENTS

A BOUQUET OF THISTLES

Lyn Stone

Dear Reader

The process by which two people become a couple has always fascinated me. Marriage, even in the best of circumstances, takes a huge amount of work, hope and determination to succeed. In medieval times, those of the upper classes rarely had much choice in the matter. How would you cope if someone else chose a mate for you? A virtual stranger? Remember that this was a business deal—divorce was not an option and love rarely a consideration. It was truly death till you parted. Would you rail against fate, or do your utmost to create a loving relationship?

In A BOUQUET OF THISTLES I give you a couple who were amiably betrothed at a very young age, but then were changed by war and circumstance into two very different and headstrong individuals. When Alys and John finally meet as adults, can they "make" love out of a young girl's fantasies and a fledgling knight's indifference? I truly hope you enjoy their efforts and mine.

Happy Reading!

Lyn Stone

In memory of my good friend, Donna Mixon.

Chapter One

Hetherston Castle, Northumberland, 1366

"He does not want you, Alys. No one expects you to honor—"

Alys of Camoy shoved past her cousin. "He is here now. I shall have a husband." Twice she had been denied that by death and circumstance. Even had she possessed a choice when betrothed, she could not have fared better this time. And her knight was home. "There will be a wedding."

"So say you. But if he did not come to claim you before…"

"Hush, Thomasine, and let go my arm. I must hurry if I am to greet him in the courtyard."

"Let him wait!" her cousin admonished. "He has kept *you* waiting long enough!"

Her kinswoman, newly arrived from London, grasped at Alys's sleeve again to slow her progress. "Do not fly to him this way. You should cry off it, Alys. The entire court makes sport of you for clinging to a ten-year contract with that half-Scottish lout!"

"One whom the king holds in high regard!" Alys snapped. Her betrothed had been taken prisoner by the Spanish usurper Trastamere while saving the king's son, Lancaster, from capture. That selfless act should endear John to the entire royal family.

Though delighted to have word by Thomasine that John was still alive and had recently arrived from Spain, Alys wished her cousin had remained at court. Thomasine reported that John cursed anyone who dared come near him there, even the king's own physicians. Untrue, of course, for that was not the genial knight she knew and loved.

She had no time to argue further. "Cease your prating and wait here," Alys ordered. Though she used a commanding voice sparingly, she could exhibit authority when need be.

Thomasine scoffed. "Go then! Act the eager pup and wriggle at his feet! I warn you, any man will take advantage if you—"

Alys did not hear the rest and did not wish to. Thomasine did not know John. She had not grown up as Alys had, feasting on the stories of his youth fed to her by his mother or glorying in the tales of his courage told by his father. No, and Thomasine had not been there at the betrothal ceremony. She did not know him.

The gates opened wide just as Alys reached the bottom step of the great stone keep. She took pride in the way she had managed since the baron's death. John would not be disappointed in her care of his estate.

Their larders were better stocked than most after a harsh winter. A generous welcome feast tonight should present no problem and there was plenty in store for the wedding celebration. Fish hatched in the holding ponds. The swine were increasing, as were the cattle. Planting had begun.

The moat had been cleaned only weeks ago and had refilled

with the spring rains. She had insisted the grounds be raked and leveled regularly and had timely repairs on the buildings made. "He can find no fault with me in that respect," she assured herself as she brushed at the wrinkles in her skirts.

Only then did Alys stop and think of how *she* might appear to her future husband. Last he had seen her, she was only eleven years old, dressed in a swathe of rich blue brocade and wearing a ringlet of spring flowers over her long blond hair. What would he think of her now?

This day she wore a plain gown of pale camlet with an untrimmed surcoat of green linen. Her hair had darkened to near brown save for streaks the sun kept light. Caught up in a day cap that refused to hold it all neatly, her errant locks did nothing to enhance her appearance.

She hastily tried to tuck the stubborn curls out of sight and tied the ribands of her cap under her chin. "La, he'll think I've become a maid of all work," she muttered, straightening her shoulders and marching on out to meet him. Too late now to mind her looks. Gallant as he was, John would surely understand.

The spiky portcullis inched its way up, creaking with each tug of the ropes. Should she have opened it sooner to signal immediate welcome? Or would he have seen that as a foolhardy measure, inviting a possible attack? Hetherston was very near the border and outlaws roamed. None had dared since she had lived here, but she thought it best not to offer them the temptation of an open door.

Alys bit her lips and moistened them, then arranged a smile upon her face. The jingle of harness and creak of leather ensued as the riders filed into the courtyard. The small party consisted of only about a dozen men.

Which one was he? Her gaze flew hither and yon, from man to man. Would she know him still? Had he changed?

How handsome he had been that day when they plighted their troth before his beaming parents and their many guests. Newly knighted, he had worn Lancaster's colors for the first time, red and black.

She remembered how he had towered over her at least a foot, resplendent with the shiny sword and golden spurs he wore. But more distinctly, she recalled the merry smile that bared his perfect white teeth. She remembered the deep blue eyes inviting her to share happiness. His dark lustrous hair had waved just so, teasing the top edge of his silver gorget. Other details of his features had faded over the years in her mind. Would she know him?

One of the men quickly dismounted and approached her. This could not be John. The fellow was nearly as short as she was. And as rotund as Father Stephen. On closer inspection of his raiment, she determined he was no knight.

"Greetings. You are well come to Hetherston," she said. The castle folk were gathering, forming a wide arc around the riders, likely as curious as she to see the returning son of the house.

"My name is Simon Ferrell, I am Sir…I mean Lord John's squire."

John had inherited his father's barony upon the old lord's death a half year past, so he was no longer merely a sir. He was lord here now. Lord Greycourt of Hetherston.

She had resumed her scrutiny of those still mounted when Ferrell cleared his throat to regain her attention. "Have you a bed prepared?"

Alys grasped the man's forearm. "Is he very ill then? She cast about for a litter but saw none. "Where is he?"

"Here," a voice growled from atop a horse nearby. He had been leaning forward in the saddle so she had not yet seen him. Now he walked his mount closer. "Where is my cup, woman?"

Alys's gaze flew to him, relishing the sound of his voice, not caring that its tone bore pique. Speechless, she took in the pallor of his skin, the dark shadows beneath his eyes and the tightness of his lips. Was he in pain?

Oh lord, she had not even thought of the stirrup cup. What sort of wife would she make if she couldn't do this least of services to a returning husband. "I shall fetch it!" she declared, turning to do just that.

"Hold!" he ordered, slipping from his saddle with some effort. "Leave it be. I would as soon take the wine in the hall." Ferrell rushed to support him.

"As you will. Here, allow me," Alys said, hurrying to lend him her shoulder on the opposite side from his squire.

He pulled back and shot her a forbidding look. What was wrong with him that he would not accept her help?

Unfortunately, little Walter chose this moment to make himself known. The towheaded imp dashed up and danced around them like a jongleur, tugging once at the hem of John's tunic. "I'm Walt!" he announced. "You must be Johnny!"

"Walter, go inside now," Alys ordered, kindly but firmly, pointing to the keep. "You may speak with him later when he has rested. Mind me well or no pudding at supper!"

The boy cartwheeled twice, showing off his newest trick, then raced away laughing. Alys shook her head, hands on her hips, as she fell in step beside the men. "Do forgive him, my lord. He's only excited to see you, as we all are. It is so good to have you home."

"Who is he?" The question sounded gruff, disapproving even, as his frowning gaze followed the child.

"Why, Walter, of course. Did you not receive your mother's letter giving you news of him?"

"Nay. Stand aside, girl, lest you trip me," he muttered,

sounding distracted, as if putting one foot before the other now commanded the major part of his concentration.

Once inside the keep, he had to deal with the steps leading up to the hall, so Alys remained silent, pretending not to notice his difficulty. Though he did not limp or gasp for breath, he did appear gravely weakened.

She rushed to the table not yet cleared from the noon meal, poured him wine and returned. He gulped it quickly as if his thirst had overcome him.

Alys watched the working of his throat with fascination, then stared at his moistened lips when he had finished. He licked them and glared at her as he handed back the cup.

When their fingers touched, it was as if he really noticed her for the first time. The sharp blue gaze raked her head to toe, then returned to her face. His expression turned quizzical, but he said nothing, not even to thank her.

Alys forgave that. He was obviously ill and travel weary. "Perhaps you would like a bath now and a meal in your chamber?" she asked, keeping her voice bright. "I will have the hot water fetched and be up to attend you when the tub is filled."

"My squire will see to the bath."

"But I...very well." She forced a smile. He was surely being considerate and only thought to spare her sensibilities, Alys decided. She was, after all, still a maiden. How could he know she had assumed the duties of his mother long ago and saw to the bathing of all guests of any import? "If you require anything else, you have but to ask."

"I am no guest here, woman. Who *are* you and where is the child, Alys? Is she here?"

He cast a narrow-eyed glance toward the hearth. Thomasine sat there with her embroidery, obviously pouting, definitely observing them from the corner of her eye. Did John think she was the one? The blond and comely cousin suddenly assumed the role of rival.

"I am Alys, John."

His head swerved with a jerk and his eyes flared. "Alys?" The word emerged in a whisper. "You?"

She grinned, amused by his surprise. "Aye. I thought you knew me. But how should you since I am much changed from the child you would remember?"

She spread her arms and looked down at herself and laughed. "And dressed no better than a goose girl, how could you guess who I am? Apologies for that and a belated greeting," she said sincerely. "I am so relieved that you survived your captivity and overjoyed that you have arrived. You can see that we did not expect you so soon."

Then she realized how bittersweet this homecoming must be for him. She had had time aplenty to come to terms with his parents' sad absence. It would take time for him to adjust to it as well. Small wonder he was out of sorts, when she had not yet offered condolences. "John, I do so regret—"

His dark eyebrows met. He grabbed on to his squire's shoulder and turned to the stairs. "We will speak later," he muttered, ostensibly to her. Then, his voice even weaker, he addressed his squire. "Get me to my chamber, Simon."

"Rest well!" Alys called after him. "The water and victuals will be up in a trice."

She watched for a few seconds as he leaned even more heavily on his man. How badly was John hurt? The war or captivity had wounded more than his body, she would guess.

This was not the young knight she had stood beside ten years before. John was a man in need now, in need of sympathy and a woman's care. *Her* care, if he would ever allow it.

She twisted the silver ring he had placed on her finger at

that time and felt the tightness of it pinch more than usual. She had outgrown it over the years, moved it to her smallest digit and even there it no longer fit. Was that perhaps an omen?

"Nonsense," she muttered under her breath. "He is simply not himself after the grueling ride in his condition. Who could expect civility?"

"There are things to be done," Alys reminded herself sternly. Food to be got and hot water to pour. With a shrug, she moved to order them from the kitchens.

Never mind that he was obviously disappointed in the way she had turned out. He had not seen her to best advantage and that was her own fault.

All she had to do was to make him glad to be home and help him regain his strength. When rested he would recover his good nature, she was certain of it. John was ever kind and considerate, a perfect knight. His current mood troubled her, but she knew it to be temporary. Meanwhile, he would have naught but smiles from her, no matter how dour his words or acts. Her future depended on it.

Her happiness hung upon it, as well. Every waking moment for ten long years, she had thought of nothing but this wonderful man and their making a life together.

John realized he had rarely given the girl a thought.

Alys of Camoy might as well have been one of the lovely tapestries his mother made to lend beauty to Hetherston's hall. Or a silver goblet his father purchased to set out on special occasions. She had only been part and parcel of the estate in the mind of a young knight anticipating lifelong adventure in service to the king's son, Lancaster. However, now the parcel had a voice. And she also possessed a presence he could not ignore. What *was* he to do with her?

"You gave the lady grave insult with every word," Simon Ferrell muttered. "Especially the ones you did not say."

"She will learn quickly enough that I have no plan to marry her. As soon as I am able, fitted for new armor and in possession of a decent mount, it is back to France to join Prince Edward's campaign against Trastamere."

"What care you which Spaniard rules Spain?"

"It is enough the king cares, that the duke has a vested interest," John reminded him. "Not to mention my own need for revenge."

Simon blew out a breath between his teeth. "Suppose you do not survive? Why not wed and sire an heir while you are here?" Simon suggested.

John sighed. "What do I know of being a lord? I fight. That is what I do and all I know. What use is a wife? Or an heir, for that matter." He winced as he stretched his arms wide to loosen his muscles. "After ignoring Alys of Camoy all these years, should I now wed her, put a babe in her belly and leave her to fend for herself? Fair treatment *that* would be, eh? Let her have her freedom and the title end with me, it's no matter."

"It might matter to the people here. Especially her."

"Nonsense. This is her third betrothal. The king will find her another man."

Simon drew off John's dusty surcoat, then tackled the heavy mail John had borrowed for the journey. With practiced effort, he removed it and laid it aside to be cleaned. "She is a beautiful woman. I have yet to see you ignore one of those."

"This one, I will." John sank onto the edge of the bed and buried his face in one hand. "I am so devilish weary, Simon. And my stomach is afire. Go and tell her—"

Ferrell unbuckled the padded gambeson. "Tell her yourself. I hate to see a woman mistreated just because your belly burns."

"Mistreated?" John asked with a huff, shoving Simon aside. He shrugged out of the garment himself and threw it down. "You do not know the meaning of that word."

Simon issued a grunt and rolled his eyes. "And you *do*, of course, languishing at the mercy of the Spanish, lo, this long, *long* year past. Are we lapsing into misery again?"

"Again?" John asked with a bitter half laugh. "Have I left it yet? My parents are dead. My strength is but that of a newborn calf. And I have wasted a decade of that poor girl's youth. Give me one good reason I should not feel miserable."

"I will give you reasons." Simon tugged off one of John's boots and dropped it to the floor. "You escaped those heathens. You are alive with no lasting damage to your person. And you have a winsome lass eager to become your bride." Simon paused but an instant, then added, "I'll give another for good measure. Self-pity does not become you."

"'Tis not self-pity, Simon, only grief and regret." And guilt and anger, John did not add.

"Those wear the same face then," Simon said.

John collapsed back upon the mattress, covering his eyes with his forearm. He could trust the ever-blunt Simon in all things, especially to spit out the ugly truth when necessary. "You are right, of course. I did behave badly. I will sleep for a few hours and then be charming."

Simon grunted again. "That would be worth a year's pay to see."

A year's pay was roughly what was owed the man in any case. That, and possibly John's very life. Simon, a farrier's son chosen six years ago from Lancaster's ranks to become his squire, had made his way alone to Spain after John's capture. Loyal to the core and practical as the day was long, Simon had done all in his power to aid John while supporting himself as a smithy and living near the castle where John had been held. Without him, there could have been no escape. "I applied to the king, Simon. I plan to knight you as soon as—"

"Meanwhile, let's get you settled."

John stuck out his other boot and waited for Simon to finish his chore. Then he muttered, "Leave me now. Let me rest."

"As you will, my lord."

My lord. John could not get used to the title any more than he could accept the fact that his father was gone, buried in the crypt within the chapel. And his mother, dead just over a year, lying there beside her beloved.

He should have come home long ago, at least for a short visit. How he wished he had, even if it had involved going against the duke's wishes. Even if it had meant wedding that infant they had chosen for him. Now he had a choice in that, having left it so long undone, but at what cost?

The news of his mother's death had come on the eve of the worst battle of John's life. Surrounded by the stench of death and the cries of the wounded, he had received the last missive he was to get before his capture the month following.

The brief letter had been penned for and signed by little Lady Alys. No fault of the messenger, but he resented her still.

How did this orphan whose very existence was owed to his father's mercy and the king's favor, think it *her* place to write of such a weighty matter?

He had not heard of his father's more recent death until he reached London. That grief was still raw as an open wound. How he wished he had returned to England during the decade past.

Had he not been so keenly intent on keeping, and even surpassing the Greycourt tradition of valor, he might have avoided the capture that now blighted his service. The Spanish had confiscated his costly destrier, armor and weapons and starved away his strength. Thankfully, they had not believed him capable of escape there at the end.

Little Lady Alys had waited all this time. Why, when it would have behooved her to set aside their betrothal and wed elsewhere? He always assumed she would. He had, in truth, counted on it. The betrothal had been but a formality, the price for his parents' entertaining the duke and his huge retinue at John's knighting.

Now that he bothered to look back, he vaguely recalled how Alys had looked then, a rosy, smiling tow-haired cherub who fairly danced in place throughout their short ceremony. Everything had amused him that day, even her. He hoped he had been kind to her, but could not remember exchanging a single sentence with the child after scratching his name on the contract.

Though she had grown taller and older—much, much older at one and twenty—she had not lost her youthful exuberance and eagerness to please. While it might have been endearing in the child, it troubled him now.

She *was* a beautiful woman despite her obvious lack of vanity. But where were her sense of caution, her dignity and righteous anger? What female with any good sense smiled so heartily at insults? Was she simpleminded?

Perhaps a lack of wit excused the fact that she had not ransomed him when the need arose. He hoped there was no other reason she had left him to his fate. Though he could hardly blame her if she believed she had cause not to save him. John had abandoned her first. The thought ate at him.

He owed her freedom. If he misliked being betrothed to gain wealth and property, how must she feel? What woman of sound wit truly accepted what amounted to being sold? Now there was an even better reason not to marry her. But would she be free to choose her life if they set aside their contract? Could he arrange something to give her some voice in her future?

Sleep tugged at him insistently and he embraced it like a welcome mistress. It provided his only escape from the devils that plagued him. And from thoughts of Alys, who stoked his guilt with her eager and blameless acceptance.

Chapter Two

"No one dared approach him, did you see?" Thomasine said.

Alys inspected the table set for supper, wishing all the while that her cousin would leave her alone and stop trotting out the obvious.

She lifted a wine cup, checked the rim for damage, then replaced it. "You put too much stock in rumor and have apparently spread it far and wide since coming here. You are the one who made everyone hesitate to greet John as they should."

"I did no such thing!" Thomasine declared, pressing a long-fingered hand to her chest. "Well, perhaps I did repeat a few tales I heard. But they were from very reliable witnesses and true." She took a deep breath and let it go in a sigh. "They say he refused an audience with the duke. Can you believe it? 'Tis said the king humored him, but only to avoid a scene. Everyone knows Greycourt is a savage. The Scots blood, no doubt."

"You should return to court," Alys suggested. "Whatever will they do there without you to stir the gossip pots?"

"I had to come and warn you he was arriving soon." Her cousin scoffed. "You will rue the day if you marry that man."

Alys turned on her, barely controlling the anger that welled up inside. "Then what would you suggest I do, cousin, ask the king for yet another? How do you think that would set with him when he has already given me three?"

"So, do not trouble the king. Cry off first, and then elope! There is Sir Ronci. He asked after you constantly."

After her *wealth,* more likely. Ronci would be Thomasine's own choice if she had a dowery. They were already lovers.

"Come with me to London. An elopement would be forgiven, all things considered," Thomasine assured her.

What was her cousin thinking? Ronci had nothing to offer either of them. Then it came clear without much deduction and Alys suddenly realized what was afoot. If Ronci were granted Alys's hand and lands—highly unlikely without an elopement for which she surely would be fined—Thomasine's future would be assured. Even as husband to Alys, Ronci conveniently could keep Thomasine as mistress and support her. Thomasine would be willing to share that man for the security the arrangement would offer her. Now her cousin's strong objection to Alys's marriage to John made sense.

For the first time in memory, Alys had needed to stand back and examine someone's reasons for a nefarious plan. What a protected life she had led at Hetherston.

She could only scoff and shake her head. Thomasine must be quite desperate. "So you say I should abandon my vows and the promises I made to Lady Greycourt on her deathbed?"

Thomasine shrugged. "She is dead and gone. Who would know? Who would care? She was nothing but a stolen Scottish bride who was never accepted by anyone who matters."

"I would know and she certainly mattered to me." Alys pitied her cousin's lack of honor. How could she make her understand? "When I was six and the plague took my father and my first betrothed, I was sent directly to Earl Hernsby's household to await my coming of age to marry him. After he declined, I spent five years wondering who would have care of me next. Certainly not *your* kin! That was made clear at the outset. Then the king saw fit to bestow me and my holdings upon the Greycourts. This is my home now. Lord and Lady Greycourt were the saving of me, and John will come to love me, too, you will see."

Thomasine raised a perfectly arched brow. "*Love* you? What a foolish dreamer you are, Alys. Can you not see how he has avoided marriage to you all these years? Why do you think he never came home to claim you?"

Trust Thomasine to raise the question that troubled Alys most.

She turned away from her cousin and remained silent for a long while, thinking, intensifying her inspection of the table.

"Forget anyone else. We must marry," she said firmly, more to herself than to Thomasine. She carefully straightened a finger bowl, wishing she dared fling it against the wall. "No matter what has gone before or what might come next, the contract is made and the marriage required. There is no setting that aside."

"Since you truly wish out of it, something can be arranged," a deep voice declared.

Alys whirled around at the words. Thomasine had gone and in her place stood John, looking much more fit than he had earlier. In fact, he fair stole her breath away, he looked so fine.

The bruises beneath his eyes were still there, but his gaze seemed clear and full of purpose. Someone, likely his squire, had trimmed his hair and shaved him. He smelled of sandalwood and cedar. She inhaled deeply, loving his scent, adoring *him*.

This evening he wore his father's colors of green and gold rather than Lancaster's red and black. The clean, rich hues suited him well. His wide shoulders no longer slumped with fatigue or weakness and, apparently, he had arrived in the hall under his own strength. Squire Ferrell was nowhere to be seen.

She pressed the bodice of her best blue silk kirtle with one hand to calm her racing heart and stretched her lips into a welcoming smile. "You are down early for supper, my lord."

"Yet here in good time to hear your lament," he replied with a wry twist to his lips. "I will release you, Alys. It will be for the best."

She met his hard gaze with one of abject sympathy. "Oh no, my lord, do not even think it."

"Suppose I insist," he said, his eyes straying idly to the table. He reached over and shifted the position of a goblet. "I do not want a wife who is reluctant."

"You shall not have one. I am more than willing. So were you when we stood here in this hall and pledged our faith," she reminded him.

He sighed loud and long, refusing to meet her gaze. "My ears still rang from the buffet declaring me a knight. I felt drunk with success and the prospect of going to war, and would have agreed to anything my father put forth to me that morn." He finally met her eyes. "Even a weanling too little to wed."

"I see," Alys said, concealing her heartbreak with a merry shrug. "And so you smiled upon a girl who would increase his wealth and provide him with companionship in your planned absence. I thank you for pleasing him then. You were a good son."

John stared at her. "Are you ever this damned forgiving? What does it take to raise your hackles, I wonder?"

She held her smile in place, making sure that it reached her eyes. "More than you have dealt thus far. Never worry, John. I understand and I love you still."

"Love?" he repeated with a laugh, shaking his head. "God spare me, you are such a child!"

Alys bit her bottom lip and refused to be drawn into an argument with him. His bitterness had a cause, but it would disperse when he felt better. He was not like this when he felt well and she knew it.

After a few moments' silence, he drew in a deep breath and turned the subject. "Come and sit with me awhile. We must talk."

"Aye, and plan our wedding," she added.

"Nay, not that." He cleared his throat, obviously uncomfortable. "I would speak of my parents. My mother…was her death a quick one?"

Alys could not lie, even to save him pain. He would find solace in an untruth, but the lady had suffered too much for anyone to deny it. "No, John. She lingered nearly a year, abed and ailing. We kept her as comfortable as we could."

He nodded as he guided her to the cushioned settle beside the hearth. They sat together, his knee brushing her skirts. "For that I must thank you," he said, staring into the fire.

She could see moisture gathered in his eyes and his voice dropped to a whisper when next he spoke. "And what of my father?"

She reached out and clutched his forearm, intending to comfort him, taking strength herself from the solid muscles beneath his sleeve. "His lordship seemed hale until he was taken from us one night in his sleep. His last words that evening at supper were of you, John, and how he prayed you were alive and safe. We had only just heard of your capture," she informed him. "I suspect that did affect his heart."

Alys devoured him with her eyes, loving the fine texture

of his skin, the way his hair brushed his brow and curled at his neck. One graceful, long-fingered hand moved restlessly over the arm of the settle as if reclaiming the feel of the home he had missed. His other pressed flat upon his thigh, probably fighting an ache there. What had happened to him? Should she ask or wait until he told her of his own accord?

He turned to her then, his gaze penetrating. "What of *your* heart, Alys? Why, with all that love you spoke of so recently, did *you* not think to ransom me?"

Shocked into silence, she simply stared at him, aghast. How could he question her loyalty? He must know very well who had paid for his release. She could not help the delay in doing so.

"Ransom was all I *did* think of from the moment I learned you were captured," she told him, quivering with sudden anger as she stood. She dared not meet his eyes lest he see the ire he had raised in hers.

"Ah," he said, nodding. "But the thinking overtaxed you, did it?"

Shocked, Alys could not think of a reply that would not involve a slap. "Excuse me," she said, just managing to keep the brightness in her voice and her countenance bland. "I must go." While gritting her teeth till they ached, she flashed what she hoped appeared as a smile.

She fled quickly, uncertain she could contain herself any longer, though she knew she must make allowances for him.

On first account, John was grieving and certainly was not himself after languishing at the hands of the Spanish. Also, even if he truly wanted out of their match for reasons she did not yet fathom, she could not afford to let him go. Hether-ston was her home, his young brother, her responsibility, and her solemn promise to their mother remained unfulfilled.

* * *

John's anger vanished as quickly as Alys did. What brain maggot had urged him to say those things to her? He could not fault Alys for what others should have done. She said she had *thought* of ransom. Perhaps she had not known how to go about offering it.

He leaned back against the rich fabric of the settle and resumed tracing the floral pattern with his finger. He recalled doing that when he was very young, while his mother sang of their history or his father spun tales of long-ago battles. For a moment, he was back there, a boy listening with rapt attention, wondering where he would fit in to the family saga.

Alys was the one who had remained here, tended his mother and consoled his father. He could see the sadness in her countenance as she spoke of them. Lashing out at her served no purpose at all.

How lovely she was, grandly fulfilling the promise of beauty she had possessed as a child. He had not realized how truly beautiful she had grown until seeing her just now, arrayed in blue silks the color of her eyes, tawny hair flowing freely, nearly brushing her waist as she walked away.

Alys of Camoy was a maid to incite longing in a man. In *him*, which made him feel even guiltier than before. And, he had to admit, vastly relieved at the sensations she had awakened.

But how could she still be merry after all he had said? She seemed concerned about him, too. Perhaps too much so to be believed. He needed to believe it, though. He desperately wanted to know someone other than a squire who depended on him for employment had cared whether he lived or died.

John realized if he had returned to England and wed Alys before his capture, her concern now might seem less false, might even have restored at least some of his faith in people. Too late.

He would set this girl free to be happy. He knew he would never make her so. Physically, they might suit very well indeed. She would surely be willing. He was delighted to still be able. Her merest touch just now, the clean sweet essence of her and the innocent yet hungry way she looked at him stirred his loins as few women had ever done with so little effort. But she would always remind him of his long years of negligence and she would endure a future filled with that, as well. He did not need a wife to worry about as he rode into battle.

She had been left hanging on the vine too long, but she still had her beauty and innocence. She could make another match with no trouble, even at her age, given her inheritance. However, the thought of her marrying another bothered him more than he wanted to admit.

Before this betrothal, she had been given a boy of six and then a lord old enough to be her grandfather. As he understood it, one had died, the other had grown too infirm. Heiresses had no say, but were given simply to satisfy some debt or favor granted by the king. John's father had thought her a prize. John had not thought of her at all until her letter about his mother.

Anyone would suit her better than himself, but still he did not like to think of it. She was his, at least his responsibility, no matter that he had no intention to wed her.

How could he do that and withstand the constant reminder of guilt she invoked? And could he ever admit and then banish the spark of envy he felt that she had enjoyed many more years of his parents' company than he had done? Sent away to foster at the age of seven and allowed only short visits with them, John felt he had hardly known his mother and father, certainly never as well as Alys had.

You could get to know them through her, a small voice in his head assured him. *And you could make up for the misery*

*and disappointment you caused her if you will only accept
your new role in life and let go of your anger.*

But the miasma and need for revenge on his captors would
not let go of him. Besides, he was a knight, born for battle,
not a lord to hang about the castle, count crops and settle
disputes. His heart felt too heavy to lift at any thought, even
the thought of the lovely maid who was his by law and had
declared she loved him.

Ha! What could this child-woman possibly know of love?
And even at near thirty, a world-weary man, what did *he*
know of it?

However, John would not deny that the very sight of Alys
this evening stirred feelings within him that had lain dormant
for a year. Her own frank appraisal of him indicated she entertained a few of the same inclinations. Not surprising since
she had blossomed some years ago and not yet been plucked.

That meant he must quickly remove himself from Hetherston or marry her, one or the other. Lust was much easier to
comprehend than love and far more difficult to suppress.

Supper last eve had proved abysmal, Alys thought. John
had barely spoken during the entire meal and made her feel
the fool for trying to fill the silence with constant chatter. He
seemed mired in the past, imprisoned by it as surely as he had
been held captive by the Spanish.

The morning had dawned bright with unusual warmth for
the month of March. Alys had decided to let the issue of their
marriage lie for a while and give John time to grow used to
his home again, to England's beauty, to freedom and folk
about him who offered no ill intent. It must have been a
horrible year for him.

Alys kept her distance, yet she felt his gaze upon her as she crossed the great hall on her way to the gardens. This morning, he had taken a seat by the fire and passed the time nursing a cup of ale.

Walter's favorite hound, Troubadour, lay at John's feet while Walter himself hung back behind the settle unobserved. She had warned the boy not to bother John until he was well again.

Alys continued on her way to gather fresh herbs for the preparation of the day's meals. Usually she sent one of the kitchen maids to perform the task, but staying busy provided the best way to avoid further contact with John.

Given time, he would lose the choler that had accompanied him home. Let him approach her next time.

She turned at the doorway and cast him the brightest smile she could muster. It faded immediately when she quit the hall and started slowly down the stone steps. No cause to hurry now. She would soon run out of busywork if she kept up this pace.

"Alys?"

She whirled around, surprised that he had followed her. "Aye, John?"

He smiled without rancor for the first time since his arrival. "Spoken exactly as my mother used to do. Where do you go?"

"The gardens," she explained, feeling suddenly shy and fluttery. She held up the basket as if to verify her errand.

"May I go with you?"

"Of course, if you feel well enough." *Oh, please, please let his heart have softened. Let him be recovered and now the happy knight of her dreams.*

Together they made their way outside. He opened the gate to the garden and stood aside for her to enter. "This has not changed," he said with a sigh, apparently glad that it had not.

"Why change things that are as they should be?" she asked,

bending to pinch back a leggy bush of thyme. She placed some of the tender sprigs in the basket and stood again.

"Why, indeed," he agreed, his hands clasped behind his back and his head bowed in thought. "Constants are comforting."

"Yet most of your constants have gone awry," she said softly, looking up at him, feeling his pain as if it were her own. "John, do not grieve so for them. They would not wish it."

"I know. It is for myself I grieve. If I had but come sooner…"

"What is done cannot be undone. And it is well-known that Lancaster is jealous of everyone's attention. If anyone is to blame, it is he."

"You excuse me so easily as that?" he demanded.

"Does that matter? You will not excuse yourself." Alys focused on her task, crouching to gather leaves of rosemary and place them carefully in one corner.

"You are entirely too good," he said, sounding annoyed.

Aye, but she could be bad, Alys thought, and how dreadfully she wanted to be. If there was naught else to be considered, she would grab him by the shoulders, shake him soundly and order him to stop flailing himself like a penitent. The past was past. He needed to look to the future.

The luster of her perfect knight continued to dim more each time they had words. Why could he not be as he was before? He should not have this fault, this horrid wrinkle in his armor. And why, knowing that he did, should she so desperately want to hold him in her arms and assure him things were not as bad as he believed? After she shook him, of course. Alys smiled at her conundrum.

With a deep breath, she stood and calmly progressed down the narrow path betwixt the herb beds.

When she glanced back to see whether he followed, he was gone. He truly needed shaking, but she could not be the one to do it. If she angered him, it would only give him greater reason to set her aside.

She knew that look he wore, one of regret and imminent rejection. She had seen it upon the faces of the people who had declined to take her in after her father and her young intended had died within days of one another. Despite how it might have profited them, not one wanted the child of a plague victim in their household. One elderly earl had consented, though he had probably been past reasoning, even then, and died soon after.

None had accepted her but John's parents, who welcomed her like a daughter and sought to make that a fact with her future marriage to their son. Her profound gratitude had soon blossomed into love for them and included their progeny. John first, because he had been the stuff of any girl's hopes and dreams. Then she loved little Walter, whom she had taken full care of since his birth. As he learned his first words, he had called her mama, too, much to the amusement of his own dear mother.

Alys had promised the sweet lady she would fulfill that role for her. But if, in a fit of misguided grief and temper, John set aside the contract, Alys would have no say in Walter's upbringing. The boy would become orphaned as Alys herself had been at his age. The other promise she had made her foster mother would also go begging. If she were not wife to John, how could she see to his happiness and well-being?

So she *must* remain good, as he had said of her. At all cost, she must appear to be good.

John nearly stumbled over the lad sitting next to the wall on the darkened stairs. "Have a care where you huddle!" he snapped, righting himself with a hand braced on the wall.

"Where is she?" the boy asked.

"Alys?"

The little fellow nodded. "I saw her leave and you went after. Did she tell you?"

John placed a hand on the small shoulder. "Tell me what?"

"That I was giving you Troubadour. I decided before you came that you might like him for a gift. She said I did not have to, but I want you to like me."

"Troubadour? You're giving me a singer?"

A fit of giggles erupted, contagious enough to draw a smile from John.

The boy pointed up the stairs. "Nay, the hound in the hall. Though he did wail a good song at night when he was a pup, hence his name."

John took a seat beside the boy on the steps. "So you would part with this treasure so I will like you well, eh? What is your name, lad?"

"Walter, sir. We met in the bailey when you rode in. Can you not recall it?"

"Ah, the tumbler. How could I forget? You are a player in residence then?" John was unused to dealing with children. In fact, he could scarcely remember ever having had an actual conversation with one, even with Alys when she was young. Somehow, this lad put him in mind of Alys. Perhaps the smile.

"So, tell me, Walter…What is the lady Alys to you? Do you foster here?" John couldn't see how that would be since his father was dead and there was no lord to see to the boy's training. However, this was no peasant or tradesman's son, judging by his speech and rich clothing.

The large blue eyes widened. "Why she is mother to me, sir. There is no sweeter one alive than she." Then the small face grimaced. "Though she does swat my hind side when I misbehave and takes away my sweets when I forget my manners."

John hardly heard the last part. *"Mother?"*

The boy nodded. "But I must call her Alys as though she is my sister, she says, so I do." The boy jumped up. "Come and meet Troubadour now. He did warm your feet by the fire earlier, but you paid him no heed."

"I saw the hound." John muttered as he got up, his weariness of heart and body increased tenfold. He needed to speak with the factor immediately, if the man could be found, and discover how it was that his parents had harbored Alys and her bastard after she dishonored them. Perhaps she had been the victim of an assault and bearing the child was no fault of hers. That would easily explain why they would have kept her.

Alys had mentioned a letter his mother had written about the boy's birth, had she not? He had never received it.

Letters had been few, brief in nature and often read by many before arriving at their true destination if they ever made it that far. All save for royal correspondence had dwindled to near nothing with the duke's army shifting from France to Spain and then back again.

"How old are you, Walter?"

"Five years, sir."

John's mother had been dead over a year. In Alys's short missive informing him of that, she had made no mention of this child. His father's few letters contained nothing personal and had dealt only with the shape of politics, keeping John apprised of the king's current sympathies and the leanings of the other barons.

John felt obliged to learn the truth about Alys. If she had betrayed him, he need not look further for a reason to end their betrothal. However, if she had not gone willingly to another man's bed, what then? His parents obviously had not seen fit to turn her out. And he could have come home years ago and married her as he should have done. That might have protected her.

"Go along and tend the hound for me, Walter," John ordered. "See that he stays clean and free of fleas."

"Then will you take him? For your own?" the boy asked in a small voice.

John felt touched by the gift, no matter how it had come about. But he would soon be leaving. "I will claim him and thank you, Walter, but since he is well used to you, perhaps you could mind him for me?"

"I will! Forever!" the lad declared and scampered away.

John trudged slowly up the stairs. He did not want to find that Alys had played him false. He wanted to believe that she was as good as she first appeared, even if her excessive cheerfulness did rankle. The trouble was, her determined effort to please him had a possible motive now. It made sense.

"That was so kind of you, John," Alys said, coming up behind him just as he reached the hall. "I heard you charge Walter with the care of his dog." She laughed. "Or I should say, *your* dog."

John figured he would settle the matter of Walter here and now. "The boy says *you* are his mother."

For a long second, her gaze searched his. The smile faltered. He saw tears form in her eyes, though they did not fall.

"And you believe this?" she asked, her voice soft, "That I would have borne a child and kept it secret from you?"

"Why would the lad lie?" John challenged. "I would have the truth from you, Alys. Is he yours?"

"Mine, precisely as Troubadour the hound is yours, my lord," she said, her words measured and careful. "A living gift entrusted to my care. Nay, I did not give birth to him, but I helped bring him into this world and I nurture him well, never doubt it. In my heart, he *is* mine."

"I shall ask others if what you say is true," he warned.

"I know. Why not begin with Father Stephen?" With that curt suggestion, she pushed past him on the steps, her stride hurried as if she could not wait to get away. Finally, he had seen she could get angry.

If she was telling the truth, he could hardly fault her for it. He had accused her outright of what amounted to fornication and then, of lying about it. Tact and subtlety had deserted him sometime during the Spanish campaign. Perhaps he had *never* owned those qualities. The women he had known thus far had not required the social niceties of a knight.

If Alys were guilty, John knew she would be packed and ready to leave when he saw her next, if he saw her at all. He went back into the hall, wondering whom he should approach first with the dreaded questions.

Why did he feel so sick at heart?

Chapter Three

"Lord John?" A very feminine voice accosted John as he was pondering the problem of asking about Alys. "A moment, if you please!"

Approaching was the woman whom he had mistaken at first for his betrothed. Though they had not spoken past Alys's introduction at supper, John had noted the sly looks this one had cast him.

She held out her hand. A fine hand it was, too, unmarred by any blemish, the nails long and buffed to a sheen. Her face, too, looked perfect. Too perfect to be natural. A court beauty, he thought, enhanced by the delicate application of potions and dyes. If she only knew how contrived was her appearance when compared to the natural loveliness of her cousin.

"Lady Thomasine," he acknowledged.

"You seemed too spent last evening for conversation, so I kept a distance," she said. "Now I am eager that we should become acquainted."

John raised her hand, stopping just short of brushing the back of it with his lips. "Charmed," he said, though he was far from it. The overly lush scent of roses surrounded her.

That, together with her brittle smile, set him on edge. He recognized a glimmer of mischief in the cat's green eyes.

He decided, on the instant, that this was not the one with whom he should begin his inquiry about Walter's parentage.

She pressed her free hand to her bosom and simpered. "It is I who am beguiled, my lord. Alys never told me how handsome you are. But then, perhaps she never noticed."

"She was only eleven when we met," John explained. "No doubt her interest then lay more in her poppets and pets."

"No doubt," the woman agreed, holding on to his hand when he would have let hers go. "Silly Alys. Even at that tender age, I knew a prize when I saw one. You, my fine lord, most assuredly fit that mold." Her gaze raked his body.

Alys's cousin was flirting with him, and outrageously. John had no experience concerning interested women with whom he was forbidden to engage. How did a man turn them away while maintaining their goodwill? Escape seemed the only answer.

"Forgive me," he said, abruptly. "I am ill." He was, no lie. She sickened him, as would anyone seeking to betray family. Forget tact and subtlety and dash her goodwill.

Questioning must wait. For now, he sorely needed to retire to his chamber and sleep. Until his mind cleared, his blood thickened and his muscles regained their former strength, he would have to measure out his efforts to be sociable. His head ached, his stomach cramped and he felt like unholy hell.

"Oh, I do hope you recover quickly," Thomasine said with a pursing of her rose-salved lips. "I—and Alys, too, I am certain—will be distraught if you miss dining with us at noon."

John's chance of escape died aborning when Alys reappeared, her determined stride headed directly for him. "Begone, Thomasine," she commanded, her words the sharpest he had yet heard her utter. Her smile was gone. So her true nature was emerging, was it?

Only when her cousin had quit the hall did Alys speak again, her voice softer now. "Father Stephen comes this way, my lord. I have given him leave to repeat to you all my confessions these last ten years."

John saw no spark of anger now in her steady gaze. There was only a faint tinge of sorrow. "I have no wish, nor a right, to hear such things of him, Alys. If you assure me you have done no wrong, then I shall believe you."

Doubt narrowed her eyes. "Then perhaps you will ask him to recount the particular occasion of your brother's birth."

John's breath caught in his throat. *Brother?*

"Aye," she answered as if he had spoken the question. She gestured with an open palm. "Sit while you await him, John. You are too pale."

Small wonder there, John thought as he lowered himself into the chair. "I was not aware…" His voice trailed off when he looked up and realized she was already halfway across the hall.

The priest joined him and soon John had the entire tale of how his mother had borne Walter, enduring great travail and almost dying in the process.

He learned how Alys had rarely left her side the following years. Then his mother had succumbed, wresting a promise from Alys to rear the child in her stead until the boy was seven and old enough to foster elsewhere. His father had been overcome with grief when he lost his wife and never was the same again.

John realized that Alys had borne the burden of managing Hetherston's household as well as caring for his brother and his parents. He still could hardly digest the news that he was no longer an only child.

What a revelation! How liberating to know he already had an heir. The boy Walter would take up the title one day and there was no need for John to feel any guilt over the barony going to some stranger the king would appoint after John's death.

As soon as the priest left, Alys returned with a cup of wine. "Here. Drink this and then you should go and lie down."

Her continued concern surprised him. He took the goblet. "How will you ever forgive the things I said to you?"

Her smile looked a bit forced at first, then softened. "You must have good cause to live with such suspicion of everyone around you. You have no trust left, have you?"

"And how would you know anything of lost trust?" John asked, genuinely curious.

"I lost mine at an early age and still find it difficult to nurture until I have known someone for a long while," she answered openly.

"You do not know *me* and yet you seem ready to trust me with your person, your estates and your future." He sipped the wine and felt it flow through his veins like warmed honey. Like the relief that filled him on finding Alys constant, even if he did not intend to marry her.

"Aye, I *do* know you, John," she insisted. "Not a day has passed since you left that your name has not been spoken, that you were not remembered to me in one way or another. I know your hopes and dreams, your very heart, and even your child-hood pranks and punishments. A man does not change much from what he is on the day he embraces manhood. I was there for that, if you remember."

Oh, sweet Alys, how wrong can you be? "A man can be altered by events, both good and ill, at any time during his life. You knew a boy then, one who had suffered nothing worse than a trouncing in the lists. I was green as new grass."

She patted his shoulder and took the empty cup from his hand. "You only need rest, John. You will not convince me you are withered from cynicism. This megrim will pass."

"You plan to see to that, eh? Shall I call you Saint Alys?"

Her smile stretched into a grin and caused a little catch in his chest. "At least I am not the great sinner you feared." She backed away, her hands clasped around the emptied cup. "Now you must excuse me. The saint has her duties."

John closed his eyes and prayed for patience. She confounded the life out of him. How could she turn everything about the way she did? Should he feel absolved now of his wrong-doing? Instead, he felt even worse. He was going to have to crush her hopes and do it soon or he would not have the heart for it.

She had to be furious with him. If only she would lash out and give him her true feelings. Above all, he valued honesty.

Perhaps he was only spoiling for a fight. Aye, that would absolve him, would it not? All he would have to do then was to storm away in anger and feel justified in forgetting her again, he thought bitterly. What a coward he was.

He needed to be perfectly honest himself and tell her now that they would never marry. John asked her direction from one of the servants and followed her to the solar for that purpose.

He remembered the room well, having spent a large part of his first seven years in it. His mother had doted on him, or so he had thought at the time. It was here, when he turned seven, that she had told him he was to go and serve Lancaster.

She had put on a false smile and said what an honor it was for her son to be so chosen. Knowing full well this was the way of things, John had neither wept nor pleaded aloud not to be sent away, though in his heart he had cried rivers. Fine, he had thought when his inner tears ran dry, he would be a knight, the best one ever. He would make it his life's work and never bother with this place again.

He stood in the doorway and watched Alys laboring impatiently over a tangled skein of thread. Her hands were so small, her fingers nimble as she worked. His skin tingled as he imagined the pleasure those sweet soft hands might offer. Impatiently, he shook off the lascivious thought.

She sat before a tapestry loom, the very one his mother had used. He had to admit that Alys looked as much at home there.

"May I enter?" he asked, fully aware that the solar was a female domain, not to be broached without invitation, even by the lord of the keep.

"Of course," she replied, intent on the threads, a slight frown marring her perfect brow. "Though you should be resting."

John crossed the room and peered down at the loom. "A monumental task you have there," he remarked, thinking he must work up to the real reason for coming in here.

She sighed, giving up on the tangles and clutching the mass in her lap as she looked at the tapestry. "Your mother began this piece. I mean to finish it for her."

Her frustration, this new aspect of Alys, delighted him. "Are you not apt with a needle?"

"Obviously not," she admitted readily with a short laugh, "though not for lack of effort."

"Where do your talents lie then?" he asked, truly interested. For all her inexperience and youth, Alys did fascinate him and he wished they could part friends. Perhaps if he brought her to that pass, she would understand.

She shrugged. The gesture made her seem even smaller, younger. "I am good at keeping others at their tasks, I suppose. I ride well. And I am a fair hand with numbers and letters."

"You know how to write?" he asked, not really surprised,

though most women were not trained in it. His father probably taught her as he had John's mother.

"Aye, and I like to make pictures with ink." She tossed the silk tangle aside and it landed in a colorful heap on the floor. "So why can I not fill in my designs with threads?"

John looked again at the tapestry that depicted a garden scene with several figures. It was beautiful, the colors nearly half-completed. "You drew this for her?"

She nodded.

"Why not hire someone to finish it?" he suggested.

Her gaze locked on his. "She charged me. It is my duty. And it will be my pleasure," she stated with conviction, then grimaced. "If it kills me."

John threw back his head and laughed. How long had it been since he had felt like laughing?

"You make sport of me, but I am resolved!" she told him, laughing, too.

He believed her, but could not see why the wall hanging was so important. "Why do it if you would rather do else?"

She pondered that for a moment, then sighed as she answered, "Women seldom have any tales of valor sung about them in the halls. Many times our quiet triumphs are all we have to mark us in the minds of those who follow."

He traced the edge of the loom with his fingers, feeling the smooth weave at the edge. "So this, then, is your legacy?"

"I mean it as a tribute to your lady mother. The better part of the work is hers."

"You loved her," he guessed, feeling a familiar stab of loss. "And she, you." John stepped closer, unable to stay away.

"Aye, she did," Alys said softly. "Though not half as much as she loved you and Walter."

How sweet of her to offer those words of consolation,

however misguided. John knew the truth. "Somehow I doubt she cared as much as you think. If my parents were living, young Walter would have scarcely two years left to enjoy whatever love they had for him. Then he, too, would be sent out to foster as I was. Perhaps they would have brought in a bride for him to keep them company in their later years. Another little Alys."

"That is unkind of you, John," she admonished. "You know full well that fostering is the custom and nothing to do with how they loved you. If anything, it shows how much they did, to want to prepare you well and see you knighted."

"Well, custom be damned. No child should be torn from his home to learn the art of war in his seventh year. Walter should remain here as he grows to manhood."

She smiled, picking up the threads again. "The second son usually goes to the Church or the king's service."

"Not this time," he declared. Walter would be lord here one day if John had aught to say on it, and here he should stay, amongst familiar things and people.

"And you think I do not know you," she said softly. "I had not even troubled myself to prepare a plea that would keep him here, for I knew what you would say."

"You agree?" he asked, surprised, even shocked by her words.

"With my whole heart. We are in perfect accord." She fairly beamed up at him.

For a moment, while drowning in those adoring, tear-filled eyes of hers and basking in her smile, John could scarcely think straight. His body reacted quite suddenly to what seemed an invitation to kiss. He wanted to, desperately, but knew that desire for her would grow apace and affect his decision about releasing her from the betrothal. So, he looked away and prayed this summer lightning storm of lust would pass.

John did suspect that Alys had again said only what she knew he wanted to hear. He was glad of his decision not to wed her. Who would want a wife who bowed to his every wish and never had an opinion of her own, or if she did so, one she would never voice? Most men might treasure that above gold, but not this man.

Somehow, he could not bring himself to tell her that, however, not in her present mood. God, why must she be so…agreeable?

Was she like this with everyone? Was that why the folk here at Hetherston held her in such high regard? They adored her. He could see it already, stranger that he was to this place.

He decided to test her mettle. What could he say that a woman like Alys would be hard put to agree with? She seemed amenable to everything. Then he had an idea that might work. This room was now hers, the solar meant for the lady of the keep and no other. Surely she would not consent to give it up.

As if assessing the place for the first time, John looked around, taking in the glass-paned windows and padded seats beneath them. "I love this place. It would make a fine master chamber."

Alys followed his gaze around the walls before answering. Now she would protest, John thought.

But she turned back to him with hands clasped together over the messy threads. "You know, your bed would be perfect there, facing the light."

"Alys…"

She stood quickly. "Why did I not think of it before? I shall order your things moved this very afternoon!"

John shook his head, pinching the bridge of his nose to hide his frustration.

God's very teeth, what must he do with her? He knew what he *wanted* to do with her, but figured she would pretend to welcome that, as well. And it would surely seal his fate as a husband.

She was already out the door, gone happily to set him up in a room he did not even want.

Other than the occasional word of greeting, John purposely avoided Alys for the next two days. The truth was, he was unsure how to deal with her. Would he break her gentle heart if he baldly declared he did not want her? The problem was, he *did* want her, only not to wife. Unfortunately, that was the one honorable way to have her and he could not bring himself to agree to that.

It would take him a while to get back his strength. He had not even been measured for armor yet or sought out a breeder to furnish him with a proper destrier. Until he accomplished that, he decided he should keep peace with her.

In order to do that, he spent most of the time in his new chamber, the former solar, exercising his limbs or soaking in the bath and reading his father's few books.

He missed the tapestry loom, gone now from its usual place. Where did Alys work? He wondered. Was the light strong enough? Had she abandoned her needlework because it was not?

Admittedly, this room proved more convenient to his needs and to those serving them, something he would never have considered had he not used the notion of taking it over himself to discommode Alys.

Instead of a grudging relinquishment of her private domain, she had happily added rich, plush carpets to warm the floor and new, heavier bed hangings to block the sun when he wished to sleep in the day.

He had been taking his meals alone since he had discovered the very sight of mounds of food destroyed his appetite. However, now his stomach's capacity was finally increasing after his long bout of near starvation.

His mind seemed to grow sharper while his grief and lassitude lessened by the hour. He thought almost constantly of Alys, still uncertain what to do about her determined devotion.

As it had in the solar that day, his body would harden uncomfortably every time he recalled the swell of her bosom above the neckline of her simple gowns or the enticing sway of her hips as she walked about the garden or across the hall. He privately thanked her for that blessed reassurance. At first he had feared the Spanish had beaten and starved away his ability to function as a man.

On the occasions when he did visit the hall, he watched her continuously, still wondering at that unfailing cheerfulness. Rarely did she raise her voice or resort to commands to have what she needed doing done. Everyone seemed to love her. Except Thomasine.

That one had cornered him only once after that initial conversation. He managed to insult her enough so that she left him alone thereafter. She seemed bound to turn him against Alys for some reason.

Odd, how the protective urge to warn Alys against her cousin deviled him so. That woman had something planned that boded no good. He could not figure what it might be, but imagined that he saw betrayal in her eyes. Given his behavior toward Alys, perhaps he entertained too much suspicion and saw evil where none existed.

John mentioned it to Simon on the third evening as they readied for supper in the hall.

"Oh, she is a witch, that Thomasine, and a talebearer," Simon stated as he laid out John's new tunic, one of several

Alys had sent in. The construction and the embroidery were excellent and the velvet rare and costly. He wondered if she had made them herself in spite of her dislike of needlework.

If she had, they were doubly precious. If not, he still appreciated her thoughtfulness in having them done. Alys would make a good wife. But not for him. He needed no wife.

However, for all she had done at Hetherston, he should be giving her gifts. "Simon, can you arrange for someone to travel back to London? Have him seek out a good armorer and entice him here. Also, I must purchase a few tokens for Lady Alys."

"Make a list. And remember a morning gift for the wedding," Simon reminded him, slipping the tunic over John's head.

"There will be no wedding, Simon. I told you that," John said firmly, shifting the garment to set better on his shoulders. "It is because Lady Alys has minded my brother and kept the house in order as well as any woman could. I would thank her." And assuage his guilt over refusing her hand.

Simon huffed. "Fine time to consider gifts when you've naught in your purse. Lancaster is a full year in arears."

"A pinchpenny." John gave an inelegant snort.

Simon shook his head and made a dismissive gesture.

"I will see the factor and withdraw funds from the estate for the purchases and your wages," John said decisively.

"Have you not met with him for an accounting?" Simon asked.

John sighed. "I have not even thought of that. God only knows how jumbled matters have become since my father's death. I should see to it."

"Just so. Your poor betrothed will have been shouldering that burden in your stead all these months."

John shook his head. "Not likely. I expect the factor has simply carried on with his former orders after Father's death."

He smoothed down the front of the new tunic and reached for the belt Simon was holding for him. As he fastened it on, he came to a decision. "I should take charge while I'm here. My recuperation is near complete."

"Thanks be to God," Simon muttered. "Here is your chain of office. Turn about."

John did so, holding the silver links in place while Simon hooked the ends together in back. His father had worn this the last time they were together. How heavy a burden it seemed.

Each day his endurance increased and now only a short rest in the afternoon hours and retiring early sufficed to see him through the day. He was ready to begin brief bouts of serious training again if he could find a worthy swordsman hereabout.

As to that, where were his father's knights? God help him, he had never had a head for business matters, but to ask who was in service here should have occurred to him sooner.

He gave his chest a firm pat with both palms, then stretched out his arms to flex his muscles. "Let's to supper, Simon. I feel like a new man tonight."

"A good thing," Simon muttered, giving a final tug on the back hem of John's tunic. "The old one needed thrashing."

"Insolent cur," John accused with a chuckle.

"And you're making that *Sir Cur* soon, you say?"

John laughed, too, and realized he did feel renewed. Soon he would be in fighting form again, back into the fray, doing as he was meant to do. This time he was choosing for himself. Neither his father nor Lancaster had a say in how he was to spend his life.

Gone were the days when others decided his future for him. Alys would soon realize her freedom to choose, as well. He would see to that if he had to pay the king for her opportunity to do it. Surely any woman would prize that boon above all.

Chapter Four

Alys struggled for patience. John had all but accused her of lying. *Again*. He sat there spearing his roast mutton as if he had not struck her to the heart.

"I tell you, John, there *is* no factor. Albert Donegal left to live with his daughter after her marriage to a goldsmith in York. His health had failed so, he needed her care."

"Donegal? Jesu, he was already ancient when last I saw him!" He offered Alys the wine cup which she refused.

"He is seventy-five," Alys declared. "Your father and I had already assumed most of his duties, but he was still good at accounts. However, after your father died, Albert gave it up."

"Well, someone has to be minding the accounts. Who tends them now?" He glanced around the tables. "I would speak with him after supper."

"*Her,*" Alys corrected, sucking in a deep breath and praying for calm. "And you may speak to me now, though I would prefer to wait until I finish the meal. You will need to see the book."

"You?" His face was a study in disbelief. "How could you do it? Rather, how could you dare? It was not your place."

"There was no one else. Someone had to and I was familiar

with it, having assisted both Albert and your father. Besides, I had no authority to hire anyone to replace him."

"Damn me," John grumbled, attacking his portion of mutton as if it were not already slaughtered and cooked.

"Everything is in order," Alys assured him, trying to ignore the doubting glare he settled on her.

"Where are my knights?" he demanded rather loudly, pointing with his knife to the lower tables.

Alys almost·rolled her eyes, wishing to heaven this conversation could wait. "Sirs Bran Copely, Robin Nithing and Royston of Gale were dispatched to travel through France to Spain and arrange for your release."

He looked astonished. "What! When?"

"Six months ago when we first learned of your capture."

"Was there a ransom involved?"

"Of course!" she replied. "How else would they have freed you? You will see the funds withdrawn upon the books. That is why our coffers are so low at present, but that will change with the next harvest."

"A ransom was never paid, Alys," John stated.

"I *paid* it, John!" she said through gritted teeth, trying to remain calm. "Who do you *think* arranged for your release?"

He pounded a fist upon the table and his thunderous expression almost made her quail. John could look ferocious. He could probably *be* ferocious.

"The ransom was paid," she repeated, keeping her voice even. "You are home. Our coffers will refill. All will be well."

Conversation around the tables had ceased and everyone watched the head table. They were naturally concerned about their lord's sudden change in mood. He had arrived at the table all smiles and now looked fit to kill.

Alys continued to eat the course set before her and

motioned for the next when it was time. She drank from their shared cup even though he neglected to offer it.

For days now she had left John to himself to recover and grow used to being home again. She had quietly provided everything she thought he would need to do that. And still, he speared her to the core with these wild accusations and unfounded suspicion.

"What is the matter *now?*" she asked.

John glared at her, suddenly laid down his eating knife, shoved his trencher away from him and leaned back in his chair. He pressed his fingertips to his brow and shook his head. "This is…*impossible!*"

Alys gritted her teeth for only a second. Then she beckoned to one of the servants. "Remove his lordship's trencher and fetch him broth. Dispense with the last course and clear away the remains of this one. Make haste!"

Her voice sounded far sharper than she meant it to, but her patience had worn down to nothing and she was done with coddling his unreasonable fits of temper.

He grasped the hand that she had fisted on the table. "Alys!"

"The rest may seek more in the kitchens if they are not full," she replied, snatching her hand from his grip. "We would have you pleased, my lord, at *all* costs."

He looked abashed, as well he should.

She bit out her words. "Your digestion will improve with time. Until then, we shall serve lighter fare."

"The food is—"

"Do not bother to thank me, John. Your comfort is paramount, for you are *lord* here." She stretched her lips wide in a smile that threatened to split them open.

"Cease this foolery!" he commanded, shoving away from the table and rising to his feet.

All eyes were turned their way. His face had grown red and his breathing rapid. "You are a feckless child and have not sense enough to—" He stopped, shook his head sharply.

She jumped up and interrupted, "To marry a fine lord such as yourself?" she shouted. "You do not want me, that is clear as springwater, sir! So you have concocted this false excuse, that I did not pay for your freedom when I should have done? Well, Lord John, good sense or no, ransom or none, you *will* marry!"

She faced him down, grasping the gown at her hips to keep her hands from grabbing his throat. "You *will* marry as promised! And you *will* do so before this month is out. Else I shall sue you for breach of promise, demand return of all profits gained from my estates these past ten years and see…you…beggared!"

She leaned closer and poked his chest hard with her finger. "Digest *that,* if you will!"

John grabbed her hand and held it fast. "Then do your worst. I will not…be…forced," he shouted back as he flung her hand away from him.

John watched her flounce away. No swaying of the hips this time. She strode like a soldier. The battle lines were drawn. At least she had exposed her true nature for everyone to see.

Perhaps she had been untruthful in matters other than her temperament. Had she really paid the ransom? Trastamere certainly had not honored the exchange if she had. John had *arranged* his own release over the bodies of half a dozen guards who stood in his way.

At first thought, John had suspected that Alys was lying to cover some gross expenditure. But the knights were gone. And she could not hope to verify their mission if it was not a fact.

This would bear further investigation, but despite everything, John wanted to believe her.

"What a temper," he murmured as he reached for his cup and took a healthy draft of wine and sat down again.

"A shrew if ever there was one," Thomasine agreed, peeking around the priest who sat at John's left. "You would do better to let Sir Ronci have her."

John turned, frowning. "Ronci? What's this? Who is *he?*"

"No one, my lord!" the cleric declared, shooting the woman a killing look. "There is no other man. And Lady Alys is all that is kind." He offered John an apologetic shrug. "The duties here have drawn her kindness so thin it has simply broken. In a while, she will be back with a smile upon her lips. You may count on that."

"Aye yes, that infernal smile of hers," John said to himself. "False as a mummer's face. She just admitted she means to beggar me!"

"Only if you deny her her rights," the priest warned. "You did agree and sign the contract." He cleared his throat and added, "my lord."

Thomasine's mention of another possible candidate for Alys's hand bothered him. He had not heard of a Sir Ronci before, but he would not inquire further of Thomasine, that sly-eyed cat. John stood again, his eyes still on the stairs where Alys had disappeared. "Where would she go?"

"The stables, most likely," the priest told him with a sigh. "I have always believed she finds more solace there than in the chapel."

John started after her. On the stairs going down he realized he had company in tow and stopped. "Remain here, Walter," he ordered the boy.

"Nay." The short legs pumped to keep up with John's stride.

"I said *stay,*" John repeated firmly.

"You are not to hurt her even if she was bad. Deny her pudding if you must, but if you strike her, I shall kill you."

John stopped in his tracks and stared down at the boy. Tears tracked down the lad's chubby cheeks and dripped off his chin. "What did you say?"

"That I would kill you. Alys has no one to protect her and you are mad with rage. I have a knife."

John noted the small, dull blade clutched in Walter's left hand. He had to admire the lad's courage, even if his lips quivered and his nose ran. "Hold it the other way round, Walt. You should stab up, not down."

John crouched so he would not loom over his brother. "I would never hurt Alys, you must believe that. Knights do not harm women or children. It is in the code we swear to."

Walter's narrowed gaze studied him for several seconds. "But you won't marry her." He sobbed a time or two and wiped his eyes with his sleeves. "Please, you *must!*"

John sighed and stood again. "This is none of your affair, Walter. You do not understand—"

"I do so! Alys will go away if you don't! What will we do if she goes away?" He plopped down on the steps and began to weep in earnest, his small shoulders heaving. The sounds his little brother made tore at John's heart.

No child should suffer so, he thought, sitting down beside the boy and hauling him into his lap. "There, there, Walter. Be calm."

The boy shook his head and buried his face in John's doublet.

"Stop weeping. I will go and speak with her. We will come to some agreement that will keep her here. My word on it." He patted the small back and brushed his hand over the boy's head. "Brace up now. Let's have a smile." He tipped up Walter's chin and looked him in the eye.

Walter sniffed, cocked his head, pursed his lips and narrowed his eyes. "I will go with you," Walter announced.

John released a breath of defeat. "Come along, then." What was he to do now? What sort of man would he be if he allowed a woman to force him into marriage with threats? And what sort of brother would he be to deny Walter the comfort of a mother's care?

Alys obviously fulfilled that role very well or the boy would not be so distraught at the prospect of losing her. John had no inkling what he would say to her when he found her, but Walter had grasped his hand and was tugging him toward the stables at breakneck speed.

Alys soothed her own battered pride as she gentled the giant horse who had seemed restless in his stall. The poor beast needed a comforting as badly as she did. She leaned over the stall gate and stroked the mane that fell behind his ears and scratched him gently. He snuffled and leaned into her touch.

Would that she could cozen John as easily as his destrier. She had tried everything she knew and that man had exhausted her patience.

No perhaps about it, she had made a huge mistake tonight. If he did not want her before, he certainly would be set against a marriage now. God save her, she deserved what he must be thinking of her at this moment. What man would want a wife who took him to task before the entire company in his own castle?

Tears of regret slid down her face. She dashed them away, cursing herself for such weakness. She never wept except with grief. However, this was a grief of sorts. She had lost all hope of happiness, of the life she had dreamed of constantly. "How could I be so foolish?" she whispered.

The great horse nudged her shoulder with his nose as if to console her. If only she had an apple to reward his concern.

"I wish your master had a bit of your good nature," she crooned to the animal. "I suppose I shall have to dig rather deep to find any there. But I will, never fear. I am resolved. No use to cry." She wiped her face dry and lifted her chin.

Alys was the one who feared, though. She knew her chances of regaining John's good graces were poor at best and she had only herself to blame.

The sight that greeted John as he entered the stables almost stopped his heart. He grasped Walter's shoulder and whispered, "Halt."

Alys had stepped upon a stool and was stroking the nose of the warhorse, Trampler. His was a well-earned name. John never mounted the beast himself except in a serious tourney or to ride into battle. If the Spanish had captured this one instead of John's favorite, they would have sent the horse back.

Was the short wall of the stall sturdy enough to hold Trampler if he spooked?

John moved forward very carefully, keeping Walter behind him. When near enough, he whispered. "Alys, step down slowly and move away."

She turned, eyebrows raised, her fingers gently scratching just beneath Trampler's right ear. "I do not plan to ride him, only to make a friend."

John sucked in a deep breath and released it with a shudder. "He is a killer, Alys."

"Nonsense," she snapped and playfully ruffled the destrier's forelock. John held his breath as she brushed her hand all the way down Trampler's muzzle. Trampler snorted, sounding almost as if he laughed. The ears went back. *Oh, God.*

"Come away, Alys. Now!" John insisted, his chest tight with fear for her.

Much to his relief, she gave the horse a final pat and nimbly hopped down. She passed him by and took Walter's hand. "Come, little man, 'tis past time you were abed."

John followed them out, his stomach still fluttering. He cast a look back at Trampler who appeared calm as a cow chewing cud. A stable lad oiling harness grinned up from his task as John passed. "She has a way with animals, my lord."

Aye, but did she mind that she had frightened ten years off *his* life? John figured his hair was no doubt gray now. He'd had horrid visions of her stomped to death on the hay-strewn floor.

Angrily, he lengthened his stride to catch up with the foolish girl and give her the sharp side of his tongue.

"You promised," Walter reminded him when he reached them and fell in step.

He ignored the little imp. "Trampler could have killed you," he told Alys.

She huffed. "And all your woes would vanish."

"That is not true and you know it! I was worried you would be hurt or worse. Why are you so angry with *me?*" he demanded. He was the one with cause to be furious.

She stopped and turned. "Did you not mean to make me so? Is that not what you intended?" She shook her finger in his face. "Since the moment you rode in, you have done naught but tweak my patience, toss my concern back in my face and attempt to break our betrothal. You have succeeded, John. Consider it broken!"

Never in his life had a woman spoken to him the way Alys had done tonight. How did a man deal with it?

"He will marry you, Alys! He said he would!" Walter announced, sliding a short arm about her waist. Then he looked up at John, his expression full of warning. "Will you not?"

John chewed his bottom lip, watched Alys fume and wondered what he could say.

If he agreed to, she would know it was only because she had threatened to sue. And she *would* sue. He had seen in her eyes that her threat was no bluff.

Strangely enough, to give in did not seem so great a concession at the moment with her tear-bright eyes shining and her color up so high he could see it in the moonlight. What a warrior she was when in a fury! How that would translate into passion. He could just imagine…

Walter tugged on his hand. "John? *Please!*"

Well, what could he do? If Alys and Walter were both so hell-bent to have the wedding, then why not? He would still go back to France. They could go on as before. "Very well, I will wed you, Alys."

"Ingrate!" she growled. "Fool!" Again she huffed and turned away to walk back to the keep. "You think you are such a prize!"

"There are others who might give you a happier life," he agreed, not at all discommoded by her name-calling. The names did fit.

She stopped again and turned as they reached the steps, probably intending to wreak further verbal havoc on him.

"*I* will wed you, Alys!" Walter declared before either of them could speak. "Do not leave us and I will be your husband!"

She rolled her eyes, clicked her tongue, threw up her hands and stalked away.

"Will I not do, John?" Walter asked in a small voice. "I know she loves me."

"You are not of age yet," John explained. "And I believe it is against Church law for brothers to have the same betrothed.

Let me speak to Alys alone. We will come to some agreement so she will stay at Hetherston, at least for a while."

Walter squeezed his hand and sighed. "Wait a bit. Then go say you are sorry and weep a little. That often works."

John raised an eyebrow, wondering if the boy's tears had been genuine. "Thank you, Walter. It is certainly worth a try."

Never in his life had he apologized for anything. Not once that he could recall. The words would fall foreign from his lips if he could even form them. He did regret how he had behaved, but so should she.

Whether he would go so far as to marry her was still in question. She probably would not have him now.

Chapter Five

"Alys, open the door."

Silence.

Again he knocked. "Alys, I order you answer me! We have much to discuss and you are behaving like a sulky child. Admit me *now*."

"The door is not locked, John."

He pivoted around and there she stood behind him. "I...I thought you were..."

"I know. Come to your solar. My chamber is quite cold since there is no fire there," she said reasonably, turning to lead the way back down the stairs.

John felt a fool to have been pounding at her door, demanding entry when she was not even inside the room. "Where were you?" he asked.

She lifted a hide-bound ledger. "I went to fetch the account book. You will want to see it."

"Aye. And I have questions for you that should have been answered the day I arrived." He reached for her arm to escort her down the steps, but she hastened ahead of him, pointedly avoiding his touch.

"You had but to ask," she said, apparently holding on to her fit of pique.

"No fault of yours. I did not mean that. I was not well and never thought to inquire," John assured her.

"I also have questions," Alys informed him.

When they reached the solar, he pushed open the door and stood aside for her to enter. It was now his bedchamber, but there was seating before the fire and also by the window. She opted for the former and laid down the book on a footstool.

"Shall I begin?" she asked, her stubborn little chin raised in question.

He stood near her, his arms crossed over his chest. It seemed the only way he could keep his hands to himself instead of reaching for her. "First I must tell you that I regret how I have behaved." He did not elaborate. "I hope you will forgive me."

"Of course I forgive you." Her words were curt. "'Tis of no great matter and already forgotten." She frowned. "My threat to bring suit against you is an empty one as you shall soon see."

"Good." John unfolded his arms, leaned over and promptly stole a kiss, marveling at the softening of her lips when they had been drawn so firm at the first. She tasted of rich spices and the sweetness of honey. When he broke the kiss and moved away, she remained still as a statue, her eyes wide and her hands clenched by her side.

"My thanks," he said with a nod. "For everything you have done for me and mine. Now ask me what you will."

The kiss had confused her. She took but a moment to recover, drew a deep breath and faced him squarely. "How ill are you? Has it affected your mind?"

John had to smile. "I can see how you might think so, but nay, not that I am aware."

She nodded, but was obviously unconvinced. "How is it a year at the Spanish court with all its rumored luxury laid you so low? Did you contract fever?"

"Not until my condition weakened," he said, not eager to recount what had happened, not wanting her to have to hear it.

"What condition?" she persisted.

"Injuries inflicted during my capture and soon thereafter."

"Thereafter? Were you not treated as a noble awaiting ransom? Did you not have run of the court?"

He looked away, staring into the gentle flames over the mound of glowing coals. "Trastamere considered me a danger within his walls so I was confined. He also wanted information."

"That is why he refused ransom for you until this past month? What changed his mind?"

"He did not change his mind, Alys. He must not have honored your appeal. You see, I was not ransomed, but escaped. With Simon's help, I managed to return to England."

"Then you thought..." Understanding dawned quickly. "Oh, John, I *did* try to have you freed. You must believe that."

He nodded and caressed her hand. "I believe you."

Alys sighed, her shoulders slumped. "But at first you did not. I do see why. We may never know what happened to the knights. Or the gold they transported." She turned away from him and wrung her hands. "It was nearly all we possessed, John, as you will soon see when you examine the accounts. Everything I could beg, borrow or steal."

"Steal?" he asked, amused. "A figure of speech, surely. I cannot imagine you breaking that commandment, Alys."

She turned and looked up at him. "But I did, if you count the wealth of coin your father had put aside for Walter's future. I shall repay that before he needs it, of course."

Alys had put her soul in peril to save him? John felt

humbled. He wanted to take her in his arms and hold her. But she was not ready for that, he could see.

"Was Simon there to serve you in your captivity?" she asked.

He shook his head. "Not those first months. During the attack on the duke, Simon, at my order, helped the others spirit Lancaster to safety while I held off Trastamere's men."

"How many did you kill?"

John shrugged. "Not nearly enough. They hauled me back to Castile, perhaps to prove to Trastamere they had made a good try at Lancaster. I thought it was in hopes of ransom to salvage something for their trouble."

"After they took you, were…were you mistreated, John?" she asked, her concern evident. There were even tears brimming in her eyes.

He released her and walked closer to the fire, bracing his hand upon the stones above it. "That is over and done."

She sighed. "Oh John—"

"Leave it, Alys. Your pity is the last thing I need."

"Pity?" she asked with a scoff. "I was thinking more in the way of sending aid to Pedro of Castile so he could overthrow the cur and do away with him!"

John laughed. "I should have guessed. The Prince will mount another campaign to restore King Pedro. I will ride with him."

"Not if I must imprison you here to prevent it!" she exclaimed.

Alys could be a delight at times, he had to admit. Why had he not foreseen what she was to become as a woman? If he had only taken more note of her, perhaps he would have. He had noticed so little that was of true importance when he was young.

"I must go back," he said. Conviction or rote?

His life since leaving his parents had become nothing more than an endless march of training, battles, drinking, gambling and wenching. It had not been to his liking at first, but he had grown into it, proved equal to it, even enjoyed it most of the time.

In all those years, he had seldom even paused for a prayer unless he did so en masse with the other knights to seek a victory. Small wonder God had punished him with a year's imprisonment and a sound scourging by his captors. Perhaps he ought to be thankful for it since that was precisely what had finally brought him to ponder his existence now.

And what came next? Could he become what Alys needed? Would she have cause to curse the day she pledged herself to him?

He could not take her. It would be too unfair. Years from now she would thank him with every breath for letting her go.

He supposed the first order of business *was* business. At least he would shorten her list of responsibilities and assume the duty of managing their properties while he was here. With that foremost in mind, John picked up the account book and took his chair. "Now to more weighty matters."

"I am not finished," Alys said as she leaned over and placed her hand on the book, preventing his opening it. "First, you must tell me why you have changed. I believed I knew you well, John, but you are very unlike the man who wrote to me five years ago with such hopes for our future."

"Wrote to you?" Unfortunately, he had not so much as thought about her.

She smiled shyly. "The letter, my greatest treasure. Your words to me then sealed my heart against all others and made it yours. Yet now that we meet again…" her voice trailed away as she shook her head.

John was tempted to take credit, but the truth would out. "I never wrote to you, Alys."

She gave the book a firm pat and sat back, clasping her

hands in her lap. "Seasoned warrior that you are, John, you should not deny your poetic side. I nearly swooned each time I read what you wrote. I still do," she admitted with a dimpled grin. "And I have never been a maid given to faints."

He cleared his throat and shifted uncomfortably. "Alys, I must say again, the words were not mine. Perhaps my mother…"

John words trailed off when Alys's face fell. Her features betrayed disbelief, then embarrassment, and finally something akin to grief. He watched helplessly as she pushed up from the chair and swiftly left the room.

Was she going to fetch the letter in question or was she merely running from the knowledge that she had been deceived?

Guilt suffused him. He hated being the one who destroyed her pretty dreams, but fact was fact. In all those years, he had scarcely remembered he had a betrothed, much less put quill in motion to declare undying love for her. If, indeed, that's what he was supposed to have done.

His mother had written the letter, he was certain of it. Who else would have bothered? Five years ago, Alys would have been a sixteen-year-old, ripe for marriage and worried with good reason that her intended had forgotten she existed.

An apology would not suffice this time. There would be no "of course I forgive you." Perhaps it was just as well to leave her with no illusions that he had ever cared about her. However, if he never had, why did he feel her pain so keenly now?

Alys retreated to her chamber feeling mortified, betrayed and such a lackwit. Not only had Lady Greycourt deceived her with that letter, she had surely made up every one of those tales of John's boyhood. Everyone knew full well he had left Hetherston when he was but seven.

Knowing Lancaster, John probably had been given no

choice but to remain with his overlord and rarely return home until that occasion of his knighting and betrothal to her. Alys wondered why she had never questioned that, never even suspected for a moment those stories of the young John's valor and gallantry were false. But she had wanted so to believe....

Oh, the mother's reasons were pure enough. She had meant for Alys to love John and remain faithful while he was away. But the fact remained, the lady was not who Alys had always trusted and believed her to be. Just like John. Both strangers Alys could not recognize.

One day she might forgive Fiona, for her lies had certainly served their purpose. However, now Alys realized that the love she had built up in her mind for her betrothed had no true foundation.

He could be a blackguard of the worst sort. At least he had been honest with her about the letter when he so easily could have let the lie stand. Somehow, she wished he had.

She pulled the covers over her head and wished to heaven she could simply disappear. How could she face him now? How could she ever marry him now even if he agreed?

Forgiving herself for being played the fool would take some doing. Never before had she doubted her ability to do a thing she set out to accomplish, but she did wonder how she would ever do that. Could she ever trust anyone's word again?

Perhaps that doubt signified her belated arrival inside the door of adulthood, she thought with a bitter grimace. One thing for certain, she was no longer the child John had called her.

Chapter Six

In the days that followed, Alys decided to act as if the letter had never existed. She was as distantly polite to John as she might have been to any stranger newly arrived, for he *was* a stranger to her.

John took to gifting her with small treasures for which she had no use. First, he sent Simon to her with a finely etched case filled with needles of steel and bone. John knew very well she did not like to sew. Next day he had given her an emerald and gold brooch, an ornament that brought memories of his mother that Alys did not wish to relive.

Last evening at supper, he had laid a small, leather-bound book of prayers in front of her place at table. She suspected it had been presented to him when he had arrived in London for it did look new. She had her own prayer book and, besides, did not wish a gift secondhand. "Read the inside leaf," he had suggested.

Love is for the asking. She read the words with a jaundiced eye for his signature beneath them was in a different hand and the ink did not match. How thickheaded could the man be, or think she was? Did he not know she would guess that some bold lady at court had given him that anonymously?

She also wondered, in spite of herself, what he would choose next to give her. 'Twas obvious he scrounged amongst the things he already had and those left to him by his mother. Then she remembered that he had withdrawn no funds from the estates' sorely depleted coffers since coming home and had been too ill to shop before leaving the city. Her heart had softened a bit, but not enough to wax poetic over his offerings.

Why was he doing this?

"Ah, your *beloved* approaches," Thomasine warned her. "And he wears a sly smile."

Alys turned, raised an eyebrow in question and suffered his greeting.

"Alys! How goes your day?" he asked pleasantly.

"Well enough," she replied, trying not to note how the subtle gain in weight this past week had improved his appearance. Gone were the sallow cast to his skin and the shadows beneath his eyes. His health was returning apace. How handsome *would* he be when fully recovered?

"I have hope you will come riding this morn for a view of the village," he said, his voice hopeful and nearly merry with anticipation.

She shrugged at the temptation. It was no use pretending that she might have what she once believed was hers by right. There was no hope of that sweet union his mother had falsely promised her. Still, she must make some attempt to close the breach between them for the sake of future peace.

In the event they did marry, she did not want them estranged. If they did not, she must see they remained friends. Otherwise, she would lose Walter, too.

Thomasine stepped forward. "You disrupt her day, my lord."

"He does not," Alys snapped, interrupting, shocking herself as well as her cousin. "I shall be glad to ride."

John chuckled, reached for Alys's hand and tugged her along as they crossed the hall. "Well done of you," he said.

"'Tis your right to ride the estate, John, and my place to show you the improvements. I will do my duty."

He laughed again. "So you will, my dear. So you will."

"What do you mean by that?" she demanded.

They stopped at the steps leading down to the bailey. "I mean that you are a creature of duty, Alys. I have heard how you love to ride and I would give you a few hours' pleasure."

She looked into his eyes and the memory of their kiss in the solar returned, as it did so often and unexpectedly. He looked as if he might kiss her again. She waited.

"So," he said, drawing out the word, dragging his gaze from hers. "We should get on with it."

"Your daily gift, I presume," she said with a weary sigh.

"I admit it," he confessed wryly as they progressed down the steps, his fingers now linked with hers in a way that sent tingles up her arm. "I mean to thank you for your care of Hetherston, my parents and Walter, but my worldly goods are a limited store at the moment." He smiled sadly. "I regret that you hate me."

"I do no such thing!" she exclaimed, yanking her hand from his and stepping away from him as they reached the stables.

"Aye, you do, and well you should. If I had written to you as I ought, we would not be having this conversation. Mother would not have felt she had to meddle."

"I understand that much more clearly than before," she assured him.

"Do you? Well, fortunately, so do I."

The stable boy cleared his throat to gain their attention. "Your mounts are ready, my lord."

"My thanks, Michael," Alys said, then noted the chestnut

mare he had prepared for her. "What is this? Where is my gelding?"

"In pasture, my lady. Lord John told me to saddle Minx."

"She's yours now," John said with an eager smile. "Your gelding is aging and I thought you might like a new mount."

Alys examined the mare, then turned to John. "She is beautiful. Where did you get her?"

"A recent gift from the king on my arrival in London. I only had old Trampler left. Simon rode him away during Lancaster's escape so we have him still. I was mounted on my own destrier which the Spanish soon claimed along with my sword and armor."

She smoothed the mare's mane as she imagined John's relinquishing of his horse and accoutrements during his surrender. How hard that must have been for him.

He reached for her waist and lifted her to the saddle. "There. She has a back like a feather bed or I should never have made it here from London."

Alys nodded, unable to speak. There was no denying John had hit upon a perfect gift this time. Nonetheless, she knew the gesture meant far less to him than it did to her. Knights viewed their mounts as either tools or weapons, not special beings worthy of emotions. The men could not afford to love them when the animals were so often lost in battle.

She noticed then that John would be riding the same stout gelding Simon Ferrell had ridden into the bailey that first day. "Do you have no other?" Alys asked.

"Only Trampler," he replied with a laugh as he put foot to stirrup. "God save me, I would rather walk than ride that one."

So John had given up his only palfrey to her? Why all the gifts? Why this desperate attempt to gain her regard?

She clicked her tongue and cantered toward the gates.

When he drew even with her, she said, "You need not give me presents, John. I swear I do not and never shall *hate* you."

"Even if we do not marry?" he asked gently.

"Even then." Alys rode ahead. Did he find her so repugnant? Was there someone else he loved?

She took a deep, fortifying breath and hardened her heart, determined not to ask him why. No matter what he said, she would move heaven and earth to make the marriage happen. She simply could not give up the only home she knew and the little boy who depended on her. Or the man who needed her, whether he knew it or not.

For the remainder of the day, John plied her with sweet words and direct attention. His very touch as he helped her mount and dismount and the way he put a palm to the back of her waist as they walked the village and met his tenants kept her in a high state of discomposure. She felt a flutter in her belly, a rapid thumping in her chest, that tingling within her center that she always experienced when he was anywhere near.

Somehow, she had lost the upper hand in this arrangement. The problem of her faltering control would not leave her as they rode back to the castle.

Again he helped her to dismount when they reached the stables. He handed off their reins to the stable lad who led the mounts away.

John drew her into the shadow of the castle wall and looked down at her. As if he had heard her recent thoughts, he said, "You have called the dance too often, Alys. Now you do not need to."

Ah, so that was it. He resented her taking charge after his mother died. In defense of herself, she reminded him, "You know there was no one else to do it, John."

"Now, there is," he replied evenly.

He cradled her face and leaned down to gently kiss her lips.

His were cool and firm and remained closed upon hers. No grand passion stirred in him that she could discern, even though her own heart thundered like a great bevy of hoofbeats on the drawbridge.

This would not do. He must want her, too, or all would be lost. To that end, Alys stood on her toes and kissed him with her whole heart. She slid her arms about his waist and pulled him close with all her strength. The heat of his open mouth on hers sent her senses swirling. She breathed him in, clung to him like ivy to a wall and explored his mouth with her tongue. She had never kissed a man so in her life. Blood sang in her veins and stars sparkled behind her eyelids.

He made a sound in his throat of pleasure or pain, she could not tell and did not care. She angled her head and renewed the kiss, bound and determined that he would feel all she felt and more. He would love her back. He *must!*

His arms enclosed her while his hands moved restlessly over her back, clutching her gown and caressing her through the fabric.

Yes! He did want her! No man could give himself this way and not want her as much as she wanted him. She pressed herself to him where she wanted his touch the most, a commanding move that seemed as natural to her as drawing a breath.

Suddenly, he broke their kiss and set her away, wearing a heavy-lidded look that made absolute clutter of what reason she had left. He removed her arms from around him and gripped her hands tightly in his. "Not like this," he muttered.

Then like what? she wanted to demand. Alys felt bereft, rejected and totally at a loss. That had been her best effort.

He let go of one hand and held the other as they walked silently into the keep. Her body was on fire for him. Did he not feel anything? What must she do now?

He stopped her before they entered the keep and turned her to him, grasping her shoulders, his fingers kneading the muscles there as if to soothe her. "The consummation would be binding, Alys, before the ceremony as well as after. If we anticipate our vows now there could be no turning back."

She yanked her hand from his.

"Listen to me, Alys," he commanded.

She looked away, containing herself as best she could. "I cling to your every word, my lord."

He blew out a breath and rubbed the back of his neck with one hand. "Come with me," he said finally. It sounded like an order, but she was just curious enough to obey.

With the determined stride of one on a mission, he led her into the keep, straight through the hall and into the solar. His chamber. Once inside, he closed the door and shot the bolt. "Sit there," he snapped.

Alys sat, now doubly curious and somewhat amazed when he began removing his tunic. Her eyes widened when he stripped off the linen chemise beneath that and stood bare-chested before her. He lowered his chausses a bit so that they rode just below his waist.

She stared with appreciation at the smooth, well-honed muscles of his chest and stomach, the enticing dip of his navel and the tightness of the fabric just below it. He was clearly aroused.

"You think to impress me, my lord?" she asked with a wry smirk. "I have seen naked men before, though I admit, none so fair. Continue at will."

"Enough of that," he snapped. He had stopped removing his clothes. His hands rested on his hips as he fastened his gaze on hers. "You do not know me, Alys. You think you do, but that knowledge is as false as the smile you put on when something displeases you." He nodded. "Aye, false!"

She dropped the smile. "I have never had anything but admiration for you, John. Surely you do not doubt that?"

"Oh nay, I do believe it. You think I am perfect. You have said as much and I could never live up to that, Alys. You must see me as I am."

She leaned forward, elbows propped on her knees and her chin in her hands as she regarded him. "You will not convince me of your flaws by undressing, John. Best take another direction."

Without a word, he turned. Alys gasped and flew out of her chair to him, her hands stopping just short of the horrid marks upon his back. "Oh, God!" she cried, choking on the words. Tears filled her eyes, blurring the awful sight of the marred skin.

He stepped away, then turned to face her again. "You see but one side of me and set your judgment. I do not think you shallow enough to mind a few scars, Alys, but I mean to use this as the example of what you cannot see."

"Wh…what do you mean?"

"Flaws, Alys. Faults. Marks placed upon me by life these last ten years. I am but a man with those aplenty." He reached for her hands and squeezed them almost painfully. "See me, Alys. See *me,* the man, not some paragon in polished armor my mother placed in your mind."

Alys drew her hands from his and placed them on his face, cradling it as she would a child's. "I see you, John," she whispered. "I feel you, the timbre of your voice, the sweetness of your breath, the longing in your eyes. You touch me even without touching." Slowly, she lifted herself on her toes until she could reach his lips with hers and pressed a kiss there. "You are in my heart."

"Alys," he groaned and took her mouth in a heated kiss that stole both breath and thought. When next she knew, she was in his arms as he carried her to his bed and placed her on it, joining her there without a pause. His hands were everywhere at once, caressing softly, then desperately, the curves beneath her gown. She writhed against him, undulating until she could feel him where her body craved him most.

"Love me," she whispered, pulling at his clothes even as he stripped hers away. In moments, they lay skin to skin, bodies urgently seeking, finding, pleasuring.

Oh, she had known it would be so. How strong he was, commanding, masterful and supplicating all at once. Her fingertips explored the firm muscles flexing beneath his skin. She reveled in the way his mouth devoured hers in a shared hunger neither could satisfy with kisses. He wanted her! And she had never desired him this way even in her greatest imagining.

Alys gave herself up to his need as she assuaged her own. She cried out to him, eager and joyous as he claimed her, making her his alone for all time. Or at least for this moment in time, a moment that swayed on the very edge of bliss for an endless golden time before crashing into it with a force she did not expect. Her body and his shook violently with shared power, surrender and a blending of souls. They were one, she thought as she floated gently down from the last tier of ecstasy.

When he quieted and lay atop her, obviously as spent as she felt, Alys smiled into his shoulder. "I did not plan for this," she murmured. "But I cannot regret it."

John sighed. "You might come to."

Dread skittered up her spine. She sighed and wrapped her arms more securely around him, feeling the scarred ridges on his back. Someone should pay for those. She understood his need to make that happen. If she were able, she would go to Spain herself and destroy the ones who hurt him so. "You think I will regret this loving when you leave me?" she guessed. "Nay, not even then. I will protest your leaving, but I understand your need to go." She lowered her gaze. "At least I shall have this."

He withdrew from her and rolled to his back, lazily trailing a hand over her, pausing to cup her breast. "What have I done, Alys? Here you lie with a man you do not even know. How can I reveal myself to you when you only glorify everything I do?"

"You speak again of these faults I should recognize?" She tangled her fingers in his hair, combing out its length and enjoying the dark softness of it. How could she help but adore him?

"Do not tell me you know of none," he said, stroking the curve of her shoulder as he looked away from her. "Admit them, Alys. Tell me what you truly know of me. Show me you are not the starry-eyed child I left behind."

She was no child. She supposed she must play this game if he was to know that. "You have a foul temper?" she muttered, glancing at his expression to judge whether that was the sort of truth he wanted from her.

He nodded, one corner of his mouth quirking up. He made a rolling motion with one hand, encouraging her to continue.

She inhaled a shaky breath. "You brood." He nodded again.

"Poor table manners," she added, gaining a good understanding now. He was giving her leave to list everything and she was not hard put to recall a few. "Comes from eating in the field, aye?"

"Do not excuse me. Just say your piece," he instructed.

Alys shrugged and inclined her head. "You scorn tradition."

"How so?" he demanded, then seemed to catch himself. "Never mind. Go on."

Alys warmed to the task. "You abhor figures." When his brow furrowed, she explained. "The account book. You never read it."

It was his turn to shrug.

"And you do…not…write…letters," she accused, then worried that perhaps he did not know how. "Can you write?"

He tightened his lips and nodded, looking slightly sheepish.

"Small regard for your servants. I have yet to see you thank one."

"I do so!" he argued, raising himself to one elbow and glaring down at her. "I plan to knight Simon."

"The others, I mean. You take them for granted, John, and they work very hard for us."

"I see," he said with a slight huff. "And…?"

"Walter, of course. You should pay him more attention. He loves you well." A thought occurred. "For the same reasons I did, of course, but let us not disabuse him yet if you intend to foster him yourself. He needs a hero."

A sad look crossed his face then. "You say you *did* love me. But now you no longer think you could? Have I gone too far with this?"

Alys laughed a little. "You *always* go too far, John. That is your main fault, I think. Sometimes you must simply let things be." She softened when he looked abashed. "The stars in my eyes are gone." Her laughter had died. "I merely clung to the one dream that offered comfort. The dream your parents provided to sustain me."

"And I dispensed with their lies," he said, his tone slightly bitter.

"Everything they said was born of love, John. Your mother and father adored you. They had no other cause to lavish me with so much attention and guide my heart to care for you. It must have been their fondest wish to have you lead a happy and contented life once you came home to settle. It was not only for my benefit they had minstrels sing praises of your feats so often. The people here at Hetherston are ready to have you govern them as lord. I am ready to have you to husband. How do you think that was accomplished?" Alys took his hand in hers. "They laid this path for you because they cared for you so deeply."

He sighed and ran a hand through his hair, disturbing its neatness. Alys could see a shadow of the young lad John had been when separated from his parents by the custom of the day. His uncertainty lingered.

"That is something to consider," he admitted, then met her gaze with one of doubt. "But perhaps it was *you* they wished happy. I do see how easy it would have been for them to love you."

"Can you?" she asked, feeling rather wistful. "Could *you?*"

John looked away, the ghost of a smile on his lips. "I do wonder how many of my mother's letters singing your praises never reached me. Or perhaps she counted upon your beauty alone to enthrall me when I returned."

Alys laughed and smoothed her hand over his naked chest. "As if you would be swayed by my looks! Nay, I am not modest, only truthful. You were appalled by me when you rode in, do not deny it!"

"In truth, I was blinded that day by my pigheaded pride and tired to death at the time." He took her in his arms. "But you wore me down."

She gave him a push, then turned from him so he would not see the hurt in her eyes. What had she done? *Worn him down?* Pestered him into agreeing to this? Even threatened him. Where was her pride? And if she loved him, how could she hold him to those early vows he had never meant?

"God forgive me, I would have done anything to remain here, to be your wife, to rear your brother as I promised. *Anything,* as you have witnessed," she admitted with a short bitter laugh.

"You said you did not regret it, Alys," he reminded her.

She shook her head. "I cannot regret the deed. I do not. But this was so wrong of me. I see that now," she whispered, realizing the enormity of what she had done.

"But we shall make it right, Alys. Never worry about that." He kissed her shoulder, his lips hot, the hand he placed on her waist an intimate caress.

For a long moment, she remained silent, then did the only thing she could do. She turned back to him, though she refrained from touching him as she longed to do. "I release you, John. We need not marry. If you will but let me have care of Walter now and again, I shall be content."

Oh, the lie, she thought. Quickly she climbed out of bed and kept her back to him. Tears stung as they gathered and fell. She could hardly bear to think of leaving this place and returning to her estate in the south. Leaving Walter would break her heart, but leaving John might well destroy her.

No matter what he thought, what his mother had done or how he had dismantled her girlish dreams, Alys loved him. The man he was, not the paragon she had idolized for so long. He had been gracious in his defeat for the most part, giving in to this loving that should seal his fate, but she knew he would come to hate her for forcing his hand.

He stood behind her now, pulling her back against him where he enfolded her in his arms and rested his lips near her ear. "You climbed into my heart and made a place there, Alys, long before today. I could not oust you if I wished to. And I do not wish to. It is your inner beauty, your fealty and constancy that have caused me to love you."

"You…you love me?" she asked, breathless with anticipation, not caring how love came to be, only that it was. If he were being honest, she warned herself. Was he lying to save face, to make her seem *his* choice and not that of his parents?

He shook his head slightly as he spoke. "I do love you, and I am glad it is not the result of high-flown praise of you written upon a page by Mother's hand. This is my reckoning, Alys. My love, bestowed upon the woman you have become. Were we not betrothed, I should fall on my knee and ask you for your hand this day." He caressed her throat with gentle fingers and placed a heated kiss upon her neck.

A shiver of pleasure rippled through her entire body in spite of her doubts. "Such a gesture I could not imagine."

He promptly turned her in his arms to face him, then trailing his hands down her arms to grasp her hands, he slowly dropped to one knee and bowed his head. "I beseech you, Alys of Camoy, do me the honor of becoming my wife." Then he looked up at her and smiled.

Alys gazed deeply into his eyes, searching for the truth of his feelings. "Nay, I cannot," she whispered, simply to see whether he would persist.

"Aye, you will," he commanded, rising and lifting her hands to his lips for a fierce kiss. His smile had flown. "And right soon," he added with a determined lift of his brow. "Plan the wedding, Alys. Now."

Chapter Seven

Their wedding day dawned bright. John hoped it boded a sunny future. Alys had agreed to release him from their contract, even after he had bedded her. He knew they must wed, though not strictly because of that. And not because his parents had wished it or that he had pledged himself to her when they were young. Nay, it was due to the fact that she had slid straight into his heart as easily as a thrice-honed dagger and he had been felled before he knew what happened. He loved the girl. The *woman,* he corrected his thought. The beautiful, spirited, persistent woman. He could not deny how he felt about her any longer. Still, he continued to worry that some cloud would suddenly descend and ruin everything.

Alys had not come to him again, nor had she made any mention of their joining. She had merely thrown herself into preparation for the wedding, giving him looks that said he had leave to stop her at any time. No chance of that.

He gave her the time to herself because she seemed to need it. Perhaps he could have enticed her into bed again, but he felt she might be suffering an attack of guilt because they had not waited. Would he ever understand her?

He ached constantly for her, to hold her again, to feel her touch and see the love in her eyes. Could it be that she no longer wanted him as a man now that she knew she would have him as a husband? Had she been that good at pretense? Nay, she loved him. Of that, John was certain. Her passion had been real.

Simon held out the elaborately embroidered tunic of forest-green with an edging of woven gold threads and the Greycourt device emblazoned on the breast of it. He wore dark, tightly knitted hosen to match and gold garters below the knee.

"You are tricked out like a courtier," Simon remarked. "Do you suppose your lady has a trunk somewhere full of these?"

"I wonder that myself. But she hates needlework."

Simon laughed. "I would bet she persists at it nonetheless. She has a right tenacious mind of her own." He straightened the flat links of John's chain. "There. Fine as frog's hair."

John took a deep breath. As he had in the past when geared for a tourney or a battle, he asked, "Shall we to it, Sim?"

"On to victory, sir," Simon replied, quite resplendent himself in a coat of dove-gray.

The buzzing sound of gathered guests reached him before he opened the doorway. The ceremony would take place on the steps of the keep so that everyone at Hetherston could witness.

Afterward, he, Alys, their attendants and the nobles present would return to the chapel inside for the wedding mass. Then an enormous wedding breakfast would be served to those within and without. A daylong feast would ensue, interspersed with hunting and games and would culminate in the wedding night. John worried how that would go. There would be no proof of her innocence for all to witness. Was she troubled about that?

Simon flung open the doors and John exited to a loud

huzzah. He raised a hand and smiled at the throng of castle folk and servants come to see the wedding. He knew most of them now, for he had taken Alys's criticism to heart. He almost felt like a lord today.

Walter, arrayed in a tunic the same color and cut as John's, nudged him and grinned. "She will be ours in truth now, John," he whispered, his young voice carrying to the crowd. Nods and bright smiles and a few laughs acknowledged Walter's declaration. John grasped Walter's shoulder and gave it a fond shake. They had become fast friends this past week.

For long moments John waited, hands clasped behind him, trying not to rock back and forth, heel to toe, and appear impatient. She would arrive in good time, he assured himself. Pray God she would not be much late.

A soft *ooh* swept the crowd and John turned to greet her.

God's breath, but she was beautiful! Arrayed in a gown of palest green, her amber locks flowing to her waist below a crown of white heather, she appeared almost ethereal, an angel come to life. He added his sigh to that of their well-wishers and held out his hand to her.

It was then he noticed she carried a nosegay made of purple thistles, the stems swathed in heavy silk to protect her from thorns. Those were hardly the sort of blooms a bride should choose. Were they a warning to him of her prickly nature? The thought made him smile.

What a wit and how unsubtle she was. He supposed the choice suited her well enough. Alys possessed a unique beauty, as did the flowers she had picked. And she did indeed show a nettlesome aspect on occasion. He quite liked that about her. She was no pale, fragile rose, his Alys, but as hardy, stalwart and adaptable as the wild flower of Scotland.

"In honor of your mother who is with us in spirit," she explained with a sweet smile and tenderly touched the spiky blooms.

John could almost feel his mother's approval embrace them. She had cared so much, he realized, and gone to great lengths to ensure his happiness. He cast a glance heavenward and prayed his parents would forgive him for ever doubting their love of him.

Alys shifted her nosegay to her left hand and grasped his right, stepping boldly to his side. Her lips trembled slightly, adding to their appeal. John could not help remembering how soft and giving they were. He must remember not to let his passion for her take hold when he kissed her. Not until tonight.

Father Stephen faced them and began the ceremony. "Dearly beloved, we are come…"

John barely heard the drone of the words that would unite them before the people. When Simon nudged him and handed him the ring, he slid it half onto her forefinger, then the middle and at last the third where it would remain. Alys made a fist when it was in place, as if to hold it there forever.

He kept his eyes upon her, unable to look away as she signed the contract placed upon the leather-bound Bible. He took the quill, dipped it and scratched his own name beside hers.

Together they marched behind Father Stephen and heard the wedding mass. As they knelt, her hand in his seemed chilled, her fingers restless. He noted a fine bead of moisture above her lips and just below her eyes.

Was Alys falling ill? Would that be the impending disaster he could not oust from his mind? Hopefully, she was only beset by exhaustion. God only knew how hard she had toiled to bring this celebration about. He would have done more to help if she had only let him.

"Take heart, 'tis nearly done," he whispered.

She looked at him as if his mind had suddenly lapsed. "Surely you jest," she snapped, her words sharp if near inaudible. They drew a glance of reprimand from the priest, though he never faltered in his chant of Latin.

"Ahhh-men," the priest droned.

At last they were free to stand. John rose and assisted Alys, turning her to face him. She lifted her chin, her lips waiting for the kiss of peace, her eyes closed.

He framed her face with his hands, sliding his fingers into the silken locks of her hair. Then he lowered his mouth to hers. He tasted her first, tracing the seam of her lips with his tongue, gaining entrance. Alys responded with a sigh of welcome John felt to the depths of his soul. In that moment, his hopes soared with hers and left behind any doubts all would be well.

Despite his intent, desire swept him like a fire to dry tinder. Her arms encircled his waist, her fingers clutching at his back. She wanted him. Her mouth welcomed him as surely as her body would.

He embraced her more fully, pulling her into him with such force, he felt the shape of her breasts right through his tunic and the buckle of his belt dig into his belly.

That, in addition to the rapid and insistent tapping on his shoulder, woke him from his fog of desire.

Well, not entirely. His breathing came in fits and starts and his eager manhood still gave clear evidence of his lapse of control. Alys was biting her bottom lip and looking up at him from beneath her tawny lashes to see what they should do next.

He kissed her again, unable not to, this time with only a gentle brush of promise. A smattering of polite applause and it was done. They were officially wed in state and church. Man and wife for all and good. Or at least they would be after the official consummation. Judging by that kiss, the success of tonight's endeavor seemed a foregone conclusion.

John grinned, took her hand and led her back down the aisle, pausing only briefly to grasp an offered hand of congratulations here and there.

They had almost reached the doorway when John saw the man he least wanted to see today. Lancaster. What the devil was *he* doing here? Had he come to order John back to the wars so soon?

"Felicitations, John," the duke said.

"Your Grace," John acknowledged.

Alys had halted in her tracks and looked anxiously from him to the duke and back again.

"My wife, Alys," John said woodenly. "Alys, His Grace, the Duke of Lancaster."

She curtsied as custom commanded, then leveled a look upon the duke that might have felled a lesser man.

John stepped between Alys and the duke and fairly dragged her forcefully out of the chapel. She relented and picked up her own pace once they were out of sight of the duke.

"He has come for you, has he not? I did not invite him!" she exclaimed. "'Twas Thomasine, I'll wager. Ronci has come, too, and I know that is her doing! I shall drop her in the oubliette and leave her there to rot!"

"Ronci? Your cousin mentioned him before. He was a candidate for your hand if I reneged, was he not?"

She turned on him, ignoring the milling crowd around them. "Only in her mind! I never considered another man. Not ever! Ronci is her lover and she only wanted me to—"

John squeezed her arm. "Calm yourself, Alys, and let it go. To salve the memory of our wedding day, I would greet the devil himself with a smile. And so shall you."

"One of my *false* smiles?" she asked.

"If need be," he replied. "Lancaster is the most powerful man in England, save his father the king."

That silenced her, but John could see how overset she was. The duke must have come to order him back to the campaign. Alys would argue about that, no matter that she had said she would understand his leaving. John would not like to see his overlord and his wife at cross-purposes.

He firmly dismissed his wondering and focused on his wife. "Are you not starved?" he asked to divert Alys from her dark thoughts. "We should take our seats at table so everyone else may find theirs. Do smile," he teased, "or else all will think our kiss set you off your feed."

She allowed him to lead her into the hall. He blew out a slow breath of relief and wondered if it would prove justified. Alys did not look appeased by his apparent acceptance of Lancaster's presence.

Alys could scarcely contain herself. Her feelings flew in all directions at once. Fear of Lancaster and what he might require of John. Wary and almost desperate hope for eventual love from John at her left. Fury skipped down the table to her cousin, Thomasine, while her immense gratitude encompassed all the Hetherston folk who considered her their own. She hardly knew what expression to wear or where her eyes should wander.

In deference to John, she pasted on a smile and signaled for the meal to begin. He leaned closer and stroked her sleeve. Alys shivered, but could not isolate the cause of it. Her whole body seemed balanced on a wire as if awaiting a fall in one direction or another.

She tasted not one bite of the pickled quail eggs or fresh

white bread. The flavor of the fine rhenish wine she had so looked forward to escaped her notice. She even ate eels, which she abhorred. Keeping her mouth filled might prevent any errant words falling out that should not, she figured.

But Lancaster seemed determined to engage her in conversation. "How is it you and John have put this off for so many years?" he asked pleasantly.

Because you demanded he stay at your side without a visit home for a decade perhaps, you selfish bag of wind? She wanted to fling that at him, but felt John's strong fingers suddenly grasp her leg just above her knee. His grip did not feel as if it had to do with wild desire for her, either. It was definitely more in the nature of a warning. So she took a deep breath before answering Lancaster. "It seemed politic to wait," she replied instead.

John rewarded her with a satisfied pat beneath the table. The warmth of his hand seeped right through the heavy silk of her gown and the chemise beneath it. She tried to hold her mind on that pleasant bit of intimacy.

Lancaster persisted. "Ah, but if he had known such beauty awaited him, I feel certain he would have headed home without my leave and I could not have faulted him for it."

Was the duke trying to charm her so he could take John away without a scene? Alys refused to look at him. "It would be hard to fault a man such as John for anything." She stabbed a portion of eel as if it were trying to escape.

"And I do not. He has been all a knight should be these many years."

She gritted her teeth. "Good of you to admit that. He did save your life, or at least prevented your capture."

"Just so, and for this happy occasion, I have written a poem set to music in John's honor describing his valor."

Was he baiting her apurpose? Did he want a charger of eels dashed at his head? If he began to sing, she would do it, so help her God. Alys could stand it no longer. She took a deep breath, laid down her eating knife and faced the duke squarely. "Have you come to order my husband away from me? On our wedding day?"

"I came to wish you well, Lady Greycourt." The duke looked past her to John. "But also to inform John that the new campaign is underway. I knew he would want to go."

"Nay, Your Grace," John said in a loud, firm voice. The clink and rattle of knives against plates and all conversation ceased. John's words rang clear in the silence. "I do not wish that. In my stead, I offer the services of three of Hetherston's knights. Do you know Sirs Bran Copely, Robin Nithing and Royston of Gale?"

The duke nodded, quite obviously shocked by John's reluctance to ride with him.

Alys gasped. If the duke knew those knights who had come to their knighthood and spent their entire lives at Hetherston until six months earlier, then he knew of her ransom attempt. He had intercepted it! "You will return the gold they carried, of course," she said.

"Gold?" the duke repeated, turning his frown on her.

"Aye, that which I sent by them to ransom my husband."

The duke swallowed hard and looked away. "I could not allow Trastamere to acquire so much. It was thrice what a knight's ransom should be and would have funded yet another foray against King Pedro."

Alys stood and shoved back her chair, facing the duke with all the fury she felt. "My husband is worth at least three knights on any occasion, Your Grace, and I would not care if Trastamere gained the entire continent of Europe if he had but let John return! You owe me for thwarting my honest attempt to gain his freedom!"

The duke stood, too, shoulders drawn back and chin up, his glare daring her to continue. For a long moment, he did not speak. Then he looked away. "Perhaps. But it is not you, a mere woman, to whom I owe a boon. What would *you* have, John?"

John surreptitiously tugged on the back of her gown, urging her to sit down, as he spoke in a calm voice, devoid of anger. "The return of the ransom gathered by my wife since it was in great part her wealth. I wish a knighthood for Simon Ferrell. And leave from the king for Sir James Ronci to wed Thomasine du Aubrey, my wife's cousin." He paused.

"Is that *all?*" the duke asked with a wry grimace.

John smiled. "And your continued goodwill, Your Grace."

The duke took his seat since Alys had plopped back down in hers, astounded that John would make the demands he had. Lancaster propped his elbow on the table and flopped his hand in a negligent wave. "Goodwill you have and you know it. Are you mad to request Ronci for any woman of your acquaintance?"

"I would have it so," John insisted, "But you should dower her first."

The duke shook his head. "Madness, I say, but a small enough favor. As for the other, Ferrell shall have his spurs. And I will return half the gold."

"Three-fourths!" Alys snapped. "You cannot have spent so much of it!"

The duke slapped his palm on the table and ground out, "Two-thirds! And do not press me further, lady!"

Alys figured that was the best she could get. "Done," she agreed with a satisfied nod.

The duke blew out a noisy breath between his lips and sat back, addressing John. "Are you certain she is not a Scot?"

John shrugged. "Trained up by one, Your Grace."

"Now do me a favor, if you please," Lancaster grumbled. "Get on with the bedding so I can quit this place. I have a war to wage."

Alys jumped up, grasped John's hand and tugged him to his feet. They barely escaped the laughing, grasping guests who hurried toward them, suspecting her intention.

Alys waved as she ran. Thomasine was jumping for joy, shouting her thanks. Ronci sat unmoving, dumbfounded, his eating knife suspended halfway to his mouth.

"Bedding for breakfast!" someone shouted and others took it up, determined to stay and make witness to the event if they could get inside the bridal chamber. At the very least they would aid in the disrobing. Not a thing to look forward to!

Dashing for the solar instead of the stairs as the crowd expected, Alys and John got clean away. He quickly barred the door to prevent intrusion, gathered her in his arms and swept her up. She laughed wildly as he tossed her onto his bed and followed her down with a rambunctious kiss.

"You were wonderful!" he declared with feeling. "Truly magnificent!"

Alys kissed him back, then drew away so she could look into his eyes. "Well, I do have faults, you know, but I shan't make you list them!"

"No faults that matter, my heart. You are perfection and I love you. I *do*, Alys, with my whole heart and soul."

"A bit late coming to that conclusion, John, but I forgive you." Totally happy, she melted into his arms and pressed her cheek to his. "What made you decide not to go with Lancaster? You said yourself you were a warrior born and knew naught else to be."

"A foolish notion formed in childhood, sweeting. It was

past time to grow up." He trailed kisses down her neck and tugged at her bodice with his teeth.

"As you have shown me so recently, childish dreams certainly can be improved upon!" Alys tugged playfully at the links of his belt and managed to unfasten it. "Welladay, now that we are both matured sufficiently, could we put our forms to better use than displaying all this silk and velvet? Help me unlace this cursed thing!"

"I've been meaning to speak to you concerning your wicked eagerness," John said with a rumbling chuckle that tickled her neck.

"Contagious fault, is it?" she asked with a breathless sigh.

"Catching as a wind-borne plague," he admitted. "Ah, my sweet girl, I shall never, ever have enough of you."

"I will see to it," she promised. And she did.

PAYING THE PIPER

Gail Ranstrom

Dear Reader

Have you ever put off dealing with a problem until it caught up to you? Or have you tried to run away, and found that it followed you? That there's no escape? If so, you'll understand Chloe Faraday's dilemma in PAYING THE PIPER.

My favorite stories are about men and women who, through adversity, find the courage, strength and integrity to face their greatest fears, no matter how difficult. I've always found it a paradox that in confronting what we fear we sometimes find our greatest reward. And *that* is a risk worth taking.

I hope you enjoy reading about Chloe and Anthony, and how, when they were willing to risk everything they held dear for the promise of love, they found each other.

Happy Reading!

Gail

Chapter One

Litchfield, Hampshire, May 21, 1814

Chloe Faraday clutched her brother's sleeve and looked up into green eyes so exactly like hers that it was like looking in a mirror. "I tell you, George, I am desperate. Our stepfather turns a deaf ear and refuses to discuss it. Last night he...he punished me. And if a girl cannot trust her own brother, who can she trust? You *must* help me."

George patted her hand on his arm and smiled reassuringly. "Dear Chloe, you are merely having wedding vapors. Is that not de rigueur for blushing brides?"

"I am not being fashionable or coy, George. I am truly desperate. I cannot imagine how I ignored the forthcoming nuptials for so long. I assure you, it is one thing to be promised to a stranger years in advance, and quite another to be scarcely a week from those very nuptials. I simply cannot go through with it, and that is an end to it."

"There, there, puss," George soothed. "You will calm as the day draws near. There is nothing to concern yourself about. I went to school with Anthony Chandler. I know him to be a reasonable man, not given to sudden angers or passions. Indeed, he has always been a most serious sort."

George was such a wag and a jester that she had to doubt him. She clasped her hands together and went to look out the parlor window. Spring was in her giddy stages. Trees wore unfurling green leaves and the buds of flowers, tightly packed now, would soon be bursting to the warmth of sunny afternoons. By the time those same trees and flowers were in full bloom, she would be walking down an aisle to join her life to a stranger's. It was untenable!

She turned back to her brother. "George, platitudes will not serve me now. If I do not have your help, I shall have to do something I'm likely to regret. Run away, or—"

"Come now. You've been betrothed to Chandler for two years. Why come down all missish now?"

"Because two years ago, there was always the chance that he…" *Oh, dear! She was going to have to say it aloud and look horrid!* "That he wouldn't come back from the war," she admitted in a rush. "And if he didn't, I could plead a broken heart and stall another match until I was considered quite unmarriageable. And I enjoyed being able to go to London for the seasons and not be troubled by earnest swains or matrons clucking their tongues over why I was not wed yet."

Heavens! When she said the words aloud, shame filled her to overflowing. Was she truly as shallow and self-centered as she sounded? She tried again. "Just two weeks ago, I was happily going my own way, and then, with the arrival of that dreadful letter to Steppapa from Captain Chandler—that he had returned to England and was posting banns at his parish church and told Steppapa to do the same, and that he wanted to marry as soon as possible—well, everything has changed now. The past three Sundays I've cringed as I've listened to the banns being read. The servants are polishing every square inch of the house in preparation for Captain Chandler's arrival. And I never actually intended to marry. Anyone."

"You've had your fun, Chloe—two years of it—and now it is time for you to pay the piper."

"The piper? Or the devil? You told me he has horns and smells of sulfur."

George grinned. "Ah, Chloe. It is a brother's prerogative to tease."

"If it is just teasing, George, why hasn't Captain—excuse me—*Sir* Anthony Chandler presented himself ere now?"

Her brother shrugged. "He had to go home, post the banns in his parish and ready his house to bring home his bride. Besides, chit, it is not like you've never met the man. *Pleasantly presentable,* I believe were your words."

Her cheeks burned. If only she had known her polite social lie would grow legs and run away with her! *Captain Chandler? Yes, I remember him, Papa Charles. He was quite pleasantly presentable.* "Oh, George. That was my first season. I danced and chatted with so many young men that they blurred together until I could not tell one from another. When you and Steppapa said that Captain Chandler was being touted as the hero of Cuidad Rodrigo and asked if I recalled him, I lied. You see, there were so many men in uniform that spring. I've absolutely no recollection of him at all. Had I known he'd made an offer for me, I'd not have fibbed about remembering him. But then Steppapa arranged the details and signed the settlements and it was too late to cry off."

"Gads!" Her brother quirked an eyebrow. "S'truth? How could you have made such an impression on him when he made no impression on you whatsoever?"

"I do not know," she confessed. Tears stung the backs of her eyes. She really *was* all those awful things—shallow, fickle and rash! "I tried desperately to recall Captain Chandler after Steppapa told me we were betrothed, but nothing would come. All the young men in uniform were presentable. Some were very amusing and some were quiet. All were excited to be going to the peninsula. I could never sort them out with their names."

George shook his head in disbelief. "Well, Anthony was always a man who knew exactly what he wanted and went after it. He'd got orders to report back to Spain the very day he met you. Looks like he was right to tie you up before he returned to the peninsula. Some other chap would have spoken for you by now."

"Some other chap? But, George, I do not want to marry. Ever. And, were Captain Chandler truly taken with me, would he not have written at least one letter?"

"Not one? Hmmm. That is a little laconic, even for Tony. And you, puss? How many letters have you written him?"

Chloe pressed her lips together to stem the flow of vitriolic words and went back to the window to watch a sparrow soar heavenward. Blessed freedom. The very thing she yearned for. Within one week, she would belong to a man she had no recollection of, lying in his bed, and expected to behave as if all this were natural—allowing liberties and feigning pleasure. Oh, yes! She knew all about what husbands and wives did. Her friend Marianne had tearfully hinted at it when she'd come back from her honeymoon.

And that was not the worst of it! No, the worst was that Marianne—and all her friends who were now married—were at the mercy of their husbands. Men whose true character was not known to them until after the wedding. Men who now treated them indifferently at best, and cruelly at worst. Why, she could even recall when their stepfather first came calling on her mother. In order to win her consent, he'd indulged her and George, and even brought them sweetmeats and played games with them every time he came. They had thought he was wonderful. But after the wedding, when her mother was subject to his control, there were no more sweetmeats and games, and her mother spent much of her time in her room crying.

Chloe swallowed the lump in her throat and spoke without turning. "It is not Captain Sir Anthony Chandler, George. It is marriage altogether. I do not want to wed anyone. And, if you do not help me, I shall do something drastic."

"Define 'drastic,' puss. What sort of thing are you plotting?"

"I shall join a convent or run away or…or ruin my reputation."

George sobered. "First, puss, you cannot join a convent since we are not Catholic. Second, if you run away, you will just be found and dragged back to the altar. As for ruining, what would you do to accomplish that?"

"If I were kidnapped, that would not make me a social pariah since it could not be my fault, but it would certainly call my…virtue into question. Since Captain Chandler has political aspirations, he needs a wife with a spotless reputation if he is to rise in government and thus would not want me then." She lifted her chin with determination—a gesture she knew her brother would recognize as her signal that she would go through with any scheme that would liberate her from marriage.

George sighed and she knew by his frown that he was thinking of their stepfather and what he might do to force the marriage. "Very well, Chloe. You'd better tell me what plot you're hatching and I'll see what I can do."

Sir Anthony Chandler, so recently knighted for valor in the Battle of Toulouse that he had not accustomed himself to the honor of 'Sir' attached to his name, stretched his stiff leg out toward the fire. The last thing he'd expected to invade his library on a stormy night was his future brother-in-law. He sipped his sherry and stared into the flames while he digested the startling news.

"Abhorrent, eh?" he asked at length. "That's the word she used?"

George Faraday sighed deeply and sat forward in his chair. "A simple case of wedding vapors. It will pass."

"So she has sent you to beg off?"

"Our stepfather has forbidden that. She has concocted some harebrained scheme to queer the nuptials. Believe me, if I thought I could talk her out of it, I would. But Chloe is determined, and when she has set her mind on something, consider it a fait accompli."

Anthony ignored the sharp edge of disappointment that sliced through him. He was not the same man Miss Faraday remembered. The intervening years had changed him, physically and emotionally. And since he was decidedly changed, well, it was only fair to give the girl a chance to change her mind.

"Is it my injuries? Has someone told her—"

"No, Tony. She knows nothing of that."

He sighed. At least she hadn't rejected him because he was in some way diminished in her eyes. "I will grant her freedom readily enough."

"That's the problem, you see. As I've already said, our stepfather has forbidden it," George admitted. "And our mother falls into vapors when it is mentioned. She fears Chloe will be branded a jilt and no one will offer for her again. Our stepfather swears he will not come up with another dowry." George held up a hand to stop the protest Anthony was about to make. "He said he will not break the contract. He's left Chloe no choice. But the lack of future suitors or dowry does not daunt her. She vows that she never intends to marry at all."

Deep in thought, Anthony cupped his crystal glass in his left hand, running his right finger in lazy circles around the rim until the glass sang. Miss Chloe Faraday—a flurry of ebony curls, sparkling green eyes, full sensuous lips and a lithe supple form swathed in virginal white—the bright and pure image he had carried with him through untold horror and hardship. His touchstone. His reason to survive against seemingly insurmountable odds. The last thing left in his life he could hold untainted and untouchable. What a great waste if she never married at all.

On the strength of one dance the night before returning to the war, and scarcely daring to hope, he'd written her stepfather and offered marriage. He could still recall opening his letter of acceptance. He'd been awash in stunned disbelief and incredible pleasure. With Chloe Faraday waiting for him, he had a reason to go on.

Society considered him a good catch because of his good looks, family connections and future prospects. But he was, in any maid's eyes, a ruined man—oh, not in the social sense. His reputation had improved, if anything. But his injuries at Toulouse had left him a parody of what he'd once been. He had hoped this would not matter to Miss Faraday, but he'd been a fool to think so.

"*I* will call it off, George. She will not need a harebrained scheme. She has reason enough to regret her choice. I am hardly the man she knew."

George cleared his throat. "That, it would seem, is part of the problem. You see, she confessed that she has no memory at all of you."

Anthony stared at George in stunned disbelief. "Ah, the final insult. How flattering." Damnation! It had been one thing to be rejected because of his injuries, but quite another to be rejected because he'd been too inconsequential to even remember! Anger, fueled by hurt, made him want to hold her to her bargain.

He placed his glass on the side table and stood. If he sat too long, his wounded leg would stiffen and refuse to cooperate. There'd be very little dancing with pretty girls in his future. Lightning struck in the orchard outside his window and thunder rumbled over Chandler Hall, rattling windows and bringing a chill wind. As he turned back to his friend, he caught his own reflection in the darkened window. The scar that ran from his left jaw to his cheekbone was evident even in that murky reflection. He traced the ridge of angry red tissue. Yes, he was enough to terrify any gently bred woman.

George, to his credit, did not try to dismiss his bruised pride. He went to the decanter and poured another sherry for them both. "May I ask why you never wrote to Chloe?"

"Pen and paper were deuced difficult to come by in the trenches, George. On the rare occasions when I might have been able to send her communication of any kind, I could not think what to say. I had acted on impulse when I asked for her hand. Since she is your sister I knew she would be of good character, and that was recommendation enough for me. Her appearance…well, you know the effect such beauty has on a healthy man. But I had no idea what we might have in common, or how to engage her interest."

His friend nodded as if he understood. "And Chloe said she did not know what to write to a man she couldn't remember." He sighed and sat again. "I could not convince her to come talk to you. She says nothing good can come from such an ill-conceived courtship, and that it is marriage she scorns, not you."

"I should not have put faith in our ability to find common ground and make a go of it. Put a rifle or sword in my hands and I am more than competent. But that slip of a girl had me tied in knots."

"She has that effect on her entire family. Chloe is an unstoppable force. Quite the little manager. That is why I despair of talking sense into her. She has been willful most of her life, but she actually means well and has a very good heart. And no, before you ask it, she has not been unfaithful nor does she have another beau in mind."

Anthony shrugged. "The wedding is less than a fortnight away. Calling it off now would make us all look foolish. Sorry to say, George, but I'm inclined to think she'll have to go through with it."

George smiled, lifting his glass. "Let me tell you Chloe's little scheme. And then my own ideas. You will have to decide if the reward is worth the risk."

Lightning struck outside the window again and Anthony hoped that was not an omen of things to come.

Chapter Two

The moon was completely obscured by storm clouds outside the coach window, giving rise to Chloe's already rioting imagination. It was too late to change her mind. From the moment George had hired the private coach and a game-keeper to hide her, there'd been no turning back. George would be planting clues to her kidnapping even now, and by morning Steppapa would be off seeking bands of gypsies or chasing strangers.

She hugged herself against the chill night air and snuggled into the plush squabs. She was exhausted. It had been the longest day of her life, secretly packing her small valise, pretending to go to bed, and then sneaking out to meet the coach. She may as well get some sleep while she could.

"Ho there! Stand and deliver!"

The coach stopped so suddenly that Chloe was thrown off the seat and onto the floor. Her musings evaporated with the ring of that imperious shout. *Stand and deliver?* Were they being robbed?

She pulled herself onto the seat again, her heart beating wildly. The door flew open and a tall man whose face was obscured by a mask reached in and grasped her wrist with one hand while the other held a cocked pistol.

"Come out, lady."

She shivered at the deep timbre of the voice, at once compelling and terrifying. "I haven't anything of value," she said as her feet touched the ground. She swayed unevenly, so used to the rocking of the coach that her legs betrayed her.

The man caught her arm and steadied her. "Where is your trunk? Your valise?"

She pointed to the coach interior. At a nod from him, she retrieved the valise and laid it at his feet.

"Thank you, driver." The man tossed a coin to the coachman. "Off with you, now."

The coach rolled into motion, picked up speed and was gone. Dull witted from dozing, she finally made sense of the scene. This was not a highwayman, but the gamekeeper George had hired. Anxious to be off the road before another coach could come along, she lifted her valise and spun toward the gamekeeper. She hadn't realized he had come up behind her and the edge of her valise caught his left thigh.

He doubled over with a muffled curse. "Bloody hell!"

Frightened, she turned to flee but had not taken more than two steps when a muscular arm caught her around the waist and jerked her back against a solid chest. "Do not test me, Miss Faraday. We still have a ride ahead of us."

She tried to even her erratic pulse. Something about this man was not in the least servile. She wondered where George had found him.

In a few terse words, she was instructed to drop her valise, and then the gamekeeper lifted her into his saddle. Once she was settled, he swung up behind her and pulled her back against him, swinging the valise across her lap. The horse wheeled and they were off at a gallop.

* * *

Anthony's left leg throbbed as if it were on fire. The little vixen had damned near brought him to his knees. And if he didn't get her to the cottage on a remote part of his estate soon, she'd bring him to his knees in an entirely different way.

Her scent, a subtle hint of lily and spring meadows, coursed through his blood, and the heat of her bottom nestled against his crotch threatened his very sanity. The gait of his horse brought her against him in a rhythmic tempo. He gritted his teeth and steeled himself for a long ride.

"Sir," she asked in a small voice, "where are you taking me?"

"Where Faraday hired me to take you. Where you won't be found. My cottage is remote—is that not what you wanted?"

"Do you do this often?"

"I've made a career of it," he said, only half lying. Ransoming enemy soldiers had been just one of the many things he'd done for king and country the past four years. The rest was considerably uglier.

"Does it pay you well?"

He coughed. What a nosy little thing she was. "Good enough."

"Then why are you still doing it? Shouldn't you have retired years ago?"

"Perhaps I'm greedy."

"Ah." She was quiet for a moment, then asked, "How much are you going to ask for me?"

"Faraday said to start at five thousand pounds. Do you think your father will pay it?"

"He is my stepfather, and he is a shrewd negotiator. You may have to settle for very little."

"That would be my guess," he muttered. He smiled down at the top of her head. He had yet to see her face clearly. And she to see his. If she truly didn't remember him, his scars would not surprise her. Ah, but they would certainly repel her. How long could he put that off?

"Whatever you are running away from must be loathsome indeed," he prodded. He felt her quiet gasp beneath his hand around her rib cage. She was not skilled at deceit. How did one get by in the world without wiles? He found it rather endearing that she was so easy to read. Such a refreshing change from dealing with enemy soldiers, generals and politicians.

"What is your name, sir? Who are you?"

"Rush." Since that is what he'd done in this situation—rush in where angels feared to tread.

"Do you have a first name?"

He chuckled. "*Mr.* Rush, if you wish."

"It's a lie, isn't it, sir."

"You can hardly expect me to give my real name. Next you'll be asking my address. This is not a social occasion, Miss Faraday, but a business arrangement between your brother and me."

"By extension, sir, that would make you my employee, as well."

"It would not, Miss Faraday. I was quite clear that I'm no lady's maid. Your brother said you'd earn your keep."

By her sputtering, Anthony guessed that George hadn't mentioned anything of the sort. Odd, how he'd set Miss Faraday up as a paragon of all things feminine and virtuous, and the reality was far from that. She was imperious and demanding, and he wondered if he'd even like her by the end of day tomorrow. But how the bloody hell would he keep his hands off her?

The problem was, he hadn't had physical contact with a woman for two years—since he'd been on leave and danced with Miss Faraday. Meeting her again was bittersweet. Bitter, because she was not what he'd thought. Sweet, because the physical pull was still strong. Too strong.

* * *

A small light coming from a mullioned window cast a faint yellowish glow in the dark, and Chloe made out the form of a thatched cottage in a wooded vale. A paddock to one side contained two cows, a goat and a small chicken coop.

The gamekeeper stopped at the path to the door and swung down. She was surprised by his groan and pronounced limp. He must have stiffened during the ride. Perhaps he was older than she'd judged by his straight back and unbent frame. And by the strength of his arms supporting and bracing her during their ride. He took her valise and then circled her waist to lift her down.

"Go inside. I'll see to the horse and be in presently," he said as he set her on her feet.

"You…you are going to stay *here?*"

The man walked away from her, laughing and shaking his head. He removed his hooded mask but did not turn back to look at her. What an odd man. His eccentricities must come from living in such an isolated place.

She retrieved her valise, walked up the flagstone path and opened the door. The plank floors gleamed with an ancient patina and a burgundy rug in the center of the room looked worn but expensive. A brown leather club chair with a matching footstool sat by the banked fire and faced an over-stuffed sofa. At the opposite end of the room, there was another fireplace, larger and with compartments for cooking set into the bricks. A worktable, two wooden chairs, a counter with a sink and pump and bins conveniently placed in prox-imity to one another completed what she assumed was a kitchen. She shivered as she put her valise down, removed her bonnet and shrugged out of her pelisse.

The door in the far wall would lead to a back garden and

a privy, another door near the kitchen fireplace led to what she could only assume would be her private room. A ladder on the opposite side of the fireplace would lead to the loft and the gamekeeper's quarters.

She sighed. Alone in a house with a male servant—truly scandalous! This was enough to ruin her reputation. But how silly—she couldn't picture herself doing anything actually *wrong* with this man—a gamekeeper, and not a very pleasant one at that.

She lit a candle from the fireplace and placed it in a candlestick, then pumped water into an empty kettle and put it over the coals to heat. Chloe had never believed she would be grateful for her stepfather's favorite means of humiliation: forcing her to earn her keep in the kitchen. But now she needed to wash the grime of the road from her hands and face—and at least she knew how to boil water! Then, blissfully clean, she would fall into bed and let slumber overtake her, praying for sweet dreams and a speedy conclusion to her little dilemma.

When the kettle was boiling, Chloe carried it into the small bedchamber. As she suspected, there was a washstand with a pitcher and bowl and clean towels hanging on the side. She poured the steaming water into the bowl and returned the kettle to the kitchen. This time she took her valise and jacket with her and dropped them on the high featherbed covered in a worn green velvet counterpane. She kicked off her shoes and stripped down to her chemise, then returned to the washstand and splashed her face with warm water, then lathered with a used bar of French-milled soap from a soap dish before she rinsed and buried her face in a soft towel that smelled of spring breezes.

Anthony was not surprised to find the cottage silent. Miss Faraday had been drooping with fatigue by the time he'd set her on her feet. He glanced at the ladder to the loft. Evidently Miss Faraday had found her way up to the quarters he and Barnes, his manservant, prepared for her. They'd converted the entire loft to a bedroom at one end and a sitting room at the other, thinking she'd have more privacy above than below. Dormered windows on all four sides would give her ample light to read, do needlework or otherwise entertain herself.

A steaming kettle on the hearth made him smile. She had heated water to wash and left the rest for him. Good. He really wasn't prepared to deal with her tonight. She was inquisitive, imperious, stubborn—in short, everything George warned she was. And his pride still stung that she hadn't remembered him, and had dismissed him so summarily. Well, she might refuse to marry him, but she'd damn well remember him this time.

He threw his jacket over a chair, rolled his shirtsleeves up and washed at the sink. He'd shave tomorrow. Tonight he just wanted a late supper and his bed. He cut a slab of bread along with a wedge of thick yellow cheese and put them on a plate. An apple from the larder completed his dinner and he headed for his room. A copy of *Life of Nelson* was waiting for him on his bedside table. He longed to rest his throbbing leg.

He stopped dead in his doorway, speechless by what he found. There, her back to him as she stood at the washstand, was a scantily clad Chloe Faraday. She was wearing a filmy white shift trimmed in narrow lace that veiled her form but did not hide it. Her curves, the delicate tint of her skin, the shapely turn of her calf, were all evident in the most erotic scene Anthony could ever remember.

As he stood there, motionless, she lifted her arms and pulled the pins from her hair. The dark lengths tumbled in a riot down her back. When she bent slightly to splash water on her face, her shift molded to the sweet curve of her bottom and brought him to instant erection. Good God! He'd dreamed about this every night for the past two years and now he was within arm's reach of his dreams. The temptation to toss her onto the bed then and there almost got the better of him.

Merely a physical response, he told himself, but a moment more and... When she straightened again and buried her face in the towel, he pulled himself from his lurid thoughts and cleared his throat. "I see you've made yourself at home."

Miss Faraday jumped and spun to face him. Her eyes grew round and she threw her towel at him.

Anthony responded with instincts honed in the trenches. He dropped his plate and caught the towel, his eyes never leaving her as she seized her discarded dress on the bed and clutched it to her bosom. His plate hit the floor and shattered pottery burst upward, scattering across the planks.

Miss Faraday's shrill scream echoed through the vale.

Chapter Three

The man in her bedroom doorway was fierce and foreboding. His dark brows lowered over deep brown eyes and a livid scar slashed across his left cheek from cheekbone to jaw. There was a strength and calm determination in his stance that caused her to step back against the washstand. This was a man who could intimidate her with no more than a glance.

She clutched her dress against her bosom. "Who...what are you doing in my room?"

"Begging your pardon, Miss Faraday, but this is *my* room."

Good heavens! The gamekeeper! He'd been wearing a mask and she hadn't seen his face before. "Yours? But this is the only private—"

"Your room is upstairs, Miss Faraday."

"Up the ladder?" she asked incredulously.

"Is there another way up that I've missed?"

She did not appreciate his attempt at humor, if, indeed, it was humor. "You would know that better than I, Mr. Rush. Could we trade rooms during my stay here?"

"No, we really couldn't. Everything has been prepared for you in the loft. And I am certain I needn't remind you that it would be the best place for you should strangers arrive, or the authorities come looking for you."

"Authorities? But this isn't a real kidnapping."

He gave a small smile and the muscles on the left side of his face twitched terrifyingly. "Your stepfather does not know that, Miss Faraday. Do you really believe he will not call for help to find you?"

"I...I hadn't thought of that."

"I would hazard a guess that is not all you have not thought of. Actions have consequences, Miss Faraday. It is called 'paying the piper.'"

This echo of George's words made her uneasy. Oh, there would be consequences, but she'd thought they would all be hers to bear. She did not like to think of her mother's tears, but if her stepfather had only listened to reason... Sir Anthony Chandler was another matter entirely. He had contracted for a bride and then promptly forgotten all about her until it was convenient for him to remember. *He* deserved to suffer. She hoped *he* was worrying.

"Steppapa is not exactly the doting sort. Do you think the authorities will come?"

"I've taken all possible precautions to insure that they will not find us. No one knows where we are. Not even your brother."

Oh, dear! She did not like the sound of that—alone, isolated, and nary a soul to know how to find her. She was surprised that George had agreed to that. When she glanced back at Mr. Rush, he was giving her a speculative look, as if he were trying to measure her reaction.

"But," he said after a moment, "if they do come, and if they find you, we shall have to concoct some likely story."

"What sort of story?"

"You will have to lie. Say we are married or something."

She looked him up and down. Were it not for his scar, he

would have been good-looking, and compared to her London beaux, he cut a more dashing figure. His chestnut hair curled nicely at his nape and behind his ears, and his eyes betrayed a sharp intelligence. But he was a gamekeeper, for heaven's sake. A common, uneducated ruffian. "I shall be very good at hiding," she concluded.

"I imagine you are very good at avoiding whatever you wish to," he murmured.

There was an insult in those words but she did not want to examine it too closely. She was still standing in her chemise with her traveling dress pressed to her chest. She glanced at her valise on the bed. "Could you at least take my bag up?"

His full lips curved in a wicked smile and he was suddenly quite attractive despite his scar. "I am afraid not, Miss Faraday. You will have to manage for yourself."

She knew her mouth had dropped open, but she couldn't think how to reply to his refusal. "But I…"

"I'll turn my back, Miss." And he did.

Confused, Chloe gathered her belongings and stuffed them in her valise. He turned to keep his back to her as she edged past him through the doorway. She scurried up the ladder, one hand on the rungs and the other dangling her valise behind her while she prayed he was at least gentleman enough not to watch her from below.

The next morning, Anthony made a pot of strong tea—such a luxury in the trenches in the peninsula that the delicate aroma could still elicit a pang of pleasure. He took two cups, bowls and plates from the cupboard and placed them on the worn plank table. Would he ever grow accustomed to fresh foods again—cream, butter, sugar, vegetables and meats that hadn't been cured in vats of salt and brine? He certainly wouldn't take them for granted again.

Nor would he take deep dreamless sleep for granted again. Last night, in his dreams, Miss Faraday had been most accommodating. Her dark hair had fallen loose down her back and her fiery green eyes had looked straight into his soul. And not shirked. God…she'd been everything he'd dreamed and more than he'd hoped. *In his dreams.*

The reality was more harsh. She would need a spot of taming, that was certain. He did not relish the idea of spending the rest of his life with a woman who ordered him about like a servant—likely not her fault, but the result of a strong will. At least he would prefer to think her strong-willed rather than quarrelsome by nature.

The soft sound of footfalls padding across the loft floorboards indicated that Miss Faraday had risen. He stirred the porridge pot, ladled the contents into the two bowls and placed them back on the table with the sugar bowl and creamer. He'd picked a handful of violets and lily of the valley on his way back from the privy this morning and put them in a teacup in the center of the table, hoping the little gesture might make Miss Faraday feel more comfortable.

He turned when he heard the scuffle of a shoe on the rungs. Miss Faraday was descending the ladder, her rounded derriere the most prominent part of her from this angle. Such tempting seductive curves. He longed to caress them, but he had no wish to face the consequences of so reckless an act. Odd, how he'd faced an entire army with less trepidation than facing Miss Faraday. He turned back to his task rather than be caught watching her.

A moment later she cleared her throat to announce her arrival. He turned and gave her a polite nod.

"Good morning to you, too, Mr. Rush," she said.

Ah, a rebuke. Did she always bite the hand that fed her? "Sleep well, Miss Faraday?"

"The bed is quite comfortable," she allowed as she sat at the table. "But I lay awake for half the night."

"Is there a problem?"

"I regret my impulsiveness. Perhaps this was not a good idea. I mean…we are quite alone. And my mother is, no doubt, overwrought."

"No doubt," he agreed.

"I should go back."

"Too late for a tender conscience now, Miss Faraday. In for a penny, in for a pound, as they say."

She lifted her spoon and dipped it in her porridge with a little shudder. "But this is not what I thought it would be."

"Did you think it would be a lark? A pleasant way to spend a fortnight whilst you confounded your friends and family?"

She gave him so dark a frown that he almost felt sorry for her. "It was my betrothed that I sought to confound."

"To force him to break the engagement?"

"Yes."

He sat across from her and attacked his porridge with enthusiasm to cover his lack of a response. So, it was *him* after all. She did not want *him*. The notion caused him no small amount of anger.

"He…he is a stranger to me," she murmured after a moment of silence.

Was that the best excuse she could manage? "You wouldn't be the first woman to marry a stranger. Was the contract made without your consent?"

"N-not exactly." She looked up from her plate to meet his gaze and a shock went through him. Was it fear he saw in the green depths? Whatever it was, it stirred something primal in him—a need to possess and protect. And he resented her for it.

"Then what have you to complain of?" he asked.

She dropped her spoon. "I wouldn't expect you to understand, Mr. Rush. There are certain sensibilities that would be foreign to you."

That was going a little far. "Because I am a gamekeeper?"

"Because you are a man," she corrected.

A man? He hadn't known that to be a slur before. "I am wondering, Miss Faraday, what I could have done to warrant your contempt."

Her eyes grew wide. "Contempt? I haven't the slightest bit of contempt for you. Why, I scarcely know you. I only meant that, as a man, you couldn't hope to understand a woman's misgivings and fears."

"Would you understand what your betrothed might feel, bound to a woman he doesn't know? Perhaps he is regretting his rash offer, but honor demands he follow through. And what do you think he will make of *you?* Will he think he's made a good bargain?"

He pushed his bowl away and went to fetch a piece of paper, a pen and an inkwell. "Let's have this done," he said as he placed them on the table and poised the pen above the sheet. "How much should I ask?"

"I want to go home," she repeated.

"Too late. Believe me, I am having my own misgivings, but we are in too deep to back out now. Besides, Faraday said the ransom would be my pay. I've gone to considerable trouble to set this up and my future depends upon the outcome. Wouldn't want to cheat me of my rightful due, would you?"

"I…I suppose not. Perhaps *I* could pay you."

"Do you have five thousand pounds lying about?"

"You cannot be serious. That would make this an actual kidnapping."

"Not when you've set it up, Miss Faraday. If charges are brought, my guess is they would be against you—for fraud. But I think it will take a while for your stepfather to come up with that amount of cash. Which will happen first, I wonder? Will the authorities find us, or will you escape your wedding day?"

She narrowed her eyes and lowered her voice. "You would not dare tell anyone that George and I—"

He grinned and raised an eyebrow. "Would I not? What would I have to lose?"

"Why you unconscionable—"

"Careful, Miss Faraday. I am a desperate man, after all. Why else would I have got myself into this quagmire?" That much, at least, was true.

She pressed her lips together in a thin line and Anthony dashed off the ransom note in block letters. "Should I consider myself a captive, Mr. Rush?"

"I believe that might be for the best, Miss Faraday."

As she watched Mr. Rush ride away to post the ransom note, Chloe wondered how her plan had gotten away from her. It had taken on a life of its own and now proceeded even against her will. She had to find some way out of this, even if Mr. Rush refused to help. One thing was certain, she couldn't allow the man to stand in her way. She would have to rely upon her own wits.

Not that Mr. Rush hadn't any wits. To the contrary. But the gamekeepers she had known were rather rustic and had the sketchiest of educations. Not so with Mr. Rush. A man who kept a copy of *Life of Nelson* on his nightstand must have the curiosity to want to read it and the sophistication to understand it. He might be brusque and border on rude, but his manners were good enough when he chose to use them.

In fact, nothing about Mr. Rush was as it should be. He was an enigma. Where in the world had George found the man?

Well, 'twas done, and she would have to deal with it. Mr. Rush might be clever, but he was no match for her. And now, with his decision to actually ransom her, she was determined to escape him. She'd noted the direction he'd taken to post his message and knew that a town or village must lie in that direction. She'd bide her time, make her preparations, and then, when he least suspected it, she'd make her escape. She had several pounds to buy coach fare home. All she had to do was find the village.

Anthony's horse shifted in the small clearing and the leather of his saddle creaked as he dismounted. The day had grown overcast with a cold drizzle soaking him through as he waited. He was chilled to the bone and his injured leg stiffened. He flexed the muscles, alternately extending and bending at the knee several times to work the stiffness out.

When George Faraday appeared through the curtain of dripping leaves, he sighed with relief. The last thing he needed was to catch pneumonia when he had a helpless female on his hands.

George dismounted and gestured to Anthony's leg. "What do your doctors say, Chandler?"

"The limp will improve slightly but is with me for life. My scars will fade and be less visible, but will never be gone entirely. My strength and stamina will return in full—and I feel the evidence of that each day. And the memories and nightmares should diminish over time. An acceptable price for the victory, I suppose."

"All the same…" George's unfinished thought trailed off as he shook his head. "I wish you hadn't risked so much."

Anthony smiled and clapped George on the back. "We

can't always weigh the reward against the risk, Faraday, but I'd have done the same if I'd have known the outcome. I'm still breathing and the battle was won."

George removed his riding gloves and ducked beneath the protection of an oak tree. "Did you bring the ransom note?"

"Aye." He withdrew it from an inner fold of his jacket and handed it to George. "Your sister thinks I've gone to the village postmaster. If she knew I was meeting you, she'd have followed me. And now that I know her a bit better, I'll be surprised if your stepfather pays ransom."

George laughed. "Already?"

"You could have warned me."

"I thought I did."

"I wasn't prepared for the reality."

"Have you found anything redeemable in my sister?"

Anthony thought of the girl in a filmy chemise. Yes, indeed. There was something redeemable there. He changed the subject to a safer topic. "What is going on at your end."

"The 'kidnapper' left a note saying that Chloe would be well cared for and untouched as long as they negotiated in good faith. That has reassured them. Now that you're asking ransom, they will assume you are a man of your word and they will be able to get Chloe back."

Anthony shook his head in disgust. "I am loath to have them suffer the uncertainty. By your sister's own admission, she had not thought of how this would affect your parents."

"Steppapa is more angry than anything. Mother is in fine fettle, though. I've never see her so animated. I'd have wagered she would be in a constant swoon, but not so. She storms about the house, cursing kidnappers, their mothers and their mother's mothers. I never would have guessed all she needed to pull her from her constant melancholy was a cause."

"All the same, I dislike to have them suffer the uncertainty."

George shrugged. "I've seen the suspicion in old Hubbard's eyes. I think he has a notion that Chloe might be behind this. I told him I was riding north to inform you of this development and to ask if you will honor your contracts."

"Then tell him to proceed with the wedding preparations."

"Truly?"

"Aye. My father has arrived from Wales to attend the wedding. I told him I had last-minute business, and he asked no questions. He says he cannot wait to meet my bride." He paused to give a cynical laugh. "He may yet have a long wait. This morning she asked to call this off and return her home."

George's eyes widened. "She cannot. Our stepfather would blister her backside, disinherit us both and bring charges against you with a suit to force you to marry. You've got to hold her until the wedding, Chandler. And don't start feeling sorry for the chit. She knew she'd be committed the instant she began."

Sorry? For Miss Faraday? He snorted. "I'll do my part. But aside from your stepfather's state of mind, how are events unfolding?"

"Nothing is according to plan, I'm afraid." George sighed. "Hubbard hired a pack of bloodhounds to follow Chloe's scent to the crossroads where she caught the coach. Then he called out the local garrison who are now scouring the countryside in a radius around Litchfield. The plan is to widen their circle until they find her, or find someone who has seen her."

"Your sister's scheme is going to finish us all at the end of a hangman's noose. The government does not take kindly to this sort of deception." He shook his head. "I cannot believe I consented to go along with it."

George threw his words back at him. "Weigh the reward against the risk, Chandler."

He raised his eyebrows. Was Faraday joking?

Chapter Four

❧❧❧❧

Sunlight poured in an open dormer window and carried with it a hint of lilacs. Chloe stretched and pushed herself up against her pillows. She sighed as she glanced about her room. When she'd first climbed the ladder, she had expected to find rough quarters and a straw mattress. She had been amazed to find a lovely room divided into two sections—a sitting area with chairs and tables, and a bedroom with high four-poster bed, puffy down mattress and an embroidered quilt.

If she were to be honest, the room was more comfortable than her own room at home. The only problem with this one was that she had to access it up a ladder. But, after seeing that the gamekeeper was lame, she understood why she'd been given the loft. Curiosity tweaked her and she wondered how he'd come by his injury. A hunting accident, perhaps?

The smell of ham and eggs wafted to her from the room below and her mouth watered. She threw her covers back and shook out a willow-green day dress. She wouldn't put it past Mr. Rush to throw her food out if she wasn't downstairs before he cleared the table.

As she dressed, she began to plan her strategy. She'd fallen asleep before he'd come home last night, so she didn't know how his errand had gone. She doubted there had been any problems. Posting a letter in the local village could not be too difficult. Regardless, she would have to lull him into a sense of complacency if she were to make an escape. She would leave him some money, though. That was the least she could do to compensate the man for his troubles. She was surprised that George hadn't paid him already. Unless…was Mr. Rush cozening her to get more money?

She made her bed, brushed her hair and tied it back with a ribbon. Assuming a pleasant demeanor, she backed down the ladder hoping Mr. Rush was not watching her inelegant descent, but his attention was focused on his plate. Thank heavens the man was so single-minded. She cleared her throat as she approached the table.

"Good morning, Mr. Rush."

He glanced up at her and she was surprised to see his haggard expression. "Good morning, Miss Faraday."

"Did you post your ransom note?"

"Everything went as it should," he allowed.

"Grand."

He'd set a place for two, so she sat and helped herself from the plate in the center of the table. The eggs were cooked through and the ham was crisp around the edges. First the porridge and now this. Cooking was not his strong suit, she decided. Ah yes, this would be a perfect way to both lull and spite him! "Mr. Rush, I have been thinking about what you said—about me earning my keep. If you will allow it, I will be pleased to do the cooking."

He gave her a wry smile. "Is my cooking not to your liking?"

Her cheeks burned as she gave her attention to her plate. How could the man see through her so easily? "There is little else for me to do," she said.

"I like my breakfast before midmorning, Miss Faraday. There are no social events in the forest to keep us up until the wee hours and therefore no reason to lie abed until noon."

Chloe gritted her teeth. "I shall rise early, sir."

He was silent a long moment, then nodded. "Shall I assume you have some experience in preparing meals?"

"None," she lied smoothly, "but how difficult could it be?" A muscle jumped along his jaw as he bit back a retort and she nearly laughed. Oh, what a perfect way to torture him for his ill-tempered remark about lying abed. She began to plan for the interesting dishes she would make him.

She ate a forkful of eggs, which were not as bad as they looked, and decided to see if she could engage him in conversation. "How soon do you expect to hear back on your ransom demand?"

"Another day or so."

"So soon? Heavens, I thought it would take longer to pass messages at this distance."

"I can see how that would better suit your plans, Miss Faraday. The longer the delay, the more effective the dodge."

"As I told you, sir, I have changed my mind."

"Not about the marriage," he reminded her. "Just about the method."

"True, but that makes no difference to my scheme."

"It does to your betrothed."

She gave him an uncomfortable shrug. "You are quite earnest in my fiancé's defense. Yesterday you said he was probably regretting his proposal. If that is so, he should be thanking me for my little scheme."

He sat back in his chair and regarded her over the rim of his cup. "What is it about marriage that disturbs you, Miss Faraday? Or is it just marriage to this particular man?"

Oh, dear. There was that question again. How could she

ever confess the truth to a perfect...well, not-so-perfect stranger? "Really, sir, you presume too much on so short an acquaintance."

"Do I?" He arched one dark eyebrow and it made his scar pull the muscles of his cheek into a devilish grin. "I think I presume just right. Are you ever likely to see me again once this affair is over and you are safely back home? No. And am I the sort of man who would discuss what you tell me? Again, no. I'd say I am an opportunity not to be missed. Really, Miss Faraday, why not avail yourself of my ear?"

There was something very tantalizing in his offer. Someone to be herself with? What would be the harm? She might even be relieved to say those things aloud. After all, she didn't really care what he thought but it might be easier if he was not quite so dangerous looking. Or if he just didn't make her feel so uneasy when he watched her.

"Come now, Miss Faraday. Can it be that difficult?"

"Perhaps if I knew more about you," she said.

"What do you need to know? We aren't going to tea, or sharing a dance at a ball. You needn't arrange a proper introduction."

Yes, she supposed that was true. And if she knew him better, she might care what he thought. Yes, it was better this way. Impersonal. "I...I shall consider it, sir."

He gave her a grin and something inside her tightened. "That is surprisingly circumspect of you," he said. "Why not jump in? Surely you don't care what I think of you?"

"No, I don't," she lied, angry that he'd guessed what she was thinking. "Very well. I object to both the man and the marriage."

"On what grounds?"

"The man because he is a cold fish, and the marriage because it is devoid of affection."

Mr. Rush folded his arms over his chest and tilted his head to one side. "Affection? You expect affection in marriage?"

"Yes. I think it is much nicer to feel some warmth for a man with whom you will, uh, share certain intimacies."

"You want affection first, and then intimacy?"

"I believe affection is necessary to any close friendship. I should hope I could regard my husband as a friend. If not, then we would be doomed to a loveless marriage. And if he is the sort of man who cannot feel friendship for a woman at all, then…why, then he is not the sort of man I would want for a husband."

"Did you ever think to go to him and learn what sort of man he is?"

"Mr. Rush, my fiancé never wrote me so much as a single word during our engagement. Two years, sir. Does that not speak of coldness and indifference? At best he is a crashing bore. I know all I need to know by his silence."

"How many letters did you write him?"

"I did not have his address."

He arched an eyebrow at her.

"Do not think to put this off on me," she huffed.

"I think you share a part of the blame, Miss Faraday. And, to be honest, don't you?"

She squirmed. "I suppose I could have acquired his address. But instead I had my news from returning officers and by way of my brother. But it all seemed…as if it were happening to someone else. It did not feel as if it had anything at all to do with me."

A fleeting look of sympathy crossed Mr. Rush's face. "I can see now that he should have written. That was a mistake. How were you to form a bond from silence?"

She sighed with relief. She had begun to think she was being unreasonable. Mr. Rush was the first to agree with her.

Even her mother and brother had not understood how the silence had separated her emotionally from her betrothed.

"Thank you, Mr. Rush. I appreciate—"

"But," he interrupted, "running away never solved anything. Have you thought that he might be too shy, too vulnerable to risk rejection by exposing his feelings in writing?"

She tried to imagine the man who'd been celebrated as the hero of Cuidad Rodrigo and who had been cited for valor in many other battles as being too timid to scratch a few lines on a piece of paper. Finally, she shook her head. "No, that never would have occurred to me, and I cannot imagine it now. The man killed people for a living, and you would have me believe him too sensitive to address a mere slip of a girl?"

Mr. Rush winced. "That is a bit harsh. And you are more than a mere slip of a girl, Miss Faraday. You are a headstrong female and a force to be reckoned with. But I sense there is more than the lack of a letter bothering you."

Yes, but she had no intention of confessing what it was! "It is your turn, sir. Tell me something about yourself."

He looked nonplussed. "I do not like to talk about myself. And, anyway, there is nothing to say."

"Then tell me how you came by your limp."

He placed his cup on the table and stood. "I have work to do. I will be gone most of the day."

Anthony did his best to keep busy until nightfall. He chopped an absurd amount of wood considering that it was nearly summer, then set to work repairing the livery barn. The property had fallen into disrepair after his deployment to the peninsula and the servants had worked around the clock two days to make it ready for Miss Faraday's arrival. They'd been told that a friend of his was going to use it for the summer as a convalescent retreat. Another of the half-truths he'd been telling lately. And, at the moment, he wasn't convalescing. He was dodging his fiancée's verbal darts.

In fact, he was still smarting from their conversation that morning. Why couldn't she have asked him something easy? About his real name, or if he'd always been a gamekeeper, something vague about his family or what he planned to do with the ransom money?

But no. Miss Faraday could certainly cut right to the heart of a matter. Leave it to her to find his greatest vulnerability and poke it until it bled. He didn't want to talk about the battle, nor his fallen comrades. He still couldn't think of the explosion that had nearly taken his leg, or of the battlefield operation to save it that, of necessity, had been done without anesthesia. Those were horrors best left unspoken.

He lit a lantern and hung it from a beam, then splashed his face with water from the trough. Lacking a towel, he lifted his shirt over his head and used it to dry himself.

This whole kidnapping scheme was ill-conceived and doomed from the start. The fatal flaw in George's plan was that all hell would break loose when Chloe Faraday found out who he really was! And once she knew, she would still refuse to go through with the marriage. She wouldn't marry him? She didn't want him? That was her decision and her right. But he'd damned well know the reason why. She owed him that much.

She'd struck a chord in her analysis of their problem. Silence did not forge bonds. Even clumsy attempts at courtship would have been better than none. Certainly she would feel no particular loyalty to a man who'd arranged a marriage without a single personal message. Even so, there was more to her refusal. There *had* to be more.

But tonight he'd have to avoid her. He needed a deep dreamless sleep without lurid unsettling thoughts.

* * *

Chloe crossed her arms over her chest as she looked at the plates of bubble and squeak she'd made with the leftover ham. They were lukewarm at best by now. Mr. Rush had not come in from his chores and she suspected he was trying to avoid her. A minute ago, she'd seen the light of a lantern through the open barn door. This morning he'd been anxious for her to do something to earn her keep, and now he was ignoring her. Of course, she didn't actually *want* his company, but she'd gone to considerable trouble to prepare his dinner and she wasn't about to let him turn it into a congealed mess fit only for swine.

She untied her apron and dropped it on her chair. Tucking a curl that had escaped her ribbon behind her ear, she marched across the yard to see what was keeping him. She opened her mouth to call to him as she entered the barn but her rebuke died on her lips.

Mr. Rush was standing at the trough, bare from the waist up. The muscles in his back bunched and smoothed again as he used his shirt to wipe his face. His dark hair was damp and scattered crystalline drops of water into little rivulets down his neck and back. For some unaccountable reason, she found the sight fascinating. The expanse of creamy flesh, taut over straining muscles, was deeply stirring. He shivered and hung his shirt on a peg next to the lantern before splashing the cold water over his chest and arms.

She wanted to say something, to retreat or to warn him that he was not alone, but she was mesmerized by the sight of him—so natural, so raw and primal. He shivered and reached for his shirt again, half turning as he did. He stopped when he saw her standing in the open doorway and dropped his hands to his sides.

He stood quietly, studying her face as she stared at his

chest. A light matting of dark hair curved in a deep V downward to the waistband of his trousers. Strong square-set shoulders and stronger arms tapered into large hands which were flexing his fingers into fists. He was tense. Was he angry?

Her attention snapped up to his face, as unreadable as always, but betraying a faint expectation. He was waiting for her to speak, but she couldn't think what to say. Nor could she move when he came toward her. She thought he would pass her and go to the cottage, but he stopped in front of her, so close she could feel his breath on her cheek.

"Did you want something, Miss Faraday?"

Heat swept through her and she looked down to break the hold of his gaze. "I...came to tell you that supper is getting cold."

He stepped closer still and planted his hands against the wall planks on each side of her. A bead of water dropped from the dark curl over his forehead and fell against her throat. She shivered as it trickled down between her breasts.

He said nothing, but his mere presence was so compelling that she looked up again. He was waiting for her, and she had the feeling he'd have waited all night like that. He bent to her and his lips were as soft and pliable as velvet when they brushed against hers. A slow tingling began at the base of her spine and worked its way upward, causing her to catch her breath. She'd been kissed a very few times before, but this was quite beyond anything she could have imagined. He nibbled her lips, urging them open, then his tongue entered to reach inside her, taste her, tease and tantalize her.

When her knees went watery and she thought she would swoon with the utter deliciousness of it, he stopped, leaning lower to trace the course of that little droplet with his tongue from her throat to the top of her gown. She gasped in shock, completely unprepared for such familiarity.

Then Mr. Rush straightened and gave her a small smile. "I hope it's still warm," he said as he passed her to the door.

Chapter Five

Anthony wasn't surprised when Chloe came into the cottage and went straight to the loft without a word. He couldn't blame her. When he had turned and seen her standing just inside the barn door, her eyes as large as saucers, he had a sudden pang of what marriage to her would mean—days of finding her at the turn of a corner or the opening of a door, nights with her wrapped in his arms and silenced by his kisses. He had definitely overstepped his boundaries. And now he'd caused another problem. How was he to resist Chloe when he knew she tasted like dark, warm honey? How would he watch her across the table without seeing that droplet of water glistening as it trickled down between her breasts?

He sat and looked at the bubble and squeak she'd made for supper. It seemed such a homey and ordinary dish for such an exotic creature to make. Almost as if the queen had made porridge. It certainly looked good. He lifted the fork and took a huge bite, anticipating the savory taste of cabbage and onion mixed with ham and potatoes—and almost choked.

He reached for the teapot and drank from the spout. Good

God! Had she used an entire cellar of salt? He should have listened when she warned that she didn't know how to cook. After he managed to purge the worst of the taste from his tongue, he went to the larder to see if there was something else to eat. Nothing simple. Not even an apple.

It was late. He was tired. He'd rather go to bed hungry than cook at this hour. He cleared the table and, just as he was about to scrape the contents of Chloe's plate into a pail for the swine, he had a sudden suspicion. He retrieved his fork and took a cautious bite.

Delicious! Quite the best bubble and squeak he'd ever had. He turned and looked at the ladder. The minx had gulled him. She'd oversalted his, but not hers. Was she up there now anticipating his reaction? How amusing! He finished the plateful standing up and watching the ladder while he mused over his guest's sense of humor. He'd have to think of a way to pay her back.

Not surprisingly, he still wanted his pound of flesh, but he had just decided to go through with the marriage. After seeing her in her nightgown, after sampling her kisses and falling victim to her practical jokes, he could not imagine marrying anyone else.

Chloe glanced around the kitchen the next morning, wondering what had become of last night's dinner. Mr. Rush had washed up and put the dishes away. When she found the remains of the bubble and squeak in the slop bucket she had to bite her lower lip to keep from laughing aloud. Since there was no breakfast on the table, she set to work. She had heard Mr. Rush leave earlier and had glanced out her window to see him heading for the barn. He was a brave man if he was willing to eat her cooking again.

She filled a pot with water and hung it over the fire to boil.

She found a basket of eggs and brought bread, butter, jam and a wedge of deep yellow cheese from the larder.

After pouring boiling water into the teapot on the table, she put the pot back on the fire, then sliced the bread and placed it on a rack to toast. She stirred the water in the pot into a swirl and cracked two eggs into the center. When they had set enough to leave alone, she hurried to the door and called across the yard.

"Mr. Rush! Breakfast is ready."

Yes, indeed. The smell of burning toast told her it was done to perfection. She hurried back to the kitchen and used her apron to place the toast on a plate. Grabbing a slotted spoon, she went to stand by the pot until she heard Mr. Rush's footsteps approach.

When he came in, all her evil intentions evaporated. The dark hair tumbling over his forehead made him look younger and vulnerable. And, though she tried desperately not to, she couldn't help but remember the feel of his lips on hers—of the seductive trail of his tongue down her throat to the V of her gown.

Oh! This would never do. He was a kidnapper! Well, a hired one.

"Good morning, Miss Faraday." He went to the table and sat. "I trust you had a good night's sleep?"

"I slept like a stone. It must be the country air." She carried the boiling pot to the table and for one brief moment, she caught a look of panic on his face. Then she dipped the spoon into the water and lifted the eggs. When she put them on his plate, they nearly bounced.

"Ah, just the way I like them," he said, lifting his fork.

What was wrong with him? Coddled eggs were supposed to be soft. Chloe sat across from him and eyed him suspiciously. As she was pouring out his tea, he took a piece of toast, scraped off the worst of the burn and applied a thick layer of butter.

She cut a chunk of cheese and nibbled on it while she watched him eat with something close to appreciation. This wasn't precisely the way she'd planned it. And when he wiped the remaining yolk up with a piece of black toast and popped it in his mouth, she was incredulous.

He looked up at her as he sat back with his tea. "Not hungry, Miss Faraday? Try to eat something. You must keep your strength up, you know."

"I'm not hungry," she said.

"Why, look at you. You're barely enough to hold on to. What will your betrothed say?"

"Nothing."

He grinned. "You are not even going to give him the courtesy of a rejection to his face? That's quite ill-bred of you. Surely he deserves that much."

Her conscience tweaked her. "I…I don't know what I will do. I suppose that once I go home he will be back at his estate. 'Twill be easier to write a letter, if he and Steppapa have not already settled the particulars."

"What if he still wants you?"

"He won't," she said with a haughty lift of her chin. "He has political aspirations, and my sullied reputation would be a liability."

Mr. Rush studied her for a moment before replying. "I would not count on that, Miss Faraday. I can see why he would not want you if he knew the lengths to which you have gone to avoid him, but he doesn't. Therefore, it would be rather mean-spirited of him to renounce you in your hour of need."

"My hour of need?"

"When your reputation is being whispered about behind fans and over brandy while all of society speculates on what your dastardly kidnapper must have done to you? Yes, you will be the ton's favorite gossip."

They would think she had...no! "What would *you* know about the ton?" she lashed out.

She could have bitten her tongue the moment the thought-less words escaped. Something hard flickered in his eyes and the words hung between them, cold and unforgiving. Oh, how unkind! How had she come to this? Demeaning those less fortunate?

His mouth quirked and he placed his cup back in the saucer with care. "Nothing, of course. But, now you mention it, Miss Faraday, I believe you may be right. Your betrothed may well count himself a lucky man to have a second chance to dust his hands of you."

Oh, why did he always have to needle her? All the guilt and sorrow she'd felt a moment ago fled. "You didn't seem to think so last night, Mr. Rush!"

"A momentary lapse in my usual good judgment," he said as he stood. "And, by the way, I have already had word from your stepfather regarding ransom."

"When?"

"This morning while you were lolling in bed, I went to the spot we arranged to leave messages and found it there."

"Then you shall soon be quit of me."

"Alas, no." He shrugged as he paused in the doorway. "Your stepfather has refused to pay. Not a farthing, he said. He made me a rather generous offer, though. For a mere five hundred pounds, he will take you back. It will take me a while to raise that kind of money."

Chloe nibbled on the last little wedge of cheese. She had left the gamekeeper's cottage at midday when Mr. Rush was busy elsewhere. It was dusk now and the fading light was already playing tricks with her eyes. When the trees shifted in the breeze, the leaves cast menacing shadows across her path. Surely she would see the village lights soon, or hear children playing—something, anything—to tell her civilization was close. It had to be!

She'd set out in the direction Mr. Rush had taken to post the ransom note and she should have encountered someone by now. Surely her stepfather would take her back. He had to, didn't he? She fought the lump in her throat. She knew her mother loved her, though.

She'd sorted through a miscellany of her many sins and, yes, she'd been quite a handful for her poor mother and stepfather to manage. Looking back, she could see that she'd been willful and stubborn. But she'd always meant well. And now it had come down to this—her family wouldn't even ransom her, and she had to rescue herself because no one else would.

How deeply disappointed they, and even George, must be in her. How horribly her behavior must have injured them. And how could she have been so blind to it all? She hadn't even realized what she'd become until she'd injured Mr. Rush with her snobbery. Tears ran down her cheeks as she thought of the quick look of pain that passed over his face before he'd covered it with sarcasm. Until that moment she hadn't realized that she *did* care what he thought.

She marched along the forest path, vowing to do better in the future. She'd be so sweet and docile that her mother would call her 'my angel' again.

An owl hooted in the gloom and she realized that night was coming on fast. Something rustled in the underbrush and she thought of the wild boar her stepfather had shot last winter. Were there bears or wolves? The trees obscured the moon, and soon she'd have no light at all. Her growing sense of unease escalated to fear, and she knew it would soon be panic.

"Oh, please," she whispered, "let me find my way, Lord, and I will be as biddable as you please."

There was a subtle shift in the wind that brought a familiar scent her way, and the hair on the back of her neck stood up. She stopped and stood very still.

"As biddable as *I* please?" Mr. Rush's voice whispered in her ear.

She gasped and whirled to face him. How had he come upon her so silently?

"I was a tracker among other things," he said at her look of astonishment.

She was so relieved to see him that she threw her arms around his waist and hugged him so tight he laughed. "I thought I was lost," she admitted.

"You *were* lost, Miss Faraday. You've been going in circles. Didn't the scenery begin to look familiar? The road is in that direction." He pointed to a path heading south.

"I…I didn't notice. My mind was full of other things."

"As interesting as that sounds, I think we'd best get home."

She let go of him and stepped back. "But why do you want me? I am a liability now that my stepfather has refused to pay ransom."

"Oh, Miss Faraday," he sighed "I regret tweaking you with that lie. I just wanted to stop you from being so smug."

"I was smug?" she asked in a faint voice.

"A little. I've noticed that the more I tease you, the more high-handed you become."

She should be furious with him but she could only sigh. That was a tendency she would have to overcome if she was to become biddable. "I am sorry I insulted you," she muttered. Tears filled her eyes. How could she have been so cruel?

"That is a credit to you, Miss Faraday," he said, tilting her head upward and wiping at her tears with his thumbs. She held her breath as his deep brown eyes grew softer. "Forgiven."

Her heart fluttered and she wondered if he was going to kiss her. He bent closer, resting his forehead against hers. His voice was half moan and half sigh when he spoke. "We'd best get you home."

He released her and she looked around, trying to reclaim her senses. She'd lost all notion of direction in the dark. "Which way is home?"

"*Home,*" he said with an odd inflection, "is another mile or two and then across a meadow. I came after you on foot so we shall have to walk, I'm afraid. Follow me, and let me know if I'm going too fast."

But he didn't go too fast at all. His limp, more pronounced than ever before, revealed that his leg was bothering him. When she suggested they stop for a rest, he offered to carry her.

"I hadn't realized you have such a delicate constitution, Miss Faraday," he said.

"Delicate?" she scoffed. "I'll show you who's delicate."

He chuckled. "I wondered how long your new resolve to be biddable would last."

Chapter Six

*P*ain ripped through his leg, slicing muscle and shattering bone. He was afraid to look—afraid of what he'd see. The odor of gunpowder, the deafening thunder of cannon shot and the clash of metal assaulted him from every direction. Then screaming and the coppery smell of blood. His heart pounded erratically. A sudden sense of his own mortality hit him with a thud in the center of his chest. He wasn't getting out of this one alive.

The night was as dark as the great abyss but for the muzzle flash of guns being fired. Crawling low and inch by inch, he dragged the unconscious O'Neil back toward British lines. It would be nothing short of a miracle if they made it.

Above the cacophony he heard Colonel Aldrich shouting. "Leave him, Chandler! Save yourself, man!"

No. O'Neil was his man and his friend. He wouldn't leave him behind. He'd lost too many men and he wouldn't sacrifice another.

A grenade exploded somewhere nearby. Shrapnel hissed around them and the percussion of the blast deafened him even as a razor-sharp fragment opened his flesh from cheek-

bone to chin. Red sprayed into his eyes and he realized it was his own blood.

He claimed another inch of ground, then another, still dragging O'Neil. A cannonball struck a nearby wagon and ignited the tinder-dry wood. Now that they were clearly visible in the firelight, he and O'Neil would be target practice for the French.

A hail of gunfire miraculously missed him, but he felt O'Neil's body jerk as if he'd been hit. Thank God he was unconscious. Finally, he gained the edge of the trench. With one last push of his good leg, he rolled into it, O'Neil tumbling with him. Exhausted, riddled with pain, he closed his eyes to rest a moment. Just a moment. Wright was still out there. As soon as he caught his breath, he'd go back for him.

The Colonel's voice flowed in and out of his consciousness. Disjointed words that made no sense. O'Neil...the poor bastard. Chandler...more dead than alive. Get...sawbones.

"Wright," he murmured, trying to make them understand that he had to go back.

The Colonel leaned over him and gripped his shoulders, pressing him down when he tried to sit. "Hold on, Chandler. We've sent for a stretcher."

"O...O'Neil?"

"Sorry, son. He didn't make it."

No! No...

"No!"

Pale moonlight filtered through the surrounding trees into the dormered windows, illuminating the open loft. Chloe had left the window panes open to the fragrant spring air and watched the ever-changing pattern of moon-shadowed leaves dance across her ceiling. Branches from the nearby tree tapped against the window pane in a soft night music.

She punched her pillows again and sat up. She couldn't sleep for thoughts of Mr. Rush. He mostly varied between abrupt and just plain rude, but in the woods tonight, he'd been almost playful. She liked that man best, when his eyes were crinkled at the corners with a laugh and a devilish smile on his face. Oh, if he could only be that way more often! And if only he could be handsome and not a common gamekeeper.

Something was troubling him—something more than her ransom. She was perceptive enough to know that, and also to know that he was not the sort to talk about his troubles.

She sighed and plucked at the blue silk ribbon of her best nightgown, a part of her trousseau that her betrothed would never see because there would never be a wedding night. Staring out at the moon, she whispered, "Oh, Lord, I've made such a dreadful mess of things. I cannot trust myself anymore. Please, guide me to thy will."

A frightful racket from below brought her bolt upright again. She could swear she heard Mr. Rush shouting "No!" at the top of his lungs, followed by the clamor of things falling or being knocked over. Had they been found out? Were they being robbed?

She grabbed the pewter candleholder as she popped out of bed, then paused at the top of the hatch, trying to see below without betraying herself. The noise had stopped, but she could hear someone breathing heavily. Had Mr. Rush been injured? When there was no further noise, she backed silently down the ladder, still clutching the candleholder.

The banked fire cast a reddish glow through the single room and she saw Mr. Rush, his bare feet and legs sticking out below the hem of a dressing robe, pouring wine into a glass he held with a shaking hand.

Her heart still racing with excitement, she dropped her arm

to her side and exhaled a deep sigh of relief. She liked to think she'd be fierce enough to hit someone over the head, but she couldn't be certain.

Mr. Rush turned at the sound of her sigh. There was a wild, haggard look in his eyes and his hand still shook as he waved her back. "Sorry I woke you, Miss Faraday. Go back to bed. All is well."

"You? That din was you?" She laughed and put the candlestick on the table. "Heavens, I was terrified! Did you lose your bearings on your way to the privy?"

He sat and held his glass with both hands as he guided it to his mouth. Three gulps later, he focused on her again. "Wasn't going to the privy."

She stood across from him and studied his face. He wouldn't meet her eyes and, closer, his face looked more ravaged than haggard. In fact, he looked the way she felt after an especially vivid nightmare. She suspected he could use someone to keep him company. "Ghosts?" she asked.

"In more ways than you could possibly imagine, Miss Faraday." Steadier now, he drank again.

She nodded and refilled his glass. "I have nightmares, too. Does the wine help?"

"Smooths the ragged edges," he admitted.

"I shall remember that." She smiled, trying to diffuse the tension. She took another glass from the cupboard, sat across from him and poured herself half a measure. "I think I could use some to calm *my* nerves. I'm still feeling unsettled."

He looked up at her. "I prefer brandy or whiskey. In truth, Miss Faraday, even rotgut would help."

"Since I do not have access to rotgut, I shall have to content myself with wine."

His lips curved up in a tiny smile. It was a start. She took a small sip and closed her eyes to savor the warmth that seeped downward. When she opened them again, he was staring at her, an odd expression on his face.

"Does it help, Miss Faraday?"

"Yes, it does." She sighed and sat back in her chair. "What do you dream about, sir?"

"Not dreams as much as memories."

"Oh!" The thought sobered her. Memories bad enough to cause him to cry out in the night and require alcohol to calm must be very bad, indeed. "Will you tell me about them?"

He glanced away from her and took another drink. "That tale is not fit for your ears."

"Try me, sir."

He shook his head and would not look at her.

She remembered how he had induced her to tell why she didn't want to marry. "Think of me as an opportunity not to be missed, Mr. Rush."

A long moment passed while he stroked the rim of his glass. Finally, he lifted his chin and looked at her. "Feel free to stop me when you've heard enough, Miss Faraday."

When he began, Chloe listened calmly, trying to imagine the horror of war that so many young men experienced in recent years. At times it had seemed that half the eligible young men in Britain had been sent to exotic locations, but she had never pondered what they might be going through, or how deeply they might have suffered. The lump in her throat grew thicker as Mr. Rush described the hail of gunfire and the cannon blasts that had left them nearly deaf for days on end. She laughed when he told her stories of his best friends and the jokes they'd played on one another.

And when his voice grew low and dark, she listened to what he didn't say and knew there was much he hadn't told her. At last, he poured another glass of wine and stared blindly into the kitchen fireplace, falling silent.

She did not like to see him in such a state and wished she could do something for him, something to take the pain away, or to help him forget. When George had made her talk about her dreams, they had lost their power over her, as if the act of voicing them had somehow vanquished them. Perhaps she could do the same for him.

She reached across the table and lay her hand on his arm. "Memories to treasure, Mr. Rush, but you have not told me about your dream tonight, or why it made your hands shake and—"

He tossed off the rest of his wine and stood. The knuckles of his hands turned white as he gripped the back of his chair. "Leave it alone, Miss Faraday."

She stood, too, feeling helpless but knowing if she did not make him talk this time, she would not have another chance. "I want to help you, Mr. Rush. I want to make those dreams go away."

He began pacing, staring at the floor, ignoring the uneven gait that must be causing him pain. "The fighting was fierce that night. We lost three-quarters of our men in the first half hour. Then Colonel Aldrich ordered us to storm the walls. He said it was our only chance. I tried to warn him… The few of us who made it that far fought until our ammunition gave out. The French were firing straight down on us and pouring boiling tar over the ramparts.

"By the time the command sounded the retreat, there were damn few of us left. I think we'd all been wounded, but O'Neil was the worst. I dragged him with me, hoping to get to the trenches in the dark and before the French regrouped. They fired grapeshot on us. The doctors said that's what tore my leg open, but that part is a blur. Then a blast set the supply wagon on fire and we were like paper targets. Later, they told me O'Neil was dead even before I got him back to our lines.

"I tried to go back for Wright, but…I don't remember anything after…the doctors trying to save my leg. By the time the fever broke, I was aboard a ship bound for Dover."

"I'm so sorry," she whispered. "I wish there were something I could do to help."

His eyes were bleak when they met hers. "I don't want your pity," he said. "But if you want to help, then help me make the dreams go away, if only for tonight."

She couldn't bear his desolation. "Anything, Mr. Rush."

He pushed his chair aside, knocking it to the floor. Before she knew what he was about, he had pulled her into his arms. "Lie *with* me, Chloe," he murmured against her lips. "Let me make love to you. Let me lose myself in you. Let me pretend, for a moment, that you love me and want me. Lie *to* me, Chloe."

His intensity startled her, and her own treacherous heart betrayed her, beating as wildly as his and urging her to accept his terms. "I cannot," she sighed.

"You can. Say *yes*. Just the single word. I will do the rest, Chloe, and we shall both find sweet oblivion in that word."

Oh, all she could think about was the feel of his lips on hers and the shocking way his tongue drew forth a wild yearning. How could she want this so much when she knew that whatever lay at the end of it had brought her friends to tears? And how could something so delightful, so compelling, cause tears?

He must have read her moan as acceptance, because he swept her up and carried her to his room, never breaking the kiss. She wanted to protest, to stop him, but instead she wrapped her arms around his neck and fell deeply into a passionate fog.

He pulled the ribbon at the neckline of her nightgown, and pushed it down over her shoulders. His hands were callused and rough but his touch was gentle as he traced a line from her shoulder blade down to her breasts. Her heartbeat accelerated and she struggled to find her voice, but his mouth was still on hers, still claiming something of her soul.

Then he pushed her nightgown lower and touched her almost reverently. One finger circled her areola and it firmed to his touch. Little tingles of pleasure coursed through her and she arched to him. He moaned and relinquished her lips to blaze a path down her throat to that firmed peak. When he took it in his mouth, the sensations made her gasp. Her nerves—her whole body—was quivering with anticipation of…what?

He lifted her nightgown now and moved lower, circling her navel with his tongue as he held her hips steady. "Chloe…Chloe," he moaned, "I knew you would be my salvation."

Her middle burned and the shock of his words recalled her to her senses. His salvation? How could that be? She caught his dark hair between her fingers and lifted his head to look down into his ruined face. Hunger, a dark desperation, and a flicker of hope burned in his eyes. And yet…

And yet, she could not be what he wanted her to be. She could not surrender herself to a disfigured, lame gamekeeper. Her life would be ruined and her future forfeit. Oh, but he was so…so strangely beautiful. So strong, yet so touchingly vulnerable. She wanted to tell him so. Wanted to say something that would banish the hurt. But she realized that she didn't even know his given name. For all their familiarity, he was a virtual stranger to her. Three days she'd known him, and in three more, she'd be gone. And at this moment—nearly naked in his arms—she could not call him by name. The shock of that simple fact brought her scrambling to her feet.

"No!" she gasped, leaving him empty-armed and dazed.

He reached out for her. "Chloe, I—"

"No," she repeated, holding back a sob as she rearranged her nightgown and tied the blue silk ribbon. "For all that I've run away, I am still engaged to be married. And I do not even know your name, sir."

"An—"

She held up her hand, palm outward, as she backed toward the door. "No! I do not want to hear it! You will seduce me if I do."

"Name be damned! You know all you need to know, Chloe Faraday. You know me for the man I am, regardless of my name."

He was wrong. She didn't know him. She didn't know who he was at his very core. She didn't know if he would be cruel once he had seduced her. She didn't know if he would make her cry as her friends had cried. And she didn't know if he would tire of her in a month, or a season, or a year. Tears filled her eyes as she backed from his room and ran for the ladder.

Anthony stood and staggered to the washstand, cursing under his breath. Damn! He hadn't meant things to go so far. He hadn't meant to get so lost in her that he lost himself, too. A mere hour of talking and laughing together without suspicion or rancor, and he'd fallen in love with her all over again. Now he recalled how she'd managed to capture him so completely in the space of a dance and a cup of punch two years ago. Chloe was still that woman beneath the surface.

But there was something else beneath the surface. Something deeply hidden that troubled Chloe Faraday, and thus troubled him. He'd commanded enough men to know when someone was hiding something. And he'd listened to enough complaints to know when there was something not being spoken aloud.

The water in the pitcher was cold as he poured it into the

basin and groped for a facecloth. He wondered if whatever fears or misgivings she'd developed regarding marriage had come in the interim, or if they'd been with her since childhood. She'd hinted that there were "certain sensibilities" that a man couldn't understand. He'd puzzled this statement, and wondered if it referred to a fear of marital intimacy. Nothing could cure that fear but the act itself.

Then she'd said she did not want to marry except for affection. He could unquestionably offer her passion, and his affection was rapidly building. There were so many endearing things about her, even when she was being prickly and trying to sabotage him. Yes, Chloe would be easy to love.

Her confession that she couldn't marry a stranger was more difficult to fix. He wasn't a stranger any longer, but he could hardly tell her that. In fact, that particular confession was growing more difficult by the hour. She was bound to resent him and her brother for their scheme. She would feel as if she'd been tricked—be embarrassed at best, humiliated at worst, and certainly angry and betrayed.

No, those reasons were all sufficient to themselves to make a woman of Chloe's spirit and intelligence shy of marriage. But there was something else eroding her trust. Something she couldn't bring herself to talk about. And that secret, he suspected, was the real reason she did not want to marry.

Anthony splashed the cold water from the basin on his face, hoping to cool his passions and clear his head. He still ached with wanting her. As he straightened, he caught his reflection in the mirror. Good God! No wonder she'd run. How could she ever love that face? How could she ever resign herself to a lifetime of looking at him across a table, of watching other women dance with their husbands while she stood on the sidelines with a cripple?

Risk and reward. Where had it gone wrong?

Chapter Seven

Morning was just beginning to cast sunbeams through the windows when Chloe turned the muffins out onto a dish towel to cool. She'd been up for hours. She couldn't sleep, couldn't even think straight. For a moment last night, she had forgotten her troubles and gotten lost in Mr. Rush's stories. He'd become so real to her, and so very appealing. She found that she liked the man, and worse, that she wanted his kisses and reveled in his touch. How would she ever explain a man like Mr. Rush to her stepfather? Impossible. In fact, the entire situation was impossible.

She opened the door of the warming oven built into the wall beside the fireplace. The bacon and griddle cakes were still warm but they'd be drying out soon. There must be something more for her to do so she wouldn't have to think. Oh, because when she thought…

A noise from the bedroom alerted her that Mr. Rush had risen. As she turned to put the teapot on the table, he appeared in his doorway, a dark stubble covering his jaw and his hair tousled from his pillow. His blue work shirt was open, revealing his bare chest, and the sight of it made her heart leap. She tried not to stare, but he was so enthralling that she couldn't help herself.

He seemed surprised to see her and oblivious to her reaction. "Miss Faraday, you are up early."

It was impossible to think straight when faced with that chest. She blinked and turned back to the fireplace. "I couldn't sleep," she murmured.

"About last night—I regret my behavior. It won't happen again."

Oddly, she wasn't certain how she felt about that. She put the griddlecakes and bacon on the table. If she looked at him, would he see her disappointment? "I accept an equal measure of responsibility, sir. I was hardly...unwilling."

In the end, his silence coaxed her gaze up to meet his. He was watching her with something akin to amazement. "I am relieved to hear that," he said with a small smile. "I feared I had misread you."

Her cheeks burned and he began buttoning his shirt. She turned away, pretending to fetch jam and butter from the larder. "But it must never happen again. I may not like it, but I am engaged to be married come Saturday morning."

She heard his chair scrape back as he sat. "Have you decided to go through with the marriage, then?"

She didn't answer. She honestly didn't know what she was going to do. Everything had been so clear back in Litchfield, and now she couldn't sort her feelings out. Duty urged her home to honor her commitment. Oh, but her heart was still mutinous!

She sighed as she sat and looked down at her plate. The only thing that was certain now was that Steppapa would punish her no matter what she did. She would wear black and blue instead of white on her wedding day. And maybe marriage *would* be a kinder fate than her stepfather. She suspected that was why George had urged her to marry anyway.

"I cannot," she said at last. No matter what Steppapa did to her, it was likely better treatment than she could expect from a stranger. Her stepfather could be kind, if he chose, and if he was not in one of his rages.

"Why, Chloe?"

That deep compelling voice when he said her name caused a shiver to tingle up her spine. *Why?* Very simply, because she was afraid of what she might receive at the hands of her husband. "Have you heard it said, Mr. Rush, that it is better to deal with the devil you know than the devil you don't?"

"What devil? Are you in some sort of trouble?"

"I am always in some sort of trouble. Just ask George or Steppapa."

"Then trouble *apart* from the usual sort," he clarified.

She sighed and picked up her fork, thinking he would stop asking questions if she were eating. With the fork poised at her mouth, she gave him one last evasion. "Alas, this sort of trouble is quite usual." And then she popped the bite of griddlecake into her mouth to forestall further questions.

He was focused on her mouth and she wondered if she'd dribbled her jam. She ran her tongue over her lips and was flustered when he gave her that sleepy smile that always left her a little nervous. She'd almost rather dodge questions.

The rest of the meal was eaten in silence while she stole furtive glances in his direction. He was watching her with open curiosity. The silence grew awkward and strained. Finally, she stood to clear the remains of breakfast.

He pushed his chair back from the table and crossed his arms over his chest. "I will find out, you know."

Halfway to the washbasin, she stopped and looked over her shoulder. "Find out what?"

"What you're hiding. What you're afraid of. And I'll know before you leave here."

She smiled. "I doubt that, Mr. Rush."

* * *

Chloe had finished washing up and had gone to the loft to fetch her embroidery when she heard the thumping of horses' hooves on the green outside. She hurried to the dormer window and peeked from behind the white lace curtain.

Soldiers! King's men by their uniforms! Oh, dear. They were surrounding Mr. Rush, who was carrying the slop bucket for the pigs. She could see the tension in his shoulders, but his expression did not change. She didn't stop to listen. She knew what they were there for.

She ran to the hatch and dragged the ladder up to the loft, then lowered the hatch. Tiptoeing back to the window, she peeked out again. She could hear conversation but could not make out the words. Oh, how she wished she'd left the window open this morning. After a moment, Mr. Rush shrugged and the soldiers dismounted. Still carrying the slop bucket, he led them toward the barn.

Soldiers circled the barn and poked into the pens where the livestock was kept as Mr. Rush and the captain continued to talk. Several minutes passed and Chloe realized they were being very thorough. One intrepid soldier poked his head out of the hayloft and called down to the captain, "Nothing here, sir."

Mr. Rush and the captain walked back toward the house, their heads bent in conversation, and the other soldiers following close on their heels.

Chloe cringed when she heard the door open and the clatter of boots on the plank flooring. She held her breath, sank to her knees and pressed her ear against the hatch.

The back door opened and closed and she suspected the soldiers were searching the back garden and privy. She made out the conversation below and strained to hear all the words.

"Kidnapped, eh?" Mr. Rush asked.

The captain's voice was clipped and precise. "Three days

ago. They could be anywhere by now, but Mr. Hubbard believes they will not have gone far. I am surprised you haven't heard."

"Is Hubbard that wealthy? How much has the kidnapper asked?"

"Moderately wealthy, I believe. There's been a ransom demand for five thousand pounds. Hubbard did not want to pay it, but his wife put up a fuss, so he is scraping it together."

"How have you become involved, Captain? I'm surprised Mr. Hubbard didn't hire a Runner to handle this for him."

"He has connections in government. Someone owed him favors. I pity the poor blighter who had the audacity to kidnap your—"

"Yes, well. I begin to see the problem."

"Those involved are going to hang or go to prison for a very long time. No escaping that, I'm afraid."

Mr. Rush said nothing to this, and a cold dread seeped through Chloe. George! Would George go to prison for her folly? How could she allow that to happen to her beloved brother? And Mr. Rush? He had only been desperate for money. It was not as if he had actually kidnapped her. No, it was more as though he'd given her sanctuary from her stepfather. Oh, dear Lord! She'd sooner cut her heart out than have them suffer for her sake. Perhaps she should give herself up now and explain the whole scheme. Then maybe she'd be the only one to go to gaol.

"Nothing in the bedroom, captain," a voice called.

The back door opened again and a rough voice said, "Nothin' in the garden or privy, sir. Riley took a quick look in the woods behind, but no trace of anyone."

After a pause, the captain spoke again. "Thank you for letting us look around, sir."

Mr. Rush's voice betrayed an edge of impatience. "No

trouble, Captain. But I have things to do. If you are finished here, I'd like to return to my chores."

"Very...rural of you, sir. Sorry for the inconvenience, but our orders are to search everywhere. No exceptions. Leave no stone unturned, as it were."

"Yes, yes. I see. I won't prevent you from doing your duty, but if you would just finish quickly, I could get on with my day."

Chloe frowned. Mr. Rush was being uncommonly firm with men who were on the king's business. And they were being exceptionally respectful of a gamekeeper. Did he have that effect on everyone?

"Yes, sir. I believe we are done here." Footsteps led toward the door, then stopped. "Oh, I see you have a loft, sir. Can you open the hatch so we can have a look?"

A tiny gasp worked its way from Chloe's mouth and she muffled it with her hand. Heavens! She couldn't push the bureau or the bed over the hatch because they'd hear her. If she sat on it, would they still be able to force it open?

"Hatch?" Mr. Rush repeated. "Oh, yes. Haven't had it open in years. I'll have to go to the barn and fetch a ladder."

"Years?" the captain asked. "Are you certain?"

"Not a thing I'd likely forget, is it, Captain? As you can see, I don't even have a ladder available."

Oh, Mr. Rush was very clever, indeed. She said a quick silent prayer that his subterfuge would work.

"I hate to put you to the trouble, sir. I shall take your word for it."

"Thank you, Captain. And best of luck on your search."

The door closed again and Chloe scrambled to the window to peek at them. Mr. Rush was heading back to the barn, and the soldiers were mounting their horses. Light-headed with relief, she whispered a grateful thank-you to the heavens.

* * *

Anthony tossed a pitchfork of hay into the horse stall. He had to admit that the physical labor in acting the part of a gamekeeper was making him stronger. But just then his stomach burned and he winced in pain. He may be stronger, but this business with Chloe Faraday was giving him an ulcer.

When he'd seen the soldiers, he'd been certain the game was up. He'd tried to divert them by taking them to the barn. Chloe, quick-witted little thing that she was, had figured out what was happening and had retreated to the loft, taking the ladder with her. By the time they'd arrived at the house, she was safely tucked in the loft, leaving no trace of her presence.

However, the captain had recognized him and he'd been afraid Chloe would overhear some snippet of conversation and discover who he was. He certainly wasn't ready to deal with that yet. He still needed to discover the reason behind her reluctance to marry.

He spread the hay over the dirt floor of the stall, tossed the pitchfork back into the hayloft and wiped his brow on his shirtsleeve. He just needed to pump fresh water into the trough and he'd be done.

Tomorrow, they'd have to leave for Litchfield for the wedding. He groaned, thinking of the fiasco in the offing if he and Chloe didn't reach some sort of understanding, but that was looking increasingly unlikely. He did not like to think what she would do when she saw him standing at the altar waiting for her. That would be a very bad moment.

She would have to know who he was before that happened. She would be all nerves come Saturday, and he wouldn't have her falling apart or fainting from shock. Yes. He'd tell her before he sent her back to Litchfield. He owed her that much.

But with so little time left, how would he persuade her to confide in him? There had to be a way.

"Mr. Rush!"

He turned to find her, smiling, framed by the barn door. The mere sight of her caused him to stiffen in all the wrong places.

She ran to him, threw her arms around his neck and planted a kiss on his scarred cheek. "We did it—we fooled the soldiers! Oh, it scared the devil out of me!"

"Would that were true, Miss Faraday." He held her away from him before she could feel the effect her embrace had on him.

She gave him a wide-eyed look. "You think they were not fooled?"

"No, I meant—"

Laughing, she nudged him in the ribs. "I know what you meant, sir. You are right. I haven't had the devil scared out of me yet, and I think it would take more than a few soldiers to do it."

He hardly knew what to make of her in this euphoric mood. She was both alluring and innocent, amusing and tender. He'd give his other leg to keep her this way always. God knows, he'd already given his heart.

"We shall have to celebrate tonight." She released him and stepped back, a flush heightening the color in her cheeks. She'd just now realized she'd hugged him.

And that gave him a decidedly wicked idea. "A capital idea, Miss Faraday. We shall open my best wine and toast our success." And anything else he could think of. He'd get Chloe foxed, or at least tipsy. Nothing like a few drinks to loosen one's tongue.

A few scruples rose to trouble him, but he put them out of his mind. After all, his intentions were the best, and if he was ever to convince her to let her guard down and confess what was troubling her about marriage, he would have to use every resource at his disposal.

Chapter Eight

After Chloe put the beef roast in the kettle over the fire, she went to the loft to freshen up and change her gown. She was feeling festive and very pleased with herself. They'd escaped the king's men. In a few more days her wedding date would have passed and she would have averted the near disaster of her nuptials. And she could go home.

That thought sobered her. Home. To Mama and George, but also to Steppapa, who would, almost certainly, whip her. She would endure his beating with as much grace as she could, because she deserved this one, even though he wouldn't know that. She *had* run away. She *had* made the family a subject of gossip. Yes, and she'd made herself unmarriageable.

And then the realization dawned on her that once she'd gone back to Litchfield she would never see Mr. Rush again. The thought made her a little sad, and she realized she'd grown to like the man. Well, a little, anyway. He'd always been kind to her, and patient. He hadn't even complained about her cooking when she'd deliberately spoiled his food. She couldn't say why, couldn't put her finger on the precise reason, but she would miss him. Would he welcome the return of his solitude, or would he miss her, too?

She stripped down, poured water in the basin and washed every inch of herself. Once clean head to toe, she slipped the only gown she'd packed that was suitable for a celebration over her head and fastened the bodice. It was a lavender silk evening gown edged in transparent white lace. She smoothed it over her hips, hoping Mr. Rush would not notice her lack of proper stays. Then she brushed her hair until it gleamed and tied it back with a white ribbon. Regretting her limited choice of clothing, she descended the ladder.

Mr. Rush had cut a small bouquet of lilacs from the bushes beside the cottage and put them in a widemouthed jug in the center of the table. They were her favorites. As she lay the table, the heady scent filled her senses and made her sigh. What sweet memories lilacs evoked—warm spring days, running barefoot through the meadow, lying back on a riverbank and watching clouds go by. Oh, for those simple uncomplicated days again!

The sound of a closing door coupled with an uneven gait told her that Mr. Rush had returned. She smiled as she spun toward him and then stopped short. The thank-you for the lilacs she'd been about to utter died on her lips.

Mr. Rush had changed into an elegant white shirt with an impeccably tied cravat and snug dove-gray breeches tucked into highly polished Wellington boots. He was clean shaven and his damp hair was combed in the fashion of the day. If she hadn't known better, and if he'd been wearing a formal jacket, she could easily have mistaken him for a high-ranking member of the ton. The ragged scar on his left cheek could have passed for a dueling scar. Something inside her tightened and she lost her train of thought.

"Lavender becomes you, Miss Faraday," he said with a crooked smile.

Her cheeks burned and she wondered at her own unexpected shyness. How many compliments like that had she been given before? And yet it took on new meaning when spoken by this uncommon man. She was suddenly tongue-tied and unsure of herself.

"You are pretty, too," she finally said.

He chuckled. She liked the sound of his laughter and had not heard it much. Certainly war and his injuries had not encouraged it. Then, for the first time, she wondered if her fiancé laughed very much. He'd been to war, too, and had fought many battles. Would he be as cautious and serious as her gamekeeper? She pushed that notion away. She did not want to ruin the evening with thoughts of Sir Anthony Chandler.

Mr. Rush took a piece of tinder from the fire to light the lanterns. She busied herself lifting the lid from the kettle and removing the roast, potatoes and carrots to a platter.

"Allow me," Mr. Rush said, taking the platter from her and carrying it to the table. He carved the roast with a deft hand and placed slices on their plates.

He brought two crystal wineglasses from the back of a high cupboard and placed them on the table. "My best wine, remember?"

He chose a bottle from the larder and uncorked it with a flourish, making her laugh at his exaggerated manners. Before she could sit, he came around the table and held her chair for her, every bit as polished as a duke or an earl.

After pouring the wine, he sat across from her and raised his glass. "To success."

She lifted hers and smiled. "And to soldiers in a hurry." The deep red burgundy seeped downward, warming her stomach. It was a very good wine, and she wondered how a gamekeeper had come to be knowledgeable in fine wines.

He lifted his fork and took a cautious bite of roast. "Well done, Miss Faraday. I must compliment you on the speed with which you have learned to cook."

Drat! Her cheeks were burning again. She pushed a potato around on her plate. "I, um, learn quickly."

"For which I am eternally grateful."

She looked up to find him smiling at her. He was teasing! He'd known all along what she'd done to spite him. She gave him a shy smile in return.

"I am pleased to see you settling in," he said. "It's a pity you'll be gone soon. We were just becoming accustomed to each other."

There it was again—that little tweak of pain at the thought of not seeing Mr. Rush again. "Did you and George make plans of how to send me home if my stepfather does not pay the ransom? Will George pay you? I have some money and—"

"No money necessary, Miss Faraday. I was, ah, paid in advance."

"Then you were teasing me about—"

"I fear we've both been guilty of that," he admitted. "Shall we declare a truce?"

She nodded and they raised their glasses to each other again. "I suppose I've been a bit of a termagant," she confessed. "I've been so on edge that I haven't been myself."

And again he gave her that half smile. "A bit high-strung, perhaps, but whoever you are, I find you most beguiling."

"You are being too kind, sir, but thank you." She attacked her food with a purpose, growing uneasy with their tenuous new camaraderie. Why was he being so nice to her—almost like a suitor instead of a coconspirator?

After a few moments, by way of dinner conversation, he asked, "Are you dreading your return to Litchfield, Miss Faraday?"

"I…I was, but now..."

"You are looking forward to it?"

"I have been rethinking my decisions. I acted in haste. No, that is not right. I allowed three weeks from that wretched man's return to pass, and my stepfather's last refusal to call it off before deciding to flee. I only regret that I did not give my betrothed the courtesy of a personal rejection, even by letter. I owed him that much, though he has not afforded me the same courtesy. Thus, I have been thinking I should return to Litchfield *before* the nuptials to clear the matter up. Perhaps tomorrow."

Mr. Rush frowned. "So you are willing to return to Litchfield to reject your affianced husband in person?"

Could she confess that his stories of bravery and courage had taught her a measure of integrity she hadn't understood before? That running away from danger or problems did not solve them? That standing up to bullies—whether her stepfather or a foreign country—was more important than winning her own way? That, because of him, she wanted to choose courage over cowardice? Would he laugh at her? "And for other reasons," was all she could say.

He refilled her glass and regarded her thoughtfully. "Would you care to share any of those reasons with me?"

Oh, she really could not look into those dark, bottomless eyes and admit that he inspired her. "We have already covered enough of this ground, so, no, sir, I would not." And then she took the last bite of her vegetables so he could not query her further.

He shrugged. "Very well, then. Let me see what we have here. To summarize, you fled because you did not want to marry a perfect stranger—one who had not even troubled to communicate with you. And because, in fact, you did not want to marry at all. And you did not want to marry because of 'certain sensibilities.' Do I have the gist of it so far?"

She nodded. "Yes. That is a fair summary. Do you take exception to any of those reasons?"

"Certainly not." He, too, finished the remainder of his meal and pushed his chair back from the table. "In fact, I agree that your betrothed is a cad and a bounder of the worst sort. He does not deserve you, Miss Faraday."

There was a note of humor to his words and Chloe tried to decide if he was teasing her again. His expression was serious, but his eyes belied it.

"But," he continued as he filled her glass, "I am a little foggy on the 'certain sensibilities' issue. I have considered it from a number of angles, and I think I may have some ideas."

She tilted her head to one side. How could he possibly know what she was thinking? She gave him a smile. "Enlighten me, sir."

"Well, were I a marriageable miss, I would lament the loss of my independence. Surely giving over your autonomy would be a difficult thing, and giving it to a stranger, even harder."

He *did* have an inkling! She raised her eyebrows in surprise and took another gulp of wine. "Well done, Mr. Rush. Have you any other insights?"

"Oh, dozens," he assured her. "Would you like to hear them?"

"Please. I am all breathless anticipation."

"Then, were I an ingenue who had been well loved and protected all my life, doted upon by parents and a brother, I might have misgivings about leaving their tender care for an unknown fate."

She gave him a reckless grin. She had him now. "If you are assuming that is true of me, then you are mistaken. My rearing was not so pampered as you would believe. Some might think I'd be better off to leave the *tender care* of my family."

He shook his head. "Not I, Miss Faraday. After all, *better the devil you know than the devil you don't*."

Her mouth dropped open in astonishment. He had listened to her—had actually understood what she had meant. Damned by her own words! She stared down into her wine. "There may be a kernel of truth in that, sir," she admitted.

"And I am just getting started."

"There's more?"

"Much more. For instance, were I a...well, you know. I'd have to admit to an apprehension of childbearing. There is, of course, the inherent danger of losing one's life, but even more so in the certainty of pain. It is one thing to endure pain with good grace, and quite another to volunteer for it."

Good heavens! She had no idea that men ever thought of such things. And, in all honesty, *she* hadn't thought of it. "I must say, Mr. Rush, that was not one of my myriad reasons."

"Really? Well, that is interesting. Even as a male, I would think twice before subjecting my wife to childbirth."

"That is very...compassionate of you," she said, a warm glow filling her as she finished her wine and he filled her glass again.

He put the empty bottle aside and went to the larder. "I have a surprise for you, Miss Faraday." He brought a bowl of dewy washed strawberries and a dish of clotted cream to the table, along with a bottle of light white wine. "I found a patch down by the stream and thought you might like some."

She chuckled to think of this rough, scarred gamekeeper hazarding a slippery bank to pick berries. The man was a paradox. If this behavior was common for a gamekeeper, she was surprised there were not more debutantes eloping with servants. "I adore strawberries and cream," she admitted.

They talked for a time about the merits of strawberries over raspberries, and whether peaches were best eaten fresh or in pies. But it was his pithy observation that apples, being a "forbidden fruit," are tempting no matter how they are eaten, that started her giggling. She realized she was growing a little light-headed.

When he raised the bottle to pour again, she held up one hand. "No, thank you, Mr. Rush. I'm quite giddy as it is."

"But this is a celebration. And if you insist upon returning to Litchfield, a farewell."

Her happy glow dimmed. It was the right thing to do. She knew it was. So why did it make her sad? She'd be back in her own bed, back to comfort her mother and back to make certain George didn't pay for her folly.

And would never see Mr. Rush again.

He lifted her chin on the edge of his hand, dipped a strawberry in cream and popped it into her mouth. "But I think there is more to your reservations than we've discussed. Will you tell me, or shall I guess?"

Her mouth full of strawberry and cream, she couldn't answer. As she struggled to chew and swallow, he leaned back again and said, "I recall you made veiled reference to 'sharing intimacies,' and that you desired friendship beforehand. Is that not so?"

She did not like the turn the conversation had taken, but all she could do was nod. She started to rise from her chair, but he clamped his large hand over her shoulder and held her in place.

"I would like to explore that word. Intimacy. Hmmm. Could you mean shared secrets? Could you mean the intimacy of living in close quarters and knowing one another's…less lovely side? Nudity? Bodily functions? Lack of privacy?"

The strawberry was halfway down her gullet and she coughed. He thumped her back with a gentle but firm pat, and kept talking. "Yes, I suppose intimacies could mean any of those things. But do you know what I think?" He paused while she cleared her throat and managed to shake her head.

"I think you mean something else entirely. I believe, in polite circles, it is called 'the marriage bed.'"

Now she really was mortified. Her cheeks burned as hot as coals.

He held her wineglass to her lips inviting her to drink to soothe her throat. "So I have a question for you, Miss Faraday. By 'sharing intimacies,' did you mean the marriage bed? Is it the act of making love that has you in a dither?"

"M-making *love?*" she managed. "But that's just it, you see. How can one 'make love' if one does not even *know* who their partner is? Or if there is anything in them to love."

"Ah, I begin to see. So it is not sex that repels you, but sex with a stranger?"

She opened her mouth and then closed it again. How could she explain it?

"So your ideal mate would agree to forgo the marriage bed until after you deem him worthy?"

"Yes! I mean, no. Oh, you have misread me entirely. Simply put, I do not want intimacy at all!" she said before she could stop herself. To cover her words, she stood and began clearing the table.

"Interesting. Now we are getting to the crux of the matter, I think. Allow me to take my musings a step further." He paused and watched her for a moment and finally asked in a soft, thoughtful voice. "Are you *afraid* of intimacy, Miss Faraday?"

Something cold landed in the pit of her stomach and the memory of Marianne's tears rose to haunt her. "I…I am not afraid, sir. But I do dread that sort of…imposition upon my person."

Mr. Rush's dark eyebrows rose and the corners of his mouth twitched. "Imposition?" He stood and caught her by the hand as she came back to the table for the remains of dinner. Slipping one arm around her and using the other to tilt her face up to his, he whispered, "I could have sworn you did not consider it an imposition last night when I kissed you and had you nearly naked in my bed. Nor this afternoon when you threw your arms around me."

His lips descended to hers, as soft and cherishing as angel wings. She held her breath as the moment drew out and when he released her hand, she brought it up to caress his cheek. She wanted to kiss him forever—just to stand there, surrounded by his warmth, safe in his arms, and willing to follow where he led.

Lifting his mouth from hers, he said, "But I can understand why you would not want to be imposed upon by me, Miss Faraday. Just the sight of me must repulse you. But to—"

"No!" she cried. Looking at him now, she realized that his ruined face was somehow noble. She saw courage and honor and integrity there. And in his rough hands and worn clothes, she found a simple pride and honesty that made him more handsome to her than any London dandy dressed in fine worsted and satin brocade. He was not repulsive in the least, and the longer she knew him, the more handsome he became. "You are not repulsive, Mr. Rush. You are beautiful in my eyes."

Oh dear! She'd fallen in love with him! How could this have happened? This was so…so completely inappropriate that it staggered her mind! Her mother would fall into melancholy, her stepfather would beat her, and George would look at her in disgust. Such an alliance could not be good for either of them.

She ran for the loft.

Chapter Nine

Anthony stared after Chloe in amazement. *Beautiful?* He was beautiful in her eyes? Then what had he said to upset her? He followed her to the ladder and called up to her.

"Miss Faraday? Chloe? Come back. We need to talk. There's something I have to tell you." No doubt about it now, she had to know his name.

"No!"

Her angelic face appeared at the top of the ladder, and just as he was about to climb it, she seized the top rung and dragged it up after her.

"Chloe! Please listen. I—"

But the hatch slammed shut. "Go away!" came her muffled cry.

Of course he couldn't go away. They were running out of time. They would have to leave here by tomorrow afternoon if they were to be at the Litchfield parish church in time to be married. He had to make her listen now, or she'd never go through with it. And God knows she still might not, even knowing the truth.

"Chloe!" he attempted one last time. Nothing.

Blast! He was hardly in shape for such antics, but only one solution occurred to him. He loosened his cravat and went out the back door. A sturdy elm stood close to the cottage and some of the upper limbs overhung the eaves. He jumped, grabbed one of the lower branches and swung himself up into the crotch of the tree.

Favoring his good leg, he climbed higher, his boot slipping on the bark once and leaving him dangling precariously over the privy. He tried not to think of the consequences of falling there. When he was finally level with the loft, he realized he was going to have a difficult time edging along the eaves to the dormer window. As it was, his leg was throbbing and felt as if he'd done some damage when he'd slipped. But this was no time for hesitation.

The branches closest to the eaves would not support his weight, so he had to climb a little higher and swing himself onto the eave. He landed with a solid thud and his injured leg gave way. As he started to slide he clutched for a handhold, finding one in the narrow rain gutter.

Finally hoisting himself into a sitting position, he edged along the eave toward the dormer window. A breeze stirred the narrow branches and they stung his cheeks and tangled in his hair. Good God! How could something that appeared so simple end up being such a trial?

The meager light from Chloe's window was all he had to go by. He had been making a fair amount of noise, so he wasn't surprised when the window opened and Chloe peered out. She'd changed to her nightgown and made a little squeak when she saw him. She ducked back inside and pulled the panes closed.

Damn. Well, he'd come all this way. He wasn't about to let a thin pane of glass stop him now. A moment more and he was on the sill looking through her window. He couldn't see her and he wondered if she'd snuffed her candle.

A sharply applied elbow and the glass shattered. He reached through the broken panes and undid the latch.

"Chloe?" he called. He blinked, trying to accustom his eyes to the darkness.

"Go away, Mr. Rush."

"What did I say? How did I injure you?"

"It…it wasn't you. It was me."

He remembered her words. He would remember them as long as he lived, because they had the ring of truth and were more precious to him than gold. *You are beautiful in my eyes.* She was not blind. She saw him as he was, and did not find him lacking. He would have loved her for that alone.

He made out her form at the opposite end of the room. Moving closer, he saw that her dark hair was loose around her shoulders, gleaming in the moonlight streaming through the window behind her. She was like a fairy princess—fragile, beautiful, ethereal—as if she might disappear if he frightened her.

"How could it have been you?" he asked. "You did nothing."

She only shook her head and backed up another step. "Go away."

"No, Chloe. I climbed that tree—" he gestured to the window he'd come in "—and you're damn well going to listen to what I have to say. We need to settle this now."

"We have nothing to settle, Mr. Rush."

He lunged at her and caught her in his arms before she could retreat again. "I think we do," he said, looking down into those green eyes that had haunted his dreams for years. "You say you want to go home. That you need to face your betrothed with your rejection. And you say that, among the many reasons, it is mostly because he is a stranger to you. But what if he were not a stranger, Chloe? What if you knew him, and did not dislike him entirely?"

"I…I cannot say. How can I know such a thing until I am

faced with it?" She looked up at him and there was a plea in her eyes. "I do not think I could go through with it, though. After all, it is still marriage."

"Ah, Chloe," he murmured into her hair. "I wish I could dispel your fears."

Her breath caught in a little sob and his heart twisted. How could he let her go? How could he allow her fears to destroy her chance of happiness. And his? This damned lie he'd been living for the past few days had trapped them both. If he told her the truth, she'd no longer trust him. If he didn't, she'd hate him when she found out.

"Chloe, forgive me," he began, "but there's something you don't know. Something that could make all the difference—"

She looked up at him and laid one finger over his lips. "I know all I need to know, Mr. Rush. You told me that once, and you were right. I know the kind of man you are."

"But—"

"I've made a dreadful mistake in thinking I could run away from my problem, and I must rectify that mistake before I can think about the future. This mess is of my own making, and nothing to do with you. Do not take responsibility for my actions, sir."

"But I *am* responsible," he said. Good God! If he'd only written her a letter or come to introduce himself, none of this would be happening now. "And if you leave, Chloe, I swear I will come after you. You see, I—"

Again, she stopped him. But this time she pressed her lips against his instead of her finger. Yes, she would have to know. But did she have to know *now?*

There was a fleeting moment when she could have stopped the way her heart was pounding. When she might have been able to step away from Mr. Rush. But it was gone so quickly that she scarcely noticed its passing. Her lips were pressed to his, and nothing else mattered. Right or wrong—gamekeeper, hermit or king—he was the man she was destined to love.

He broke the kiss and tightened his arms around her. "Chloe, you are making a mistake if you think I can let you go. I cannot. I warned you what would happen next time."

Had he meant that to be a warning? To her ears, it was a benediction. She gave him a shaky sigh and rubbed her cheek against his crisp linen shirt. "I won't turn back this time, Mr. Rush."

"My name is—"

She raised on her tiptoes and spoke against his lips. "Hush. Not now. If I do not know it, Steppapa cannot beat it out of me."

He groaned and lifted her in his arms. "Chloe, how can I make love to you when you are calling me Mr. Rush?"

Why was he so insistent? What did his name matter anyway? "Find a way, sir, or *you* will have to turn back."

"Never," he growled as he carried her to the bed and laid her on the coverlet.

He stood beside the bed, tossing his cravat aside, then unfastening his shirt and lifting it over his head. Her heart leaped to her throat as his chest came into view, every bit as stirring as it had been in the barn.

He looked awkward for a moment and she realized he could not remove his boots standing. He would have had a bootjack in his own room to help. Sitting on the edge of the bed, he drew his good leg up to rest on his knee and tugged at the heel. She had assisted George once when he'd pulled a muscle at cricket, and she knew she could help Mr. Rush. She slipped to her knees before him. Cupping his heel in one hand and the toe in her other, she wedged the boot off and tossed it aside.

When she turned her attention to the other foot, he placed his hand on her shoulder. "You do not have to do this, Chloe. Give me a moment, and I'll be done."

Was he embarrassed to need her help or ashamed of his crippled leg? She smiled at him and shook her head. Gripping this boot like the other, she gave it a firm tug but stopped when he winced.

She tried again, using finesse this time, and the boot slipped off easily. He stood and lifted her to her feet. He looked as if he would say thank you, but he kissed her instead—her forehead, her temples, down the line of her cheek to the corner of her mouth. His tongue traced her lips, urged her to accept him. And she moaned when he drew the very breath from her, calling up all her hidden secrets, all her buried desires.

He stroked her back, his strong fingers pressing her closer until she could feel the length of him against her—the solid planes of his chest, the strong swell of his thighs, the hard bulge that pressed into her belly. Her knees went weak and she pushed her fears back. She wanted this. It was all she'd ever have of him and she would not cheat herself of it.

He fumbled with the ribbon of her nightgown and then pushed it over her shoulders, allowing it to drop to the floor. She shivered in the night air seeping through the broken window. When she looked up at him, he had frozen, just looking down at her, his lips parted and a soft smile playing on his lips. She returned his smile, her confidence restored.

He bent to nibble at her earlobe and she suddenly lost patience. She fumbled with the waistband of his trousers and he responded with a sharp intake of breath.

"Chloe, no—"

Too late. She had them unfastened and was pushing them, along with his drawers, down over his narrow hips. He grabbed for them, but they were already beyond his grasp. She was a country-bred miss, and was not shocked by the sight or size of him. Or the fact that he was already in a full state of arousal. But she was shaken at the sight of his mangled leg. Livid scars ran up his thigh from his knee to his groin. A bandage still covered a small section at midthigh and was stained with a ragged patch of fresh blood.

"Your leg," she murmured. "You've reinjured it."

"Believe me, Chloe, that is the least of my problems at the moment." He scooped her up, placed her on the bed and came down beside her.

"But I had no idea your injuries were so…fresh. I should be careful of you."

He laughed and gathered her into his arms. "I'm the one who needs to be careful, my dear."

"Oh," she sighed as he kissed her. The heat of his body against hers was so seductive, so encompassing, that she could not think of anything else. She was still a little dizzy from the wine, and the taste of it on his tongue made her hunger for more. She tightened her arms around him, wanting to drink him in through every pore.

He stroked the length of her back, causing her to arch against him and moan. With her head thrown back, he bent to kiss the hollow of her throat, running his tongue along her collarbone to the dip beneath her ear. She shuddered with the pure deliciousness of the sensations that caused, and she became aware of a throbbing and a growing dampness between her thighs.

"Oh!" she gasped, wishing now that she knew his name.

He groaned as he inched downward. He circled her nipple with his tongue, causing her to shiver with delight as the peak hardened to a small pebble. And still, he gave it attention.

Seeking to be closer, to somehow meld into him, she lifted one leg to straddle his hip. The shift afforded her the opportunity to push her mons against his and suddenly his shaft was pressed to her entrance. She should be shocked, but she only wanted to deepen that contact, so tantalizing that she could scarcely bear it.

He took a deep shuddering breath and released her. "Not yet, Chloe. Not yet. I want you writhing with your need to have me inside you. I will not take you if you are trembling in fear. I want all your doubts dispelled, all your fears vanquished."

"But—"

"Shh! Let me savor this moment. Let me sear you into my memory so that I will carry you with me always."

Tears stung her eyes and she squeezed them shut. Yes. That is what she wanted, too. To keep this moment in her heart, to make it a part of her, private and untouched by the world, so that in the long cold days ahead, she would have something to give her comfort for having gone back to Litchfield to do the right thing.

She fell deeper into a world of his making, a world of sensual pleasure. His exploration dissolved the memory of Marianne's tears. How could anything so delightful, so sweetly undeniable, cause pain? There was, shockingly, no part of her forbidden to him, no part he left untouched, unknown, unkissed or untasted. And, when he was done, he knew her more intimately than she knew herself.

At last content that he'd discovered all of her, he returned to her breasts and settled himself between her thighs. She tangled her fingers through his hair and held him to her, too overcome with emotion to speak. The lump in her throat prevented it. She was tingling all over and gooseflesh rose on her arms when he moved lower again to lap at her core.

A trembling came upon her and she could not stop. She was burning up. She had stopped breathing and was now gasping with every stroke of his tongue and every touch of his hand. "Please," she begged at last, "please..."

He moved upward again and covered her with his body. She drew her knees up to enclose him. At the first tentative prodding of his shaft, she moaned. Yes. That was what she had been waiting for. He pushed gently again and she was ready. She lifted her hips to meet him and something burned deep inside her as his thickness invaded her. It was both pain and pleasure. Innocent and erotic.

He withdrew and came into her again, establishing a rhythm that ached and aroused, propelling her forward, sending her careening into a sudden heart-stopping burst of pleasure that left her shattered.

"Chloe, Chloe," he whispered into her hair as he shuddered against her. "I always knew you'd be heaven."

Chapter Ten

Anthony winced as sunlight penetrated his eyelids and urged him to roll over. He reached out for Chloe and found only tangled sheets. She must have gone to the privy, or be making breakfast.

He sat up and blinked to focus. He'd lain awake long into the night, watching Chloe sleep and making plans. He had thought he loved her before, but that was a pale imitation of what he felt now. She was his heart and soul, his very reason for being. He was not naive, nor inexperienced. He'd been with women before, but none who engaged him as she had.

And now he knew the depth of her fears, and the courage she'd possessed to oppose her stepfather. She'd said nothing, and only hinted at it in passing, but ugly bruises, faded to greenish yellow now, marred her creamy back. When she'd said she had defied her stepfather, he hadn't realized what that had cost her. And now he realized why Chloe feared marriage. If all she'd seen of it was scorn and occasional brutality, then it was no wonder that she would not want to risk worse at a stranger's hand. *The devil she knew...* But whatever she decided, whichever future she chose, he would see to it that Mr. Hubbard never again touched his stepdaughter.

He swung his legs over the side of the bed and stood, wrapping the tangled sheet around his waist. The sight of the clothes he'd discarded the night before draped over the back of a chair brought a grin to his face. That little act of domesticity warmed him.

The chill morning air drew his attention to the broken window. He would have to fix that today, before he put Chloe on the coach to Litchfield. Then he'd go home, pack a bag, collect his father and follow in his own coach. And tomorrow—

A folded sheet of paper tented on the bureau and bearing his name caught his attention. He retrieved it with an uneasy feeling. A line or two penned in delicate script. He glanced at the bottom.

With Regret, Miss Chloe Faraday

He sat in the overstuffed chair. Bracing himself for the worst, he read from the top of the sheet.

My Dear Mr. Rush,
Forgive me for leaving this way, but I could not bear to say the word "Goodbye." I shall miss our arguments and, even more, our friendship.
You have made me see that I was a coward in running away from my problems. Now, because of you, I am ready to face them. Alas, this means I must leave you.
With Regret, Miss Chloe Faraday

With regret? Good God! After what they'd done, she could just walk away from him? Had it meant so little to her? Well, he'd find her and bring her back. He'd make her listen to his name, and they'd damn well get things straight this time.

He dropped the sheet and started for the hatch, but a small stain of blood on the snowy linen stopped him. Her blood?

Or his? He glanced down at his leg to see the raw wound. He'd lost the bandage somewhere in the night. Had Chloe seen the lesion? Is that why she could turn her back on him so easily? Lord, she'd grown used to the scar on his face, but his leg had repulsed her.

Damning himself for pointing out the south path to the road, he went down the ladder, ignoring the sharp pain slicing through his thigh. That would heal eventually. It was Chloe who had to be dealt with now.

Still weary from the coach ride that had brought her back to Litchfield last night, Chloe stared at her reflection in her dressing table looking glass. There were violet smudges beneath her eyes and no blush to her pale cheeks. Her mother stood behind her, twining a rope of pearls through her dark hair. She looked more like a cold marble statue than a breathing being.

"This is too much trouble, Mother. A complete waste of time. I am not marrying the man."

"So you say, Chloe, but I think you must. Mr. Hubbard is set upon it."

Mr. Hubbard. Papa Charles. Her stepfather. How could her mother refer to her husband, with whom she had certainly shared many years of trials and intimacy, the same as any stranger would? But then she thought of Mr. Rush, with whom *she* had shared—no, she couldn't think of that now. She'd only cry. She pinched the bridge of her nose to prevent tears from forming.

Her mother cupped her shoulders. "Dear, please do not cry It will make your face all puffy."

"I must see Mr....Sir Anthony Chandler before the nuptials."

"Mr. Hubbard has forbidden it. He believes you will offend

the man or beg off. He says it is a miracle that Sir Anthony has agreed to proceed, given the unfortunate circumstance of your kidnapping. Sir Anthony may be your last chance of a respectable life and a home of your own. Please be reasonable, dear."

Her last chance for a home of her own? That was a sobering thought. Without a home of her own, would she ever be free of Papa Charles?

She stood and watched in her mirror while her mother lifted the ivory silk gown over her head and laced the bodice up the back. She looked wan and frightened to her critical eye, and when her mother added a small lace veil, she fought her tears. "I want to talk to George," she said. "He will listen to me."

"George is with Sir Anthony at the inn, Chloe. He will not be back until it is time to escort us to the church."

She glanced at the clock on her dressing table. In less than an hour, the vicar would be waiting at the altar. And so would Sir Anthony Chandler! Her stomach churned. Would she have to refuse him at the altar?

Anthony arranged the triangular points of his collar and the folds of his cravat as he watched George Faraday in the mirror. He repeated George's question. "What happened at the cottage? I wish I knew how to answer that. We got off to a rocky start, but then I thought we had reached an accord on certain things. I certainly believed we had got to the bottom of her dislike of marriage and had forged a friendship. But then, yesterday morning, she was just gone. No explanation. She left a note thanking me and saying she would miss our friendship. That is all."

"Miss it? But she has been railing against you ever since she walked through the door last night. She has renewed her insults and says you must be a crashing bore."

Anthony squirmed. "If it is Chandler she is cursing, then it isn't me. If it is the gamekeeper she loathes—then I will have to own it. I never had the chance to tell her who I am. She thinks my name is Mr. Rush. I intended to tell her the truth yesterday, but she was gone before I was awake." He sighed and shrugged into his navy-blue tailcoat. "I wonder if there is any point in going to the church."

"I cannot say what Chloe will do at the altar, but I am certain she will arrive at it. Our stepfather will see to that."

Anthony combed his fingers through his hair and sighed, a feeling of loss coming over him. "Well, I suppose I cannot leave her standing there alone, even if it is to reject me. Is there any chance at all of having a private word with her in the vestry before the ceremony?"

"None, I fear." George went to glance out the window at the church across the green. "The doors are open and the vicar is sweeping the steps. Sorry, Anthony."

"Bad enough to be rejected, but to be rejected before witnesses…well, we did our best to smooth this out, George. No regrets, eh? You were right. It was worth the risk." At least it would be a small ceremony—not too many people to witness his humiliation. He retrieved a large square box from the end of his bed and handed it to George. "Give this to Chloe, will you?"

"Oh, George!" Chloe buried her face in her hands as the coach started the short distance to the church. "Why, when I have wanted so badly to do the right thing, has everything gone awry?"

"That's the way of it, dearling. The gods never make it easy to do the 'right' thing."

"*Nothing* has gone right since that wretched man returned from the peninsula. You were with him mere minutes ago, were you not? What does he say?"

"That he is looking forward to taking you home. I gather his house and servants are waiting for a mistress."

She groaned. "Did you tell him the truth of my supposed kidnapping?"

"Why would I do that?"

"So that he would know the lengths to which I have gone to avoid this day."

"And yet you are the one who has come back for it. Why is that, Chloe? I thought you planned to stay away until after the wedding day had passed."

She heaved a sigh and looked up at her brother. "Oh, George. The gamekeeper you hired…was quite extraordinary. He had been wounded in the war, you know. Fighting in the trenches when men like Sir Anthony were likely directing the fight from afar. He has such integrity, such courage. He quizzed me almost daily and made me see how cowardly I'd been. When I learned what he had done, all he had risked, for his comrades…well, I was inspired to emulate his courage. Whatever sort of scoundrel Sir Anthony Chandler is, he deserves better than to be abandoned at the altar without so much as an explanation."

George laughed. "I wouldn't be too sure of that, puss."

"Yes, but he was kind enough not to abandon me when I was 'kidnapped.' I cannot marry him, but I have no wish to humiliate him."

George's eyebrows shot up and a skeptical smile lifted the corners of his mouth. "Did you like the gamekeeper, puss?"

Heat rose to burn her cheeks. How telling! She did not need to speak for George to know the truth.

"Then why did you run home? You could have stayed with him."

"Oh, George! You know what that would mean." Such a shocking event would shame her mother, disgrace George and even her stepfather. She'd been headstrong her whole life, thinking only of what she wanted and not what was best for the ones she loved. If she followed her heart, society would tar her family with the same brush they used for her because they had failed to "control" her. Could she do that to them?

And, frankly, Mr. Rush hadn't asked her to stay. Hadn't even mentioned love or "forever." The closest he'd come was to say, once, that if she left, he'd come after her. But he hadn't. And now she was home, with nothing but her determination to stand between her and disaster.

George took a deep wooden box from the seat beside him and handed it to her. "This is from Chandler."

She glanced at it and shook her head. "I cannot accept presents from him when I am about to jilt him."

"For heaven's sake, puss, just see what it is."

She lifted the lid and gasped. There, nestled in white tissue, was a bouquet of fragrant pale lavender lilacs. Their stems had been wrapped in white ribbon and tied together in a beautiful bouquet. She caught her breath on a sob. "Oh! That man is infuriating! If he thinks he can make me like him, he is mistaken."

George raised a single eyebrow. "It's only lilacs."

Only lilacs? "It is not that they are lilacs, George. It is that Sir Anthony Chandler presumes to know me. He is insinuating himself into my life with little gestures made too late. He will not worm his way into my affections."

George sat back, crossed his arms over his chest and regarded her with a weather eye. "Perhaps you are right, puss. The blackguard deserves to be left at the altar. What do you say we pay the coachman to take us to Glasgow where we can board a ship for Canada? They'll never find us there."

She smiled in spite of herself. "Oh, George, how have I arrived at this day in such dire straits? I've stalled. I've run.

I've tried to do what's right. And still I find myself arriving at the church to marry a perfect stranger."

The coach pulled up in front of the church and George threw the door open and hopped down. When he turned to lift her out, she almost panicked.

He knew her so well that he merely smiled and kissed her cheek as he set her feet on the ground and handed her the bouquet of lilacs. "It's almost over, Chloe. A few more minutes and, for better or worse, you'll have settled your future."

Yes, she would tell Sir Anthony she would not marry him as they stood at the altar. That was bound to be a very bad moment. Mama and Papa Charles would be outraged, Sir Anthony's father would be incensed, and Sir Anthony, himself, would be either angry or hurt. How had one simple lie landed her in such a predicament? *Captain Chandler? Yes, I remember him, Papa Charles. He was quite pleasantly presentable.* Oh, if only she could take those words back! Now, instead, she would have to say, *No, Sir Anthony, I am sorry, but I cannot marry you.* She would utter those words, then take the consequences.

George offered her his arm and led her up the steps to the wide double doors, open in a welcome. Her heart beat wildly as she entered the vestibule and looked up at her brother for reassurance. He smiled and patted her hand where it lay across his arm.

Glancing back down the long aisle, she noted a cluster of people standing at the altar in muted conversation. She recognized the vicar, her mother and her stepfather. Even Marianne and her husband had come—a reminder of all her fears. Two other men, taller than the rest, faced the vicar and turned slowly as the conversation hushed.

Her step faltered. George steadied her and continued the slow walk to the altar. She couldn't catch her breath and she felt light-headed. The brave scar slashing the handsome face was the dearest, most welcome sight she'd ever seen. How had she ever thought him frightening? And his eyes, when they met hers, spoke more eloquently than words. He *had* come for her.

And then reality set in with a shock. Her betrothed and her brother had tricked her! She glanced sideways up at George and narrowed her eyes. "You will pay for this, George. And so will Sir Anthony," she whispered.

He grinned. "You left us little choice, puss, and he and I already agreed that it would be worth the risk. So what are you going to do now?"

She turned back to Sir Anthony, remembering all the times he tried to tell her who he was, and remembering, too, all the unkind things she'd said about him to his face. She would marry him—there was no doubt of that—but he would have to give her satisfaction. And she would have a lifetime to see to it.

And at last she knew who Anthony Chandler was. He was a hero. He was a man who'd risked all he was, all he had or would ever have, for strangers. He was a man who had placed his very life on the line to protect and defend people like her. He was a man who had faced unspeakable horrors for the good of civilization and to halt tyranny and aggression.

And he was the man who had picked her lilacs, had endured her ill humor with good grace, had climbed a tree to talk to her, and had cared enough about her to risk losing her in an attempt to win her. He was a man who would never hurt her.

They arrived at the altar and George halted. Smiling down at her, Sir Anthony stepped forward, took her hand and lifted it to his lips. "Forgive me for my tardy introduction, Miss Faraday. My name is Sir Anthony Chandler, and I have loved you for years." He cupped her cheek and wiped a tear away with his thumb. "Will you marry me?"

She was lost in his eyes, aching for his touch and drowning in those miraculous words. He loved her. Oh, and she loved him, too. It had never come to mind in all her planning, that she would meet the perfect stranger. "Does it occur to you, Sir Anthony, that if I marry you, you will be paying the piper for the rest of your life?"

"Worth the risk, my dear, and a price I'm willing to pay."

"Then, yes, my love. I will marry you."

BATTLE-TORN BRIDE

Anne O'Brien

Dear Reader

I wrote the love story of Richard and Beatrice from a true happening in the Wars of the Roses, when lovers were parted by a diplomatic marriage arranged by the lady's father. The elderly husband met his death on the battlefield at the hands of the lover. Against all the odds, the lovers were reunited and were able to marry. The stuff of high romance indeed!

This led me to wonder how many lovers were torn apart, their love shattered by the callous indifference of an arranged marriage, or by the tragedy of national events which led to bloody and heartbreaking deeds on the battlefield. So Richard and Beatrice suffer brutal separation brought about by influences and treachery far beyond their control. It would take a particular strength of understanding, love and trust between the lovers to overcome such potential heartache, and I set myself to explore it.

I was delighted to create for Richard and Beatrice a true fulfillment out of tragedy and loss.

Do enjoy it,

Anne

Look for
THE RUNAWAY HEIRESS
Coming August 2006

Prologue

"I loved you. I looked for marriage with you. Yet you betrayed me, Richard. You betrayed our love."

"Betrayed? What is this…?"

"I think you never loved me at all. It was simply a Twelfth Night flirtation to be cast aside by Candlemas."

"Beatrice…how can you think that? My heart is yours—has always been yours."

"I expect you forgot me as soon I was out of sight."

"Never that. You dishonor me!"

"If that is so—if you truly loved me—how could you abandon me to a marriage with a man such as William Somerton? You have broken my heart, Richard Stafford."

Chapter One

July 1460: Great Houghton Hall, a golden-stoned manor house.

Lady Beatrice Somerton followed one of her serving maids, who was skillfully balancing tankards and a flagon of ale on a heavy tray, into the Great Hall. Two more of her servants, hastily borrowed from their kitchen duties, came behind her with platters of bread and cheese and slices of cold meat. Another with a dish of mutton pasties. In the Hall were some half a dozen gentlemen, sitting or standing, engaged in deep conversation. Newly arrived, their clothes and boots were covered with dust from a morning's hard riding. It could be noted from their swords and slim-bladed daggers that they were well-armed.

Their conversation, of a political content and subject to some ribald comment, dried as the lady entered. She was clearly the mistress of the house despite her lack of years. Young and slight of figure she might be, but she bore herself with unmistakable dignity and calm authority. Her manner was forthright, her whole demeanor used to obedience from those who served her. The gentlemen who were seated on bench or stool rose to their feet. Bowed with respect and not a little admiration. Lady Beatrice Somerton was quite beautiful and a force to be reckoned with.

"Be at ease, gentlemen." She swept them with a smile. "I think ale will be welcome here."

"Very. We are grateful, my Lady Somerton." One of the gentlemen stepped forward to bow before her with practiced gallantry. A most attractive lady and not as one would have expected in this household, having met the lord, Sir William Somerton. This lady was many years his junior.

The lady directed her maids who began to pour the ale, watched as they placed the platters, put out pewter plates and knives on the oak table. Looked round to ensure that all was in order.

"If you require anything more, sirs, Betsy will remain within call." She nodded to the maid at her right hand who dimpled with pleasure and expectation.

Then Beatrice turned to go—but where? To her own chamber or out into the garden, she supposed. She would not be required to attend her husband and his most important guest who were now closeted, alone, in the parlor. That had been made very clear. Any further needs of the visitors could safely be left in the capable hands of the steward, Master Lawson.

Another gentleman entered the vast room with its beamed roof and gleaming paneled walls, after seeing to the deployment of the armed retinue that had accompanied them to Great Houghton. Drawing off his gloves, removing his hat, he placed them on the coffer by the door, then ran his hand through dark hair, which waved around an arresting face. Approached the table with its promise of a long draft of ale to wash away the dust of summer roads.

And came to a halt in the center of the room.

As, at exactly the same moment, did Beatrice Somerton.

His face was suddenly smoothed of all expression, the thought of the ale wiped from his mind. His body went still. His hands tight-fisted at his side.

Her eyes widened, lips parted in shock. The blood drained from her face to leave her skin as pale as the lace decoration on the bodice of her velvet gown. Her fingers tightened on the edge of the empty tray that she would have carried back to the kitchen.

Tension wound the emotions between them to near breaking point, as taut as an expert Glamorgan archer would stretch the waxed-hemp bowstring as he prepared to loose an arrow with deadly accuracy. Surely the tension was obvious to everyone in the room as a living breathing thing? Except that, as Beatrice was faintly aware, the conversation behind her ebbed and flowed as if nothing were amiss: the visitors continued to concentrate on the food and ale and their own comforts.

At last the lady and gentleman found words. But not of any importance or significance for those who might overhear. Nothing to indicate the rapid leap of pulse, the thud of heart against ribcage, the surge of heat through the blood. It was as if their wits had been stripped away in that one moment of meeting.

"My lady. I had not thought…"

"Lord Richard. I did not know…"

Beatrice dropped the tray she was still holding onto the table beside her with a loud clatter. She discovered that she had been holding her breath. When the day dawned it had promised nothing new, nothing out of the way. No occurrence to disrupt her uneventful life, day after day, here at

Great Houghton. Surely there should have been some warning. Some indication, some premonition. In the weather perhaps—a violent storm—or in the presence of a magpie, strutting in the kitchen garden, with all its dire warnings and omens. There had been no heralding of this—this *disaster!*

And yet here in her home was the one man who had the power to turn her life on its head, with a single look from those eyes with their hooded lids, dark and watchful as a hovering raptor, that were even now intent on hers. The one man who could have turned her life to pure gold, causing her heart to throb with joy, her blood to heat with passion at his slightest touch. And what had he done? Why nothing—except to forsake her. Abandoning her to a cold, lonely existence with a man who disliked her, ignored her, humiliated her. To an existence without love.

The day, a warm midsummer's day when bees flooded the lavender stalks and swallows darted through the gaps in the stable doors to feed their offspring, had indeed started normally enough. Then, perhaps an hour after the midday meal, Sir William Somerton strode through the courtyard and into the stone-flagged entrance hall of his elegant but strongly defended manor house. He stood there, squinting in the sudden gloom, hands fisted on hips.

"Beatrice!" His voice rebounded off the warm stone. "Beatrice!" His frown deepened as he raised his voice further.

No response. The house remained silent around him. The tapestried hangings absorbed the sound.

"Beatrice. In God's name, where are you, girl?" He was halfway to the foot of the staircase with a hiss of ill-temper, when a lady appeared on the half landing, and came to a halt, looked down over the carved balustrade.

"There you are. What are you doing? Why are you never around when I need you? We have visitors, it seems. Perhaps a score or more, so the sentry reports."

"I have been folding linen and storing it with herbs against the moth," the lady explained to answer her lord's first question. Her voice, composed despite her peremptory summons and its rough tone, contained no apology. She descended the stairs slowly, not quite to the bottom, so that her eyes, the deep purple of the heartsease in her herb garden but on this occasion lacking their tender gentleness, were on a level with Sir William's. Her gaze was direct and did not fall before his fierce stare.

"Who is it who visits, my lord?"

"Lord Grey de Ruthin, by my soul." Somerton's grizzled brows merged into one heavy line at the prospect. His thin lips thinned further. "A black ragged staff, clear enough to see emblazoned on all the livery of the escort and on the standard. All very fine and imposing! He is accompanied by a number of gentlemen as well as an armed retinue. Quite an entourage, in fact." Sir William stared at his wife. "What in God's name will de Ruthin want?" A demand, as if Beatrice would know the answer. "I warrant I have paid my feudal dues to him this year."

"I expect he will tell us soon enough."

Beatrice recognised the name. A powerful magnate with influential friends. A Lancastrian, as were they, prepared to lead his retained army in the name of his Majesty King Henry VI against the traitorous might of the Dukes of York and Warwick who would seize the Crown and make York king.

William turned on his heel to stalk to the door at the sound of the gates being opened and the first of the mounted escort entering the courtyard. "Make preparations. Immediately!"

"What do you require?" Quite unruffled, Beatrice stepped down into the Hall, well used to speaking to her lord's back.

"Ale and food for Lord Grey and the gentlemen. Tell Lawson to arrange ale for the men-at-arms in the courtyard." He stepped outside, fists still on hips, to oversee the arrival. "I doubt they will stay long."

Lord Grey de Ruthin and his undoubtedly impressive following clattered across the bridge over the moat and into the enclosed courtyard. Beatrice watched them from the open door. Glossy horseflesh, smart livery, the glint of sun on polished weapons and harness. The black ragged staff floating arrogantly over all, was imprinted on the breasts of the armed retainers.

William still stood and waited on the steps, very much the master of the Hall. He would not be intimidated in his own home, even though he realised the danger of antagonising this man to whom he owed feudal allegiance for the two prosperous manors of Letcham and Rosedale.

Beatrice had issued instructions to Master Lawson and was now tempted to linger to watch and listen. Something out of the way, something of importance to intrigue and interest, far more entertaining than folding linen and chasing moths. But, sensing her presence, William turned on her.

"Go about your work, madam. This is no place for you."

So she withdrew a few steps, not bothering to hide the flounce of resentment, the swish of skirts. Not that William would notice. How dare he address her as if she were one of the servants! This man who was her husband, though not of her choosing, a man who was older than her own father would have been, had he lived. A man who treated her as nothing better than a chatelaine to manage his household and see to his comfort, in spite of the substantial dowry she had brought him, not to mention the alliance with the

Hattons of Mears Ashby, her own influential family with their high-bred connections. The truth was that he had no need of her other than as a housekeeper and certainly no liking for her. Patience was not often in evidence in Sir William's manner. He even preferred the ample figure of one of the serving maids to warm his bed. For which Beatrice realised she should be grateful, of course. William had an heir from his first marriage—two full-grown sons to carry on the family name. So Beatrice Hatton was an irrelevance—other than as a source of wealth and influence in local affairs.

She showed her teeth in nothing like a smile, but stepped back into the Hall, unwilling on this occasion to court her lord's unpredictable wrath. Withdrawing, however, no farther than the shadows in the doorway from where she could still listen.

The gentlemen, perhaps six of them, dismounted in a flurry of activity and sharp orders. Lord Grey approached. His authority lay on his shoulders as evident as the heavy cloak, which he now discarded with the increasing warmth of the sun and draped over his horse's withers. Stern of face, he was clearly not a man to brook disagreement with his demands.

"My Lord Grey. Welcome to Great Houghton Hall." Sir William inclined his head in brusque recognition, managed a wintry smile at odds with the warmth of the afternoon.

"Somerton. I am grateful." De Ruthin responded in like manner, equally cool. The noble visitor made it abundantly clear that here was no time for the niceties of extended greeting. "I would speak with you. A matter of urgent business—to be settled without delay."

"All business is urgent with armies in the field, my lord."

"And particularly when a battle is imminent."

A taut silence hovered over the courtyard as if no one cared to acknowledge the possibility of another battle. Only the clink of horse harness, the stamp of restless hooves.

"A battle?" Sir William raised his chin. "Do you say?"

"The king is at Northampton with his army." Lord Grey clamped his hands around his sword belt. "He is camped between the town walls and the River Nene."

Northampton! So close! Beatrice angled her head to hear more of the present state of affairs as de Ruthin continued.

"We have been given warning that the Earl of Warwick is approaching from the south with a considerable force. There will undoubtedly be conflict unless Warwick chooses to retreat. I think he will not."

"What do you need of me, my lord?" Sir William frowned. "My loyalty to the Lancastrian cause and my fealty to you has never been in doubt."

"As I am aware. King Henry is grateful." De Ruthin removed his leather gauntlets and slapped them against his leg, releasing a cloud of dust. "I would speak with you alone, Sir William, if you will. A matter for your private ear only." It was a request but a flat stare compelled Somerton to accede.

"Very well." Sir William resisted a shrug. "If you would come with me…"

"My thanks, Sir William. These gentlemen who accompany me—perhaps some refreshment—we have been on the road for a lengthy time this day and have not eaten."

"Of course." Sir William stepped aside to allow Lord Grey to precede him into the house. Who knew when the ironfisted support of Lord Grey de Ruthin might not be advantageous in this never-ending conflict between the fluctuating powers of the royal houses of York and Lancaster. "All is prepared in the Great Hall for the gentlemen of your party. There will be ale and food for all…"

Beatrice had already vanished to take up her duties. Whatever the purpose of Lord Grey de Ruthin's visit, she doubted that it would have any bearing on her existence in this cheerless house.

Chapter Two

Beatrice Somerton found herself face-to-face with the last man in the world she expected to see here. The man whom she had not set eyes on since that day in January, now well over two years ago, in the royal palace at Westminster. A face that haunted her sleeping and waking hours.

Lord Richard Stafford. A supporter of the legitimate Lancastrian claim of King Henry VI. A man with a notable reputation for his skills as a knight, both in the mock warfare of the tournament and in the grim reality of the battlefield. Men spoke of his prowess at Ludford Bridge when the Lancastrians had swept all before them and the Duke of York had been driven into exile in Ireland. Lord Richard had become recognised as one of the foremost adherents to the Crown, close relative of that most powerful aristocrat the Duke of Buckingham, who was the Commander of the king's armies.

And now that Lord Richard stood before her, she was lost for words beyond the most distressingly mundane. At last, aware of some interested glances around her and through sheer force of will, she resorted to the polite smile and polished manners of the Lady of Great Houghton Hall.

"Lord Richard. Welcome. Some ale, I think."

Whilst Lord Richard Stafford equally grasped at his disordered senses. With a perfectly bland expression he found enough presence of mind to execute a formal and graceful bow to the lady who had just dropped the tray on the table from unusually clumsy fingers. She was looking at him as if she were facing an other-worldly apparition in her home. He could not read the emotions that darkened her eyes and drained the delicate color from her skin.

"My thanks, Lady Beatrice. Ale would be most acceptable."

Beatrice collected a jug of ale and a pewter cup. Then by common consent the lady and gentleman moved a little aside to the relative privacy of a window embrasure. The newly installed glass and enlarged openings, indicative of Sir William's wealth and position in the locality, awarded them a most attractive view over the informal gardens that Beatrice loved and tended. The tumbling blooms of Rosa Mundi, the sweet upturned faces of the gillyflowers might waft their heady perfume, the lilies might flower with regal grace. But neither Lord Richard nor Lady Beatrice was aware. Neither did they so much as glance through the window at the tempting scene. She poured the ale and presented the goblet with lowered gaze. He accepted it, his eyes never leaving her face. If his hands should brush her fingers, the slightest of caresses in the acceptance, no one would notice or find room for comment. But Beatrice noticed, held her breath as the butterfly wings of physical awareness fluttered in her belly. For him the effect was a powerful blow to the gut. Desire for her, strong, unexpected, shuddered through him.

"Beatrice," he murmured after a gulp of ale to ease the dryness of his throat that had nothing to do with the heat of the day. "Are you well?"

"Yes. And you?" Now she looked up.

"As you see."

And he looked amazing. He filled her whole horizon so that she could not take her eyes from him, all other in the room fading into insignificance. Tall and loose-limbed with the well-toned muscles of a soldier, Richard stood before her with all the elegant grace she remembered as being so characteristic of this man whom she had met at a Twelfth Night celebration at the royal court. His hair was the same dark brown with rich glints of gold and russet when caught in the sun's rays. It fell heavily to wave around a face not conventionally handsome. Narrow and austere with a straight nose and firm chin, it was the face of a man who would command his own destiny and who would command others. A face of sharp angles and flat planes. There was the touch of arrogance she recalled so well. The dominance and the aura of controlled male power. And also the carved aestheticism, almost the face of a scholar, but the body of a man of action. A lethal combination for those who would look and admire. Beatrice found her eyes drawn to his once more. Clear and piercing beneath dark brows, their depths, somewhere tantalisingly between grey and green, gleamed with golden lights. Ah, yes. Just as in her dreams. So fierce and direct as they were, guarded by slightly heavy lids. An arresting face, to be sure. To draw the eyes of any woman and make her wonder.

"Are you happy?" His voice was also as she remembered. Cool and deep. Beautiful. Its silken tones stroked her senses so that memories shivered along the length of her spine to spin her back into the past. But this must not be! Shaking her head, she forced her mind to concentrate on the meaning of his words.

"Are you happy, Beatrice?"

She could not answer. Shook her head. Then, because

honesty demanded it, replied, a little sharply because it touched on the heart of the matter between them. "I must not complain. Life is comfortable enough here. I have all I need and more. I lack for nothing of material wealth."

There was a little silence that hung in the warm air.

"Have you married?" she found herself asking. His answer could not possibly have any bearing on her life, yet she found herself tensing against his reply.

"No. I have not." Then, "Your parents. Are they in good health?"

"My father is dead, last year of one of the pestilent fevers. Ned, my brother, is now head of the family. He is settled at Mears Ashby with his wife and an infant son. My mother, Lady Margery, lives with them." A deliberate hesitation to halt the rush of unimportant detail. Then in a low voice. "Ned would never have forced me to wed William Somerton just because his estate marched with ours."

There was nothing Richard could say. He stretched out one hand as if he would touch her cheek, then let it fall. He could not. Too public. Too compromising.

"Does he—does Somerton treat you well?"

"He does not beat me." Which said it all. Beatrice raised her head. Pride stiffened her spine.

"You deserve to be loved. Does he love you?" Richard persisted.

"No. He acquired an excellent dowry. And the Hatton connection. That is all he wanted. He has no need of me." She could not prevent her fingers linking together. They were white with pressure but she was careful that her face should express no emotion.

Lord Richard knew he should not ask her—but equally knew that he must know the answer.

"Does he treat you with consideration?"

She looked up at him, taken aback at so forthright a demand. She knew his meaning, and answered with all her usual openness. She could not lie to this man who owned the very breath in her body.

"He does not come to my bed, my lord." Her voice was low so that none other might hear, but her reply was devastatingly clear to him.

"Ah, Beatrice…" There were no words that could be said. Neither in pity for her caught in a loveless marriage, nor to explain the strange relief that relaxed the tension in his muscles.

How beautiful she was. The years had given her a gloss of experience and maturity, polishing those immature charms that had first attracted him. As Lady of Great Houghton, her dark hair was drawn back from her forehead, to be confined under an elegant and most fashionable transparent veil. He knew that if she released it from its confines, it would curl, would reach well beyond her shoulders. Would wind around his fingers if he allowed it. Soft as satin, strong as silver thread. Her height he considered perfect, reaching just to his shoulder. Her head could rest so comfortably there, his arms fit so easily around her slender waist. Her innate quickness and agility had first caught his attention in the foolish and energetic games at Twelfth Night. Her fair skin, which he wished to touch, was now flushed with delicate rose. Those dark eyes, almost the deep purple of the stately monkshood, with their dark lashes could appear quiet and composed, until they flashed with temper or passion, as he knew to his cost. Until she stared down that straight nose, as she had only minutes ago, with an hauteur that could sit so strangely with her youthful years. Not a meek and mild lady, then. No gently charming heartsease. He found himself wondering how she had responded to Somerton as her husband. Not well, he thought. She would resist his attempts to curb her energies and her spirit, would kick against the traces. As long as Somerton did not choose to apply the whip… Lord Richard turned his uncomfortable thought from such a direction. Beatrice's relationship with her lord, elderly and coldly self-interested as he was, was not his affair.

He forced himself to focus on the lovely face turned up to his. A pretty mouth with a full bottom lip, quick to smile. To laugh. Her voice low and a little husky. The deep blue of her overgown caused her glorious coloring to glow.

He had wanted her then; he wanted her now. His body was hard for her, forcing him to take a breath against the hot urgency. But matters had not changed between them in essence. Her father had rejected his offer of marriage. Now she was within the dominance of her husband. There was no future for them. He must not even contemplate it.

"Beatrice… I must not speak what is within my heart. It would not be honorable."

"Then I will speak what is in mine." There was the confidence he remembered, the spark of light in her eyes, the bright spirit that had charmed and intrigued him. She would not hesitate to declare her love. For a moment Beatrice glanced away across the garden. But when she turned back there was no pleasure, any love in her face obscured. Her lips were compressed into a thin line, her eyes full of pain and anger. Her reproachful words were as a sharp slap against his flesh.

"I loved you. I looked for marriage with you. How could I have been so mistaken? You betrayed me, Richard. You betrayed our love."

"Betrayed? What is this…?"

"I have had a long time to think about this—and I think you never loved me at all." Her voice broke a little, then was quickly controlled. There were certainly no tears in those snapping eyes. "I think it was simply a Twelfth Night flirtation for you."

"Beatrice… How can you think that?" He was astounded. "My heart is yours—has always been yours." He seized her hand, regardless of those who might see.

The lady was unimpressed. The slap became a sharp blade twisted in his heart. "I expect you forgot me as soon I was out of sight. I expect my family was not sufficiently important for you to pursue the connection."

"Never that!"

But she was implacable. Dragged her fingers from his clasp as if his touch burned. "My mother warned me that it would happen. I should have known that men are not to be trusted."

The blood ran as ice in his veins—over a shiver of righteous anger. "How can you make so outrageous a claim? How can you think so little of me?" He sought in his mind for something to say to prove his love, to extricate himself from this bottomless crevasse that had yawned before his feet without warning. Thrusting his hand within the furred neck of his tunic, he drew out a small velvet-wrapped package. He held it out, the velvet falling away.

"If I did not love you, Beatrice, if I do not still love you, why would I carry this next to my heart? Why have I treasured it and kept it by me if the giver meant nothing to me?"

It was a swan, small enough to fit into the palm of his hand, large enough to see clearly the clever workmanship. It had been fashioned of ivory, now warm and cream with age. Its feathers on wing and breast had been carved by the hand of a master, a delight of soft curves and hard edges. A masterpiece of observation and skill. Gold had been used to pick out its beady eye, its beak and feet: its neb and claws were equally striking in black enamel. It was a Lancastrian piece, intended for one who would support his Majesty for the swan proudly bore around its neck a golden crown. Whilst attached to the crown was a heavy gold chain, perhaps a symbol of the binding of its wearer to the cause. The chain ended in a ring for securing to a garment with a pin, as a safety device.

A wonderfully distinctive jewel, as suitable for a man as for a woman.

"I remember the day you gave this to me. A Hatton legacy, you said, and yours to give. You gave it to me as a symbol of your love. I have kept it—a priceless keepsake from the lady who holds my heart in her hands."

"So do I remember. But I did not know that my devotion would outlive yours."

"Beatrice!" Lord Richard was astounded. "You are the light of my life. Do you not know that?"

But Lady Beatrice Somerton would not be soothed. "No, Richard. What use in denial? If that is so—if you truly loved me—how could you abandon me to marriage with a man such as William Somerton? You promised that you would come for me—and yet you did not."

"No! That is not so…"

But she would not listen, the misery of two years of blighted marriage a tight band around her chest. "You have broken my heart, Richard Stafford!"

"Beatrice…"

What more Lord Richard would have said in his own defense Beatrice was not to know for there was the sudden eruption of movement, the heavy impact of booted feet, of opening and closing doors, and then Lord Grey strode into the

Hall already pulling on his gloves. His lips were tight-pressed, his spine rigid, his eyes alight with temper but he kept a grip on his words. His gaze searched the room.

"Stafford!" He signaled Lord Richard to his side. "The horses. We leave immediately."

"Yes, my lord."

Lord Grey beckoned in impatience when Richard would have hesitated beside the lady, then turned to his host. "I must thank you for your hospitality, Sir William." His voice denied his words.

"It was my pleasure, my lord." But anyone seeing Somerton's expression would not think it. "I am sorry that my reply was not to your liking." Stiff disapproval sat weightily on him.

"No. It was not. I clearly misread the strength of your sentiments. I trust you will not come to regret your decision."

"My decision is not final, my lord, as I made clear. I have to consider carefully where my duty might lie—and my loyalty."

"As do we all," Lord Grey bit off the words. "I trust that you will also consider *carefully* where your best interests might be. It would be a foolish man who aligns himself with the losing side."

Sir William remained silent in the face of this enigmatic response. Then, "Are you so certain that there will be a battle, my lord?"

"Without doubt. In two or three days." Lord Grey gestured sharply to the gentlemen who still watched and listened with ill-concealed interest. "The two armies are too close to retreat."

"Is negotiation not possible?"

"Warwick might, but Buckingham will not allow him near the king." Lord Grey made no attempt to hide his contempt for King Henry. "Our anointed king is, unfortunately, not always in charge of his wits."

Sir William ignored so treasonous a comment but his reply remained conciliatory enough. "I shall make my decision, my lord, and inform you of it."

"Very well. I advise you not to disappoint me." Lord Grey turned his back. "My lady." A brusque bow in the direction of Lady Beatrice. "Gentlemen. Come."

Without another word, Lord Grey turned on his heel and strode to the door, leaving his words to echo and re-echo in Beatrice's mind. A battle. Within the week and close at hand.

"So you will be engaged in the fighting?" Her heart told her to go to Lord Richard, to touch him, as he gathered up his sword and cloak, to follow him to the door. But she would not. Could not. Had she not told him that her heart was broken and he was the cause?

"Yes." The bite in his voice struck home.

"It will be dangerous. You could be hurt."

"Undoubtedly." The edge in his reply became more intense. "I would like to think that you cared. I am no longer certain."

For a long moment she closed her eyes to erase the terrible images. How was it possible for her to want him to touch her and yet at the same time to accuse him? Yes, he had broken his promise to her. But for him to be in danger in battle within an arrow shot of her home, perhaps to be taken prisoner, to be wounded, even suffering a lethal blow that would cost him his life. And she would not know of it… It was almost more than she could bear.

Richard saw her conflict but was at a loss. Her husband and Lord Grey had both made their way out to the courtyard. The horses were being led from the stables, the escort already mounted. He could hear Lord Grey's raised and impatient voice calling his name, demanding his presence.

He stopped in the doorway, looked back over his shoulder.

"I must go, Beatrice. But I cannot leave it like this. We need to talk. There is no time now. But after the battle, God willing, I will return." Too late now. Too late for explanations. "I neither betrayed nor abandoned you. I would that it were possible for us to be together. That I could find a way to make it so…" No. By God! He would not leave her with this matter lying so viciously between them.

Against all the dictates of common sense he strode back across the room to face her, to curve an arm around her waist and drag her close in a kiss. It was not a gentle meeting of lips, contained no tender reminiscence or soft promise of fulfillment for the future. Rather it was a devastating statement of need. At first Beatrice resisted, pushing against his shoulders, her mouth cold and unresponsive, indignant that he should treat her so. But he would have none of it. His hold tightened pressing her close, breast and thigh, until she was aware of nothing but the hard strength of his body against her softness.

"Beatrice, I want you…"

And she knew it, trembled at the raw physical response in his body that was instantly mirrored in her own. Relentless, shockingly intimate, his mouth claimed and owned, until her lips warmed and parted beneath his demand. It was an assault of sheer ungoverned passion, speaking wildly of pain and loss and a terrible uncertainty. Of a possession that could never be. Of a divide that scored both to the bone. It seared through his veins to hers, to the very heart, leaving them both scorched by the heat of it. Then he released her, as suddenly as he had claimed her, afraid to prolong the intimacy.

"I will come to you. I will not allow this misunderstanding to remain between us. Remember this, whatever the future holds. My love and devotion are yours. On that promise, I shall keep the Hatton swan."

Then with a curt bow of the head as his only acknowledgment, he placed the velvet-wrapped brooch back into the breast of his coat and strode from the room, unable to say more.

"Richard…" Anguish heavy in her breast, Beatrice stretched out her hands, swamped by a need to beg forgiveness. But he was gone beyond her recall.

Which left her with no choice but to stand and watch, his words etched in her mind, as he seized his reins from one of the grooms and swung into the saddle of his splendid dark bay destrier. Richard turned the animal and without a backward glance rode through the gates and across the moat. Against her better judgment she climbed quickly to stand on the battlement walk, to continue watching as the cloud of dust gradually swallowed up the little party of horsemen in the distance.

She pressed her fingers to her lips as if she would retain the memory of the imprint of his mouth on hers, the bright fire of it. It still burned there, as it did through every inch of her body. She could taste him in the lingering heat. The threatened tears came at last, only to be quickly wiped away. She would not weep, neither for herself nor for him. But, "I am afraid for you," she murmured. "I love you, Richard Stafford," she admitted. Because in spite of everything, she could not deny that she still wanted him, still longed to be with him to feel the power of his body, experience his bold caresses. And that made his casual desertion of her so much worse. Now he had left her. She doubted that she would ever see him again. She had not even bidden him farewell, only left him with the memory of her harsh words and bitter accusations.

I will come to you.

God grant that he would. Because he had kept her gift and his kiss spoke to her heart. All she could do was hold tight to the hope that his love for her was as strong as ever.

* * *

"Beatrice!"

All emotions quickly governed, her face a blank mask, she descended to the courtyard where Sir William waited for her. His temper had clearly not improved. If anything, it was stoked by some occurrence in Lord Grey's visit to an even higher temperature.

"Bring more ale to the parlor. And a flagon of the best Bordeaux. Quickly now." Then as he stalked inside, "Tell Lawson to bring it. I have no need of you."

Without a word she went to do as she was bid. It no longer seemed to matter. Nothing very much mattered when measured against the loss that gripped her heart in its painful fist.

Lord Richard Stafford rode away from Great Houghton, the grooves beside his eyes and mouth very much in evidence. His mind was full of nothing but the woman who had just questioned his honor and integrity.

Some two years or more before, he had by chance attended the traditional gathering at King Henry's court at Westminster. And there he had set eyes on Beatrice Hatton. How long had it taken him to fall in love with her? As long as it took to plunge headlong into the depths of her violet-blue eyes, as soft and velvety as a pansy, and willingly drown there. He had watched her, distantly at first, admiring her joyful participation in the dancing, her fearless skill when riding a horse to the hunt. Her shining happiness in all that she did. And he had been drawn to her, the sharp tingle in his blood giving him no rest. Until the archery contest when he had made his first approach, encouraging her to respond to his subtle flattery, enjoying her innocent response. Being captivated by the indomitable life force, the translucent charm. Vivid and unquestionably beautiful, she had drawn all eyes, but it was to *him* that she looked. On *him* that she smiled and granted her hand in the succession of round dances.

Now as he rode from Great Houghton, Lord Richard found himself remembering her as she had sat between her smiling mother and glowering father, watching the dancing, her desire to participate clear in every line of her body, the tapping of her foot against the tiled floor. She had been wearing, he recalled, a high-waisted gown of figured silk trimmed with fur at hem and low neckline. The full skirt, which flowed into a train, would not make dancing an easy task but that would not hinder her with her gifts of grace and agility. Her hair had been covered by a long veil secured by a jeweled band, that did everything to emphasise the lovely clear oval of her face as the pale silk drew attention to her glorious eyes.

Then the music from flutes and horns and drums had struck up a popular tune and Richard had known that he must dance with her. So he had approached Sir Walter Hatton, stern and forbidding despite the lighthearted occasion.

"I would ask your daughter to partner me in this dance, Sir Walter. With your permission."

Sir Walter had frowned, pursed his lips in sour thought, · misliking the smooth elegance of the young courtier who bowed so gracefully toward Beatrice. But he could not so openly refuse without comment. Stafford had powerful connections. Besides, Lady Margery smiled her agreement and Beatrice gave a little tug to her father's sleeve. So he would comply, if grudgingly.

Sir Walter hunched his shoulders. "If she wishes it, sir."

Of course she did. Her face was alight with it. She was on her feet before her father could change his mind, her hand in Richard's as he led her to join the other dancers.

"Did you think I would refuse?" Her fingers curled into his, her teeth glinted in a smile of sheer delight.

"No, lady. But I thought your father might."

She glanced over to where her father continued to grimace at the merriment in general and at her and her partner in particular. "He has no love for the Court. He is here out of duty only, and in loyalty to the king. He suspects all courtiers of empty smiles and false words. But why would he refuse something so trivial as a dance?"

"He might have other ideas for his beautiful daughter."

Her brow furrowed in a little frown. "I do not take your meaning, my lord. Ideas other than what?"

"Of you being my lover. Of being my wife."

Her eyes flew to his face. Her pretty lips opened in a perfect O of shock.

"My lord… Indeed…"

"I would never have believed it possible for me to fall hopelessly, helplessly in love with you—with any woman—with so little acquaintance. But now I do, Mistress Hatton. What do you think? Can such a thing as love at first meeting exist?"

"I…I think you flatter me, my lord." She turned away from him in the dance, only to return a moment later, to put her hand trustingly into his.

"Of course I flatter you," he continued, noting the deepening color in her cheeks with appreciation. "How could I not flatter so lovely a lady? But it comes from a heart which you hold within these pretty fingers." He tightened his clasp on her hand as they moved closer together in the dance.

"Lord Richard!"

"Mistress Hatton!"

Perforce they separated again. But she never took her eyes

from him. And then they were together once more, one of his arms firmly around her waist as they trod the lively steps.

"I think I have fallen in love with you. What do you think?" He whispered the words against her ear.

She glanced up. "Is your heart beating as fast as mine, my lord?"

"Undoubtedly, lady. It beats for you."

"Then I think you could very well be right."

And he had been. Somewhere between the festive carol-dance and the intricate steps of the sprightly pavane, he had fallen in love. As effortlessly and completely as that.

It had presented a soldier adept in military tactics with no difficulty at all to organise any number of private meetings with the lady. Where eventually he could persuade her compliance in a kiss, a close embrace. Although, as he recalled, she had needed little persuasion, only reassurance for her innocence. Her emotions were as engaged as his and they had yearned for more than a stolen kiss. He had wanted marriage, and so had she.

They had discovered one particular gallery, little more than a corridor between one reception room and another in the vast Palace of Westminster. But it was blessed with window seats, and too cold for most to brave except through necessity. It had been witness to their exchanged vows of love. When she had shivered in a brisk draft he had taken off his fur-lined cloak to wrap it round her, to envelop her in its heavy warmth. She had sighed with pleasure and leaned in to him. Until a lady and gentleman had walked past, with slanted glances, knowing smiles.

"We must go. I think I should not be alone here with you. My mother would not approve." She had tightened nervous fingers on his arm.

"And your father would probably have me whipped from the palace!" He had smiled his understanding. "My lovely Beatrice—will you grant me one privilege before we go?"

"I might." Her teeth gleamed in the shadows.

"Your hair, lady. Will you let me unpin your hair?"

"What would my mother say? She would assuredly disapprove." But Beatrice laughed at the prospect, not caring. "Very well, dear Richard. If you can. But I warn you—it is no easy task."

So he had wrestled with the thin gold wires that held the butterfly headdress together. Removed it carefully, laid it aside. Then the transparent veil, as light as gossamer. Finally the pins that secured her hair.

"It is easier to get into my suit of armor with all its separate plates!" he remembered muttering as he dropped the pins on the floor and she tutted tolerantly at his clumsiness.

"I thought you would have some skill in this, my lord." Her eyes had twinkled under his ministrations.

"Perhaps." His shoulders might lift in a careless denial but he could not prevent a smug smile. "But on this occasion, lady, you should know that my hands are cold and my fingers less than agile." A soft kiss had effectively silenced her.

Then her hair had been free. Had fallen to her shoulders and beyond. He had curled his fingers into it as it glimmered in the cold light from the window behind them. Soft waves of it, a deep rich brown as lustrous as his sables that wrapped her around.

"I shall remember this." He bent his head to press his lips to it, to turn his cheek against it.

"Someone is coming!" Beatrice had tugged on his arm at the distant clatter of feet against the paving. So compromising a situation should be avoided by a carefully brought up girl.

And so Lord Richard had hidden the wires and the veil beneath her full skirts, pulled up the hood of his cloak to disguise her from inquisitive eyes. She was young and he was mindful of her unblemished reputation.

It was the last time that they had been alone together. The last time they had been able to speak together, apart from the terrible constraints of that final meeting in her family lodgings in Westminster.

He never did ask what excuse she had made to her mother for returning without her butterfly veil.

The smile that now touched his mouth as he rode away from Great Houghton was bitter indeed. Because he had also been correct in his initial reading of Sir Walter Hatton. That gentleman would rather give his daughter to a man from his own narrow world than to a frivolous courtier, even though that courtier was a Stafford, with all the blood and connections of the name, and with a name as a soldier to his credit. So Beatrice Hatton, who had stolen his heart, was spirited away from Court with its shallow influences and had then been given in marriage by her family to a man who did not deserve her as his wife. Sir William Somerton, aged before his time, selfish, impatient, with a fine streak of self-importance running through his every gesture, his every word, was no fit husband for a young woman of Beatrice's demeanor, full of life and spirit.

As good as his promise to Beatrice, he had made his farewells at Court and taken himself to Mears Ashby, determined to face Sir Walter, pursue his lady and carry her off to his own home. He had got no farther than the courtyard, hardly dismounted from his horse. Sir Walter had been less than welcoming.

"I am here to ask you to reconsider your decision, Sir Walter."

"Lord Richard. You were not expected. Much as I admire your tenacity, my decision is made. I will not change my mind."

"I would offer a substantial settlement for Beatrice as my wife."

"I care not for the Stafford name or for any settlement. Somerton is an influential man in these parts."

"May I see your daughter?"

"No, you may not."

"Can I not at least make my formal farewell." By now Lord Richard would have grasped at any opportunity to see her.

"No. She is not here. She is staying at the home of her new husband."

"What? Married so soon?" He could still remember the bitter blow that he was too late.

Sir Walter's brusque reply had held no compromise. "No. She is there at the invitation of her lord's family. Sewing bridal clothes, and such. Women's work. She will remain there until the ceremony. All has been settled between Somerton and myself and the agreements signed. My daughter will not return here."

Which had left Richard adrift, with no case to argue. And no action to take, unless he intended to beat on the door of her prospective groom and demand the bride for himself. To carry her off on horseback and wed her in the face of strong opposition and legal settlements. It might be appropriate behavior, and romantic at that, for minstrels' songs of chivalric love and eternal devotion, but it would bring scandal down on his lady's name as well as on his own. He had returned to London in a sour mood.

So it would seem that her father had not told her of his renewed request. Well, he could put that right. But there was nothing that Richard could do to change the situation, either then or now. Beatrice was still as far removed from him as—well, as the maidens of ancient mythology who stared down on him with lustrous eyes and unsmiling mouths from the tapestries stitched by long-dead Stafford women at his own home at Elton's Marsh. Richard cursed the memory of her dead father who had rejected his own undeniable reputation, his position at court and his highborn Stafford blood in so cavalier a manner. Choosing over and above these advantages the Somerton connection and the expansion of local power, since the Hatton and Somerton estates marched together. Local politics had most assuredly been weighed against Beatrice's own wishes and her happiness. Lord Richard tightened his fingers on the reins, causing his stallion to toss its head and fidget at the unusual treatment.

Which brought him to his senses. Deliberately he attempted to force his thoughts into more immediate channels. Such as his strengthening suspicion of Lord Grey de Ruthin's interests and motives. The reason for Grey's presence at Great Houghton. His obvious fury with Sir William's response. There had never been any real suspicion of Grey's loyalty to King Henry but perhaps it would be wise to keep a close eye on Lord Grey de Ruthin in future. Lord Richard must report his suspicions to his cousin, the Duke of Buckingham, who had been instrumental in his own presence here today in de Ruthin's entourage. He stared with narrowed eyes at de Ruthin's rigid shoulders up ahead as if he might read the man's ambitions through the velvet of his tunic. In recent weeks de Ruthin had been very busy in his meetings and close discussion with a surprising number of Lancastrian lords.

Lord Richard sighed, breathed out slowly. With a battle so imminent, it was imperative that he concentrate on his duty to the Crown. He had no right to place Beatrice Hatton, her present and future happiness, before the security of his king. Or to consider his own happiness of paramount importance, for that matter.

Lord Richard proved to be the worst of company on his ride back to the Lancastrian headquarters at Northampton. His noble companions eyed him askance after a few short replies. They left him to brood.

Chapter Three

On the morning following the visit of Lord Grey, Sir William began to make preparations for the imminent battle. Rickerby, the Commander of the small garrison at Great Houghton was in receipt of a list of terse instruction. His men-at-arms must tend to their weapons, their leather jacks and helms. Beatrice was similarly instructed to oversee the liveried surcoats that would proclaim their allegiance to the Somerton family. The silver gryphon, wings spread in flight, shining out from a deep blue background made a bold splash of color. Messengers were sent out to William's retainers in the surrounding manors to inform them that their lord would require their feudal service in battle.

Somerton's own suit of armor was unpacked from its wrappings by his squire, cleaned and placed ready in his bedchamber. Beside it, the great visored bascinet with throat and neck guards. His sword was honed to a lethal edge.

Then all they had to do was to wait. Which gave Beatrice far more time than she needed to worry and think and remember.

It was inevitable that the images to crowd her mind were those from the occasion when she first saw Lord Richard

Stafford. Overawed as she had been by her visit to the royal court and the splendor of the occasion, yet still she had noticed the handsome figure of the influential Stafford lord. Had watched and admired him from afar. Discreetly, of course. What interest would a young girl from a small estate hold for this man when his family had the ear of the king? Still light in years—indeed, he was only some few years older than her own brother, Ned—Lord Richard bore his authority and his shining reputation as effortlessly as he rode his destrier in the lists at the Christmastide tournament—and with equal success—a subject of envy and admiration from both men and women. No! Lord Richard Stafford could look as high as he pleased for a bride, or for a lady to share his bed in a more temporary and carnal arrangement if that was his choice.

But still her eyes were drawn to him. She was aware of his presence whenever he entered a room. His figure carried the fashions of the day so extremely well. She could still see him, bright painted in her mind, standing within a small group of royal advisors in a thigh-length tunic of rich patterned damask, his knee-length boots in the softest of leather, his hose of finest wool. A low-crowned, draped hat with a gleaming jewel pinned to the upturned brim called attention to his face. She thought that it was his fine eyes with their dark brows, reminding her of the peregrine falcon in her father's mews, that had captivated her. When he claimed the hand of one of the court ladies to dance, she knew for the first time in her adult life the unpleasant slick of jealousy over her skin.

But of course he would not look at her. A Stafford would not look at a girl who had barely left her lessons at her mother's knee!

Until one day. Beatrice could not but smile at the memory of the day, brighter than the rest and with a gleam of sunshine, when archery butts had been erected in one of the courtyards to allow the assembled company some outdoor activity other than the hunt. All who wished, including the ladies of the court, were encouraged to take part.

Beatrice could see it now. Well taught by her brother, she was quite confident in selecting one of the smaller long bows. All she needed were the arrows. And when she would have gone to collect a sheaf for herself, she had found Lord Richard suddenly there, standing at her side. He made an elegant little bow. His fine lips curved in pleasure at her surprise.

"Mistress Hatton. Allow me to be of assistance." He presented her with the first of a sheaf of arrows.

He knows my name! She could feel her face flush, her mouth become dry. Prayed that her hands would not tremble at his proximity.

"Thank you, sir. You are kind." She lifted the arrow from his elegant hand.

There was much jocular comment and friendly laughter from the knots of bystanders around them; that perhaps it was necessary to keep a fair distance now that the ladies were to participate.

"And should I step back?" Lord Richard asked in all seriousness, his eyes on hers. It was the first time that she had noted the flecks of gold that warmed his cool regard.

She angled a glance. "Do you not trust me to be true in my aim, my lord?"

He smiled more widely at her deliberate flirtation. The lady might be youthful and innocent but she undoubtedly had a pretty manner. "I think I might trust you very well, Mistress Hatton."

"With the first arrow? First arrows are notoriously unpredictable, my lord."

"Perhaps. Do you need to find your range?"

The undercurrent between them, the swirling current that wrapped itself around her senses, was so strong it had almost choked her as she sought for a reply.

"I think I know the range very well."

"Then let us try it."

"Would you wager on the outcome, my lord?"

"Indeed I would." He was watching her, as she knew. Could not take his eyes from her animated face. "For what is a contest without a wager? A gold noble says that you hit the target. With the first arrow."

"And at the very center?" Her eyes widened along with her less-than-innocent query, allowing him the full impact of her direct gaze.

Charmed beyond belief, Lord Richard laughed. "You drive a hard bargain, Mistress Hatton. I will respond as any gentleman must to so confident a lady. Two gold nobles if you achieve such magnificent accuracy."

Beatrice nodded. Her mother would be truly horrified if she could overhear her well-brought-up daughter. Wanton indeed!

"Very well, my lord."

She positioned her slight body sideways to the target, drew back the bow-string with a fine grace and considerable expertise to her ear. Sighted calmly along the goose-feathered arrow. And let it fly.

It buried itself in the center of the target. Which, after all, she silently acknowledged, was not so very distant.

There was a ripple of applause and comment around them, but neither was aware. Lord Richard took her hand, raised it formally to his lips.

"Your accuracy is magnificent indeed, Mistress Hatton."

"I warned you." She knew that her fingers closed tightly over his.

He leaned a little closer so that his next words were for her ears only. "Would your lethal arrows be as fleeting and deadly in piercing my heart, do you suppose?"

"I could hope so, my lord." She understood his meaning perfectly. And had no hesitation in answering him in like form although she blushed with deep color. "For my heart is also touched. I would not wish to suffer the torment alone."

And when Lord Richard Stafford later had the opportunity to hand over the two gold nobles to the fair archer, he did so in a private corner of the inner garden, with a kiss. Not a formal, chaste caress to her cheek, to which no one could take exception. But with his arms holding her close, breast and hip and thigh molded against his, and a pressure of mouth against mouth that both possessed and promised everything. A kiss that left her momentarily stunned and speechless and set anticipation humming through her blood.

Now in her bedchamber at Great Houghton, she sighed as she remembered. And folded the two gold nobles close within her hand. She would never part with them.

And she remembered also that in that inner garden Lord Richard had drawn a glowing picture for her of his own home. Elton's Marsh in Norfolk. Made it live for her with words that spoke of his deep love for it.

"Is it large with drafts that whistle down long corridors?" Beatrice had been skeptical of his description. "And dark corners where it is impossible to see to set a stitch or to write a letter?" She knew both inconveniences from her own home at Mears Ashby

He had grinned at her disbelief, giving his often stern face a youthful charm that caused her to tingle with awareness of him. "Yes, it is large but less drafty and certainly lighter than most.

"And how can that be? Do you boast, my lord?" She had rewarded him with an arch look and raised brows.

"If I boast, it is of my grandfather's doing. You should know that he fought in the war in Europe and came home a wealthy man. In France he had seen castles greatly different from our own and was attracted. So he built Elton's Marsh with them in mind."

"And you are proud of it." She could see it in his eyes, hear it in his voice, as he described it for her.

"It is splendid." Lord Richard had drawn her hand through his arm as they strolled down a damp path in the garden, skipping the puddles, brushing through wet branches that overhung the path. Caring nothing for the silver drops that might soak their clothes. "It is built of brick and shines red-gold in the sunlight. In an evening after a fair day it glows with warmth. My grandfather had larger windows put in and many small chambers rather than a single Great Hall. It has a garden as extensive as this one."

"But would it not be easy to attack and destroy such a house?"

"Why, no. My grandfather was a prudent man, so Elton's Marsh has a moat and a tall lookout tower. Ramparts and a gatehouse, of course. I can repel anyone whom I do not wish to receive at my door."

Beatrice could not resist the question. "Would you be willing to receive me at your door, my lord?"

"I should be delighted to do so," Lord Richard replied promptly. "Indeed, I think I will insist."

And oh! how she had hoped and dreamed that he would, lured by his kisses, awakened to the needs of her own body by the knowing finesse of his mouth and clever caress of his hands. Even now her blood heated at the memory of his tongue tracing the outline of her lips, teasing the sensitive corners, encouraging her to allow him access to explore the inner softness. So intimate a possession. As intimate as the pressure of his hand on her breast so that her nipples tightened and her breath sighed with the glory of it. How could she not have fallen in love with him and believed his every enticing picture of their life together.

Instead her dreams had been shattered. Her family left the Court, her father full of plans to wed her to William Somerton. Lady Margery, her mother, could only advise her daughter that she would forget any festive dalliance as soon as she returned to the normality of life far away from the palace of Westminster. That she suffered from mere infatuation with a man of experience and glamour. Beatrice's hand clenched hard around the shining metal of the coins. The love had remained at the center of her heart, tightly locked there, even when the days passed and he did not come. Even when William had pushed the ring onto her finger.

But Richard had forgotten her. Although he had denied it, perhaps it was simply that he had not loved her enough.

She placed the coins once more into the coffer that held her jewels, sore of heart.

For she must learn once more to live without him.

On the fourth day the inhabitants of Great Houghton Hall awoke to stormy skies and heavy rain that showed no immediate sign of abating. Then they became aware of the unmistakable sounds of an army on the move. There was no doubt. It was the Earl of Warwick's army in support of the royal claim of the absent Duke of York, very close and making its ponderous way toward Northampton.

The battle would begin as Lord Grey had predicted.

Beatrice expected Sir William to gather his men and leave

immediately, to avoid the Yorkist troops and join the Lancastrian flank. To her amazement, the courtyard remained silent with no activity beyond the movement of the servants between dairy and kitchen. She found Sir William seated on the dais in the Great Hall, frowning at the rain, which still rattled with summer ferocity against the windows. He tapped his fingers on the table with a hideous and persistent monotony, a dark thundercloud on his brow, saying nothing, unaware when Beatrice stepped in.

The hours of the morning ticked by. Rickerby hovered outside the door, muttering at the delay, awaiting orders that never came. Master Lawson watched from the shadows. Sir William remained where he was with now a tankard of ale at his elbow.

The troop movements without continued.

Finally Beatrice could stand it no longer. She took up a position at her lord's elbow.

"That clamor is surely the Yorkist army under the Earl of Warwick," she stated, unnecessarily.

"Yes."

"Will you not go?"

"No."

Sir William continued to sit in sullen silence, his face deliberately turned away from her. Almost, she thought, as if he did not dare meet her critical gaze. Which she found impossible to believe.

"Will you not join the Lancastrians and fight for your king against those who would usurp his rightful power? Both Warwick and York have been declared traitor by Parliament."

"It is not a simple decision." The sharp snap of a reply could not hide the anxieties in her lord's eyes, in the heavily scored lines that bracketed his mouth. He looked drawn, as if he had not slept well, and older than his years by a good decade.

"But His Majesty will look for you, for your standard. Have not Somertons always stood for the Crown?" Beatrice lifted her hands, then allowed them to fall in total incomprehension.

At that, Sir William surged to his feet, pushing away his chair so fiercely that it rocked back on its legs. "Oh, yes! Somertons have a fine reputation for their loyalty! Without question we cleave to Lancaster. But you have no sense of the choice put on my shoulders, girl." He swung away from the lady, who so innocently masqueraded as his conscience, and stomped from the room, leaving her to look after him in appalled amazement.

The midday meal was served, where no one showed any appetite. The spiced rabbit casserole, a favorite of Sir William's, congealed in its dish. The delicious Lombard chicken pasties, bursting with meat and spices, went untasted. The waiting continued. The manoeuvring armies had fallen silent. The brittle silence also continued in the house. This time Beatrice chose not to break it.

Then at two o' clock, the rain still falling steadily, distant shouts and cries again drifted to them through the heavy air. Laced through it all was the heavy crash of cannon fire.

"It has begun." Sir William paced the Hall, teeth gnawing at his bottom lip.

"My lord…" Beatrice did not know what to say.

But Sir William had finally made his decision and raised his head. "We leave immediately." He signaled to his steward. "Tell Rickerby to attend me here."

"But you cannot go like this—you are not wearing your armor—you will be in danger…" Beatrice's words died as her husband lifted his hand to silence her.

"No. I think it will not be necessary." His expression was grim indeed and it was, she thought, not from fear of the battle or of death. "I should have been gone from here some hours since. I know what my conscience dictates but I dare not…" The words were bitten off. "This will be protection enough. Help me." He began to shrug into a leather brigandine jacket, lined with metal plates to give some basic protection, such as his archers might wear.

"At least take your helm. You cannot go without."

"Very well." The squire was dispatched. "Listen!" Sir William's hand closed round Beatrice's wrist, fingers digging in with sudden intensity. "I fear the outcome… I shall not be gone long, but, God help me, I must give my allegiance to Lord Grey de Ruthin."

He rode out of the gate at the head of his liveried retainers, a proud little army, leaving Beatrice to watch in mounting horror, not understanding the direction of his words.

On the flat expanse of ground before the walls of Northampton, the Lancastrian forces on the right flank under the command of Lord Grey de Ruthin, broke their tight formation to allow the Yorkists to charge through unhindered. From where he controlled the center, the Duke of Buckingham stood aghast, unable to believe what he saw.

"What are they doing? In God's name, we are betrayed! If Warwick gets through our lines, the king himself will be open to attack and capture."

"Do I attack?" Lord Richard Stafford at his right hand signaled his men to come up.

"Yes. Give no quarter. If Warwick takes possession of the king, we must fear for his life." Buckingham slammed his visor down. "We must protect His Majesty at all cost."

So Richard Stafford led his liveried men-at-arms toward the unfolding disaster. The Stafford banner, red and black

with its proud silver lion, flew bravely overhead. The deep cry
of *A Stafford* rent the air above the thud of hooves and the cries
of the troops. As he drew his sword and prepared for some
fierce hand-to-hand fighting Lord Richard cursed the war,
the outrageous ambition of the Duke of Warwick, and the day
when it had become impossible to determine friend from foe.

Then there was no time to think at all.

Beatrice waited for the rest of that endless day. A prema-
ture dusk fell, the rain turned to drizzle. William did not
return. But fleeing soldiers, some of them bearing obvious
Lancastrian colors, began to pass along the road outside the
castle, making haste and in disarray. Of their leaders there was
not a sign.

"What news?" The sentry at Great Houghton called the
enquiry.

The reply chilled Beatrice's blood to ice in her veins. "The
king is defeated. Warwick's troops are running amok. King
Henry is taken captive."

Beatrice sat in her chamber throughout a long night. She
had no thought of sleep, worried for the safety of her husband,
of course, as a wife must be. But also swamped with a slick
wash of guilt that her true anxieties were elsewhere.

For she knew not the fate of Lord Richard Stafford. The fear
for him held her in its vicious talons, too hot to allow tears.

The glorious sunshine of the following day, so cruel in its
beauty after the torrential storms and the bloody massacre,
beat down on the somber cavalcade making its way to Great
Houghton Hall. Beatrice watched it approach, scanned the
faces and then, its meaning heavy in her breast, ordered the

gates open. She was waiting in the courtyard as they entered. Some of the Somerton men-at-arms led the party, but not all who had departed with Sir William returned. She was relieved to see Rickerby in their midst. There was also Sir Edward Hatton, her brother. And at the rear, the supply wagon bearing a shrouded form.

"Ned." Beatrice came to stand at his stirrup, her face as white as he had ever seen it against the deep red damask of her gown. "Is it William?"

"Beatrice…" Ned dismounted to stand before her, similar in height and coloring. Similar in temperament, but maturity had brought him a calmer outlook. He took off his hat and scrubbed a hand over his face where the strain of the previous day's activity showed clearly. He took his sister's hand in his. "Beatrice. What can I say…?"

"It is William, isn't it?"

"Yes."

"You saw it happen?" Her lips felt stiff, as if pronouncing the words was difficult.

"Yes. I was there."

"Let me see him."

She walked to the side of the wagon. Ned leaned in to cast aside the wrapping from the body and Beatrice looked down on the face of her dead husband. His clothes and hair were filthy from where he had fallen in the churned mud of the battlefield. The fading red of his grizzled hair was almost obliterated by the deeper rust of dried blood that streaked his face and matted his clothing. His eyes were closed but his mouth was set in a twist of pain or perhaps fear. She touched one of the cold hands folded on his breast.

"William…"

It was difficult to feel grief for this man who had treated

her with such callous indifference and contempt. She could not weep for him.

Ah, but she could weep for Richard Stafford.

Was Richard Stafford lying somewhere wounded? Dead even? She had sent him into battle, refusing him the words of love, of concern and tenderness that were in her heart, driven instead by his rejection of her. But what if he were dead, his final thoughts of her only that she had condemned him? She would never forgive herself.

Remembering her duties, she gave orders for the men-at-arms to disperse, to be given ale and food. For the chapel to be readied to receive Sir William's body. Then turned back to Ned.

"Tell me what happened. We learned from men passing the gates that our forces were overrun by the Yorkists."

"It was a disaster," Ned answered, his voice thick with sheer disbelief. "They drove us from the field and put to death every one of the Lancastrian lords they could lay their hands on."

"And William was cut down, too."

"Yes. He was not wearing his full armor. A brigandine such as his would never stop the heavy blade of a sword. What was the man thinking to risk his life so?"

Beatrice shook her head but did not explain William's strange delay on the day of the battle. What did it matter? William was dead.

"Oh, by the by, I found this." Ned broke into her thoughts as he began to dig in his pockets. "I recognised it immediately. I suppose you gave it to William as a charm, a safeguard. Although I would consider it far too valuable to risk in a bat-tlefield." His lips twisted in a wry grimace. "It was pure chance that I saw it…"

She saw what he held in his hand. Impossible! Her heart tripped from its normal beat, her throat dried as she recalled where she had last seen it. She struggled to find her voice. "Where did you get that?"

"In the mud. I saw the gleam of gold. A little way from Somerton's body. It must have been torn from his clothing when he fell."

Beatrice could not find the words. She took the object from Ned's hand, turned it over.

"Did you give it to your husband?"

She looked at Ned in sheer horror.

He did not understand her response. Saw only the pale skin, the white shade around her mouth as she compressed her lips, the deep color of her eyes as they took in the meaning of his revelation. It was simply grief and shock, he decided. A political marriage did not mean that she would not mourn her lord. No need to tell her of William's ignoble deeds on the battlefield. That would only serve to bring her more grief.

Then Beatrice closed her hand over her brother's arm, nails digging in. Her voice was low but with an intensity. "What did he look like? The man who struck William down? You said that you saw him."

Why does something so inconsequential matter? If a man falls on a battlefield, what does it matter whose hand wielded the sword? But Ned would tell her this, if it would help to ease the pain that shivered over her flesh, vibrating through her fingers into his arm.

"I never saw him without his helm or even his visor raised—I was too busy defending my own skin—but the standard and the livery of his retinue was one of the Staffords—a silver lion rampant, on a half red, half black background. It is one of the most recognizable arms in the country. So it would have to be Lord Richard Stafford."

Beatrice merely stared at him, lips parted, unaware that her fingers had tightened like claws, until her brother winced in discomfort. Her mind could not take it in. The facts jostled in her brain, seeking any explanation but the one that hammered at her consciousness.

Richard Stafford had slain William.

How could this be? Were they not both fighting for the Crown?

One answer worked its insidious path into her thoughts. One answer only, as Richard's words as he had left her dropped clearly into her mind.

I will come to you. I would that it were possible for us to be together. That I could find a way to make it so.

Was that it? She had accused him of allowing her to be sold into a cruel marriage. She had made it abundantly clear that she was unhappy, had she not? Could Richard have acted on that? Could he have taken the opportunity of chaos on the battlefield to bring about William's death and so rescue her and perhaps redeem himself in her eyes? To leave her free for marriage to himself? Surely not. Surely not! And yet…it could be so. The pieces fit together far too well to be carelessly discarded.

And if so, then she was as guilty as Richard.

She turned away from Ned's concerned gaze so that he should not see her shocked agony. That the hand of the murderer should be the hand of the man whom she loved more than life itself. And that she, too, had had a hand to the sword hilt.

Oh, God! Let it not be so!

Inner conflict swept through her. The terrible relief that she was free forever of William Somerton. The delectable chance, a bright shining possibility that she could now win her heart's desire and be united with Richard. But had

Richard acted on her own promptings? Guilt pricked her skin, a greasy shame. She was implicated in that deed. And Richard. A forsworn murderer, without honor. If Richard Stafford had released her from her marriage in such a manner, he had damned forever any future they might have together. She had accused him of betraying their love. Now, between them, had they not destroyed any possibility of its ultimate fulfillment? For how could love stand up against guilt and shame and murder?

Ned left Great Houghton, reluctant to abandon his sister in her wretchedness but with a need to reassure his own family at Mears Ashby of his safety. Besides, there was nothing other he could do for her. As for the rest, the wicked and unbelievable treachery that had all but destroyed the Lancastrian army, well!—he would tell her of that when her grief was not so sharp.

Beatrice went about the necessary arrangements for the burial in the village church, all in a paralysis of grief and despair. Her actions were automatic as her thoughts swung wildly from severe doubt to a terrible certainty. When she had the opportunity, she took the little swan to her chamber, cleaned the mud from its feathers. One foot had been twisted, perhaps struck by a horse's hoof as it lay half-buried, giving the little figure a whimsical quality along with the grave dignity of its golden crown. She closed her fingers over it, holding it against her breast and at last allowed the tears to fall.

She loved him. She loved Richard Stafford and would love him until the day of her death, but could never condone this terrible deed. How could the man she loved have done something so completely dishonorable? To deliberately make her a widow so that he could marry her. How could he ever believe that a relationship between them, built on the foundations of

William Somerton's blood, might bring them happiness and fulfillment?

There was no peace for her, only hurt and wretchedness and bitter tears.

Chapter Four

William Somerton was buried with due formality in the church of St. Michael and All Angels beside generations of Somertons. His two sons and their families came to witness the occasion without undue grief. Sir William had not made himself loved by his family. Not least, Beatrice was forced to admit as she intercepted sidelong glances, by his taking a young bride. Because William's will had left her a wealthy widow. She had expected—because she knew the terms of her marriage as negotiated between William and her father—to retain full rights over her original dower. But William's settlement on her in his will could not but astound her. Overnight, with William's death, she had become a woman of more than considerable wealth and property. The house at Great Houghton, all its land and all the household goods were hers to hold for her lifetime. Yet her good fortune left her numb. It was Richard Stafford's dark features that brought the gleam of tears to her eyes as William's body was lowered into the vault.

Eventually the Somertons went home, leaving her alone at Great Houghton. She walked the silent rooms. Refused to accept the kind invitation to join Ned, his wife, Alice, and her own mother at Mears Ashby. She was the first to acknowledge that she was not good company.

In the following days the pattern of Beatrice's life remained as in William's lifetime. But her thoughts were wayward. They sometimes strayed to Lord Richard Stafford. Often were with him. Almost every moment of every day! She covered her eyes with her hands as she rose again from her restless bed. Sometimes she was swamped with an impossible love for the man. Sometimes with an uncontrollable fury that his actions—and her own ungoverned words—should have put their love so entirely out of reach.

Did she even know that he had escaped alive from the bloody aftermath of the battle? He could be dead, lost to her for all time. Her fury dissipated as mist in summer sun at the prospect of never seeing him again and pain swept through her whole body, keen as a January wind. She threw down the tapestry at which she had been unenthusiastically stitching and stalked the chamber.

This was no good! If he was alive he had blood on his hands. An unforgivable, unpardonable crime. The sparkle of temper returned to her eyes as her feet tapped along the oak boards of the floor. She drove herself about her work with an enormous energy that only flagged when she went to her bed. Then the anguish returned and, although she would have denied it to anyone foolish enough to inquire about her state of health, she could not restrain the tears. The soft skin beneath her eyes became imprinted with violet shadows, the only testimony to her anxieties that she could not prevent. It seemed to her that there was no end to her hopelessness.

Until one afternoon

"A gentleman to see you, my lady." It was Lawson, her steward, who stood at the door of her solar, who had set himself to keep a fatherly eye on his young mistress.

"Who is it, Lawson?" She looked up from the tapestry, which was once more in evidence for want of anything better to do with her mind. "Do I know him?"

"Yes, my lady. He visited here with Lord Grey de Ruthin. It is Lord Richard Stafford."

"Lord Richard…" She sat, her hands suddenly frozen on the stitchery. That he should come here to her…

"Yes, my lady, Lord Richard," Lawson replied after a little while, receiving no further orders. He prompted her. "Do I show him up? To the solar?"

"No! Not here!" Her fierce response amazed him, as did her denial. "I cannot see him." Too private. Too intimate.

"Shall I perhaps tell Lord Richard that you are indisposed, my lady?"

"Yes—no, rather. I *will* see him."

"So shall I show him to this room?" What a strange mood the lady was in today.

"No. The Great Hall. I shall come down immediately."

"Do you require some refreshment there, my lady? Lord Richard looks to have traveled some distance."

"No. We do not." She stood, braced her shoulders beneath the velvet cloth of her gown. Was it at all possible to mend the rift between them? It seemed to stretch black and dangerous at her feet.

"Very well, my lady." Lawson left, shaking his head.

Leaving Beatrice to conduct a silent conversation, a conversation between her heart and her mind, which achieved nothing but further heartache as it gave obvious victory to neither side.

He is here. He is alive. Her heart leaped with joy. I can see him, touch him. Shiver at the sound of his voice. The touch of his fingers on mine when he greets me. He is not dead in spite of all my fears.

But he killed your lord! Her logical mind frowned its disdain at the obvious delight.

I have no proof that his hand wielded the sword. A foolish clutching at straws.

What more proof do you need than that you already have? That Ned saw him do it? Her mind was relentless.

So I will ask him—and I will ask him why?—and I know that he will answer me. Her heart sighed within her, with hope that all could so simply be put right between them.

Perhaps you know why! Her mind destroyed her hope with sly insistency.

Be silent! she snapped silently and descended to the Great Hall with measured steps as if the visit were of a casual acquaintance who had merely come to pass the time of day. And she promised herself that she would remain calm and composed. Listen to what Lord Richard Stafford had to say. Refuse to judge him before he could stand in his own defence.

There he stood by the windows, where they had held their last conversation, looking down into the garden as he waited for her. She could not see his expression. He lifted his head at her entry, sensing her presence. Smiled, his dark brows lifting in pleasure at seeing her, warmth spreading across his face to dispel the cool austerity, rendering him instantly more approachable. The stern lines between mouth and nose softened, his somber eyes reflected glints of sunlight. Tall and straight, he stood before her and she could not deny her reaction to him. The blood throbbed in her body, to her very fingertips. It would be so easy to walk across the distance between them, to touch his face, to allow him to take her into the safety of his arms where the death, the destruction and loss of war would hold no sway. Where the guilt and the blame could be scoured away in the heat of passion. She was free now to allow such desired intimacy between them… For one moment Beatrice almost acted on that impulse. Ah, no. She must not forget. She stopped just inside the door, the whole expanse of the room still between them.

Beatrice! It struck him immediately that he could not read her expression with any certainty, with any accuracy. Yet here, as he knew well, was a young woman whose emotions were wont to shine in her eyes, in the curve of her lips, evident to all who saw her. In the proud manner in which she carried her head. But now… He had lived for this moment through the long days of grief and loss to his family since the battle, determined to mend her shattered trust in him. Yet there was no welcome here for him. No smile, no warmth. Nothing but a cool appraisal, almost a condemnation. She made no move toward him but stood, severe in her black gown an air of deliberate withdrawal wrapped around her. When she still did not approach, he took a step toward her but something made him preserve the distance. A faint line dug between his brows. Something was amiss here, something responsible for quenching the light in her eyes. Did she know of his own involvement in William's death, that her lord had died at his hands. Not for the first time since that appalling event, an insidious finger of guilt slithered down his spine.

Beatrice was the first to speak, emotions carefully masked.

"Lord Richard. You survived the battle."

"Yes. I was fortunate to escape Warwick's massacre." How formal she was. How reserved.

Richard's voice vibrated along her nerve endings. Deep and masculine. How often she had longed to hear those firm tones that shivered along her skin. She set her teeth against the ripple of pleasure and faced the truth.

"My husband did not survive. He was not fortunate at all."

"I know." Richard chose his words carefully and with difficulty. "I have come here to… I had to come. To explain—to beg your forgiveness." Sighed. "I am sorry that you have been made to suffer, Beatrice."

Her lips parted to reply. Before she could, he made the admission that confirmed all her mind's gleeful arguments and drenched her in grief and guilt.

"I need to tell you, Beatrice—Somerton died at my hands."

So easy to say. So destructive in its repercussions. Now Beatrice approached, but not near enough that she could touch him. That would be her undoing.

"I know," she told him. "Ned saw the attack, he saw you and the Stafford banners. He told me of it. And he brought me this—he found it in the mud near William's body." She held out her palm where the little swan winked innocently in the light.

Now he understood her reserve. "Beatrice… What can I say to you? I had no choice. I wish it had happened any other way."

"No choice?" Her voice had dropped to little more than a whisper. "That is what I do not understand. You were both supporters of Lancaster, both engaged in defence of our king against those who would capture and depose him. How could this have happened?—that you should be responsible for William's death?"

Richard drew in a breath as he watched her stricken face. *So she does not know what William had done. Do I tell her? That her lord committed treason against the king?*

But her next words brought him up short.

"I do not understand but I would like to. Richard—will you tell me this?" Her hands gripped convulsively around the ivory swan and her voice was controlled against the threat of tears. "Can you reassure me, in all honesty, that you did not strike William down to release me from this marriage and so leave me free to marry you? Can you swear that you never considered that your sword would grant me that freedom?"

He felt the blood drain from his face. She had hit on the one nub of this disaster, as an arrow direct to its target, that had destroyed all his peace of mind in recent days. In that moment as he stood facing Beatrice, the words drying on his lips, the debacle at Northampton came back to him with vivid clarity. William facing him on the battlefield, instantly recognizable by the Somerton livery, the fierce fighting around them, the need to keep King Henry safe from Yorkist clutches. Somerton coming at him with sword and dagger. His own automatic response when faced with death.

And the thought that had flashed through his mind as he raised his sword, that his next action could release Beatrice from her despicable marriage. His sword had parried Somerton's lethal lunge, beat aside another deadly blow, and then his dagger had driven into the man's body, between his ribs. Somerton had fallen, dead at his feet.

Yes, he had thought about it. What man would not? But to take a life to fulfill his own personal desires? It would be an action both unjustifiable and contemptible. He would not do it. Yet still the deed lay heavy on his heart.

Richard returned to the present to hear Beatrice repeat the question, a desperate plea in her voice. She had noted his hesitation and it confirmed all her worst fears.

"Richard. Tell me, I beg of you, that you were not aware that your action that day would free me from a husband I despised."

And being a man of honor he could not lie to her but his lips were stiff with it, his muscles and sinews braced.

"Beatrice… I cannot deny it—I knew what I was doing. I could not draw back from my engagement with William Somerton but, no—I was not unaware."

Eyes wide, her face paled in the dimness of the room. "Oh, Richard. What have you done?"

"Only what was necessary to do on the field of battle."

"To murder my husband to achieve our happiness together?"

"My own happiness was not my motivation in raising my sword against Sir William." *Do I tell her? Do I excuse my own actions by casting the blame on Somerton? Destroy any lingering respect she might hold for him, her memory of his being true to the Lancastrian cause, in the name of my own desires?*

And again he could not do it. All the tenets of chivalry in which he had been raised demanded that he should not. What happened on the battlefield should stay there. When he saw Beatrice hold out her hands to him in hopeless anguish and entreaty, his heart broke for her.

"Tell me something that can give me hope," she begged.

"I cannot change what happened on that battlefield. Or that Somerton is dead."

Tears now streamed unhindered down her cheeks. Her heart was torn apart with helpless grief. "Then how can I come to you in a new marriage, set free by the murder of my husband, when you are responsible for that death?" In utter despair, she covered her face. "If only some other hand had done it."

"But it was my hand." His bitter words reflected his thoughts. "I killed Somerton, and that fact can never be altered."

"My lady." Lawson stood in the doorway, had been there for some little time, unashamedly listening, aware of the needs of hospitality, despite his mistress's uncharacteristic refusal. He carried ale and goblets and a platter of little mutton pies. "I thought I should bring refreshment for Lord Richard."

"No, Lawson." She turned her back so that her steward should not see her distress. "Lord Richard will not be staying."

"Very well, my lady." Lawson turned and left, but his mind was working furiously. He had heard Lord Richard's reply and came to a halt in the passageway. To consider. The atmosphere in that room had been suffocating with claim and denial, beyond bearing. So Lord Richard Stafford had cut down Sir William in cold blood, had he!

Lawson abandoned the ale and pasties on the nearest cupboard and hurried across the courtyard to the stables to speak with Rickerby. Perhaps it was the duty of the Somerton retainers take revenge in the name of their dead lord. To gain justice and reparation for his death.

Unaware, the two in the Great Hall made an end to it, their words and actions painfully compromised, as a butterfly caught and held in the sticky binding of a spider's web.

"You must leave me, Richard. It does no good for you to remain here." She grasped at pride and raised her head, mindless of the tracks of tears on her cheeks.

"If that is your wish, lady." Every movement harshly governed, he accepted the cost of his actions.

"It must be. I am afraid." She dare not speak of love. Dare not contemplate that she was shutting him out of her life forever.

"Of what?" Drawn to her distress, wanting only to give comfort in his arms, because it was all he could offer, he moved close.

"Of my own sin. That the blame for William's death is as

much mine as yours. That you acted because I had accused you of doing nothing to stop the marriage. That if I had been by your side at that one moment of decision on the battlefield, I might have encouraged you to make that lethal blow." She saw his intent, stepped back. "Don't touch me, I beg of you. It will destroy me."

Which brought him to a halt. When he stretched out his hand she hid hers behind her back. In desperation at her admission of culpability, he dropped to one knee at her feet, ignoring her little cry of distress and lifted the hem of her gown, with bent head pressed it to his lips. "On my oath, I would do nothing to harm you, to force you against your will. All I desire in this world is your happiness. But I would ask you to reconsider, Beatrice. Would you allow Somerton still to stand between us?"

"He must." Ah! How her soul cried out as she condemned their love. "Because my guilt, Richard, is as strong as yours. I am as much to blame for William's death as you." But her determination wavered at his closeness and the banked passion in that gesture. It was beyond her powers to resist touching the dark waves of hair, soft and vibrant, the lightest of caresses. Until she drew back her hand as if burned.

And so he understood at last. Beatrice's own transgression, as she saw it, effectively cemented the wall between them. They both had a weight of guilt to carry, undeserved, unnecessary perhaps, but still present as a dark cloud to cover the sun. He knew that it robbed him of all choice, even as he felt the brush of sensation against his hair. Rising to his feet, he took possession of her hand whether she wished it or not. And pressed his lips to her cold fingers. Despite her rejection, they clung to his as if she feared to let him go. Then he turned the hand that did not still clutch the brooch and pressed his mouth against the soft palm.

"Farewell, Beatrice. God bless you and keep you. You will ever be in my thoughts."

"I would not want that we should part like this."

But he had already moved away from her.

"Nor I. But what hope is there if love is bought at such momentous cost?"

He walked from the room. And, she acknowledged as she pressed her palm against her heart as if to preserve forever his final caress, from her life. When he had gone and there was no one to hear she sank to the floor and sobbed out her wretchedness, devastated by the barrier that she had helped build between them.

Richard Stafford stalked in potent despair from the Great Hall, down the shallow steps and across the courtyard toward the stables. He was devoured by it, a frustration so outrageous that it compromised his self-control, threatening to ignite into a blazing and violent outburst. Silently, viciously, he damned the twist of fate that had led him—and her—to this.

When she had looked at him… He swore at the memory. He could tell her, of course, that Somerton had broken his sacred vows of allegiance to his Majesty. But what value in that? Would it not make her pain even harder to bear? Somerton's blood was still on his hands. He loved her too much to inflict that on her and so would take the burden on his own shoulders And how could he refute her accusation? That he should deliberately widow her to take her to wife? A callous act, but what man in his circumstances would not consider it? Had he acted on such a shameful thought? No. But he had known what the end result would be, had he not?

He grasped the reins of his horse from the groom in the stableyard, without his customary word of thanks, prepared to mount.

And suddenly it came to him that he was surrounded by a ring of Somerton men-at-arms. Within the circle stood Rickerby, and Lawson, the steward.

"What is it? Would you prevent my departure? I think not!" His question was a challenge to those who would impede him, a clear statement of his standing as a Stafford lord. But one glance round the faces was enough. The implication of the scene lodged heavily in his belly. There might be no weapons yet in sight but the plan was threateningly clear.

The steward took on the role as spokesman. Unlike his usual deferential manner, there was no respect for authority in his voice. Rather that of judge and executioner.

"Lord Richard. You were responsible for the death of Sir William Somerton on the day of the battle."

"Yes. My blade killed him," Lord Richard replied. He kept his eyes steady on those of the steward, but his senses were aware of the dire threat from the circle around him. He dropped the reins, swept his accusers with a stare that contained as much arrogance as conviction.

"Sir William owed his allegiance to the Crown. Somertons have always been loyal to the Lancastrian cause." If it was possible for Master Lawson to snarl, he did so now. "Yet you, in the name of Lancaster, killed him. What treachery is this? You will not leave here alive, Lord Richard. You will pay for our lord's untimely death with your own."

"No! It is not as you think…" Suddenly, it seemed that his life might depend on his revealing the circumstances of Somerton's death. But with a sharp rasp of metal, enough to grate along his stretched nerves, Lord Richard faced a bright ring of steel.

There was no hope. They would not listen to reasoned arguments, hot for blood as they were. He knew it as he measured his first move. Far outnumbered, he could not hope to repel so well-armed a band of trained soldiers, men who were out for revenge. But he would not make it easy for them. So because there was no other means of escape, he drew his sword with his right hand in one long, slow movement. His left hand plucked from his belt the long-bladed dagger. He would not die easily. To do so would be an acceptance of his guilt as a cold-blooded murderer.

It crossed his mind, fleetingly, to wonder if Beatrice was aware of this ambush.

"Come, then. Or are you too cowardly to face one man alone?" He swept his sword around the circle with lethal grace, grim and resigned but his courage unwavering. "I wager that not all of you will leave this place unscathed."

Then the time for speech was gone. Rickerby was the first to advance. With a skillful defensive movement on his right side, Richard Stafford parried the first thrust.

How ridiculous, he thought, before he became too occupied to think of anything beyond the immediate, how supremely ironic that he should escape the carnage of the battlefield, when the Yorkists had sought to slay every one of the Lancastrian nobility they could set their sword against, only to die at the hands of these Somerton retainers who owed their allegiance to the woman he loved.

The eruption of noise, quite unmistakably that of hand-to-hand fighting carried to Beatrice indoors, broke through the tremors that still shook her slight frame. She leaped to her feet, ran in the direction of the clang and scrape of metal against metal.

And stopped with a shriek of horror at what she saw by the

stable archway. Richard Stafford, still holding his sword but beaten down to one knee, his dagger in the dust at his feet. Hemmed in by five of her garrison, who might respect the skills of their quarry, but would still force the issue with sword and poignard to the death. The outcome was in no doubt.

"Stop." Her clear voice rang out with all the assurance and command that she could muster. She would not let her fear show, that their desire for blood and death might be stronger than her control over their allegiance. "Lower your swords! Stop!" She ran forward, praying that they would obey. When they still remained fixed on their prey, a fox's single-minded stalking of a rabbit, she pulled on the arm of her steward. "Lawson. Make them stop! I will not be responsible for this!"

"He killed your lord. He should be made to pay." The steward slid her a glance, his eyes a little wild. "I heard your accusation. He did not deny it."

"Stop them, I say." Her face blazed with determination, bright color slashing along her cheekbones. "Rickerby! You will put down your sword. I will not have this. You will do as I command."

All her awareness was centered on Lord Richard. He was hard-pressed, beyond recognition of her intervention. All his will was focused on the need to watch and react, to offer stroke and counterstroke, to hold the deadly steel at bay. Blood streaked his temple and cheek from a heavy blow to the head. His left arm hung loosely, carrying a brutal slash, dripping blood down his fingers into the dusty cobbles. Every thrust and parry was weaker than the one before. How long would it be before one of those swords found its way to pierce his chest or his belly? Sweat ran down his face to mingle with the blood; his breathing was labored. He shook his head as if to dispel the darkness that crept around his brain. It could not be long.

Beatrice's fingers dug painfully into Lawson's arm. Now she was every inch the Lady of Great Houghton, demanding obedience. "We will not stain the Somerton name with this man's blood. It would dishonor your lord's name. This must stop at once."

The steward might still hesitate, but the lady's temper and her stark words did the trick. With his own sword drawn he advanced, knocking away, beating down those who would finish off their attack. They fell back as the lady's orders cut through the bloodlust but not before a number of heavy boots made connection with the prone figure.

So Beatrice was free to sink down beside Richard Stafford, now forced to the floor, hardly conscious yet he still struggled to push himself upright, against the pain and the fast-encroaching blackness. The sword hilt was still grasped in his hand although he had not the strength to lift the point of the blade from the stones. She looked over her shoulder to her retainers, composed and full of authority, no evidence of the churning emotions inside.

"I understand your reasons. That you would be revenged for Sir William. But we will not take another life. Too many have died in these past weeks, without adding another name to the list." She swept them with her gaze. "You will accept my judgment in this." Only when she was sure that she would be obeyed did she turn her back to where Richard lay, still attempting to rise to his feet and face his tormenters.

"Beatrice…" His voice was a mere groan. "What have you done?" Before he slid silently to the cobbles, releasing his sword at the last, his face hidden in a tangle of dark hair.

She wasted no time to even consider that he might be lying dead at her feet. "Lift him," she ordered. "Take him into the house. Prepare one of the rooms, if you please, Master

Lawson. Gently, now. There is no blame to be meted out here but you will not take his life."

Without comment, they did as she bid them.

Beatrice followed. She shuddered at the closeness of brutal killing but forced her knees to bear her with strength, her shoulders to remain firm.

He is alive. I will not allow him to die.

With all the twists and turns of fate, Lord Richard Stafford's life was now in her hands.

He was carried to a bedchamber, quickly made ready on the orders of Lawson who found himself unaccountably the object of his mistress's wrath. Had it not been justice to exact revenge? But the Lady would have none of it. She sent two of her maids at a run for water, linen, herbal salves as Lawson saw to the immediate problem of cutting away his lordship's ruined coat and shirt and applying pressure to the most serious of the damage to stop the bleeding. His ministrations revealed to Beatrice's anxious gaze an array of blemishes and wounds.

The splendid body, its muscles toned to perfection, had suffered. Guilt and pity rose to choke her. Her words, overheard by chance, were undoubtedly responsible. But not all had been inflicted at the hands of her men. The battle at Northampton, too, had taken its toll. The multicolor of heavy bruising, now beginning to fade, along one side from shoulder to thigh could be evidence of a fall from the saddle. There was a superficial sword slash, again partially healed, along one arm. A deep gash down one calf, the outside of one thigh. And the reddened chafing of armor around neck and shoulders, now fading, after that long day of intense activity on the battlefield in humid conditions and driving rain.

And then, if that were not enough, there were the recent

wounds. Nothing life threatening, she thought. Relief flooded through her, a cool draft to relieve the worst of her concerns. But a glancing blow from a sword edge to his shoulder had torn the flesh so that it was bleeding freely. New, livid bruising had sprung up along his ribs—probably from the viciously aimed boots of her men-at-arms—which could be broken ribs. Most serious was the blow to the side of his head that had rendered him unconscious. It was deep, along his hairline on his temple where his hair was matted with blood. It would leave a scar—but as long as it proved not to be fatal. Head wounds could be dangerous.

She took stock of his injuries with quick eyes and solemn face. Then she and Lawson exchanged looks. Until Lawson's fell when he read the sharp concern, the self-condemnation in her face that she was unable to hide.

"Forgive me, my lady. Perhaps we should not…"

"No." She sighed a little. "You should not."

"I thought…"

"I know. I know of what I accused him—and what you overheard. But whatever the truth of my lord's death, Lord Richard did not deserve this at our hands. The fault is mine."

"But, my lady…" His eyes flew to hers again. "I heard you accuse him of my lord's death…"

"Yes I did. I can no longer think…" Panic rose to rob her of calm thought. All she knew was that if Lord Richard died because of her, she would have to live with the guilt until the day she, too, died. The prospect was beyond contemplation. But she knew that she must think. And act. She drew in a deep breath as one of her maids entered the room with the linen, a bowl and an ewer filled with water. Beatrice took the bowl and approached the bed, looked down at the ravaged and motion-less figure, using every ounce of self-control to fight back the nightmare that he might not live. To any onlooker she succeeded admirably and her voice was calm.

"The best we can do is restore him to health."

"Of course." Lawson lifted the ewer and poured the water. "I can take care of this, my lady."

"No. It is my burden, too." She managed a wry curl of her lips. "I think I need to make amends. I will help you all I can."

So Richard Stafford, within the hour, was washed and cleansed, the blood soaked from his hair. His wounds bound in clean linen, soothing salves applied to give relief from pain. And throughout their ministrations, Beatrice prayed that he would regain consciousness. How would she tolerate it if he slipped from this lack of awareness into death, without her ever being able to speak to him again? Setting one of the serving girls to sit beside him for if—*when* he awoke—she went to her own chamber to remove her bloodstained gown and blame herself anew for her impassioned words. He was still her love. Nothing could ever destroy that. As long as he would recover…that is all that she could ask. He would still leave her, of course. Guilt would still lie heavy on both their souls. But as long as he was alive and well, she could accept the inevitable.

She returned to his room when the soft summer night was falling.

"How is he?"

"There is no change, my lady." The maid rose to her feet.

Beatrice laid her fingers against Richard's forehead, the lightest of caresses. No fever, no heat. No obvious cause for concern, except that he did not stir. She could not resist allowing her fingers to smooth back a lock of hair.

"Go and eat. Get some rest." She smiled her thanks to the girl. "I will stay a little while."

Beatrice sat in the high-backed chair and watched him. Dark lashes on shadowed cheeks. Tanned skin stark against the heavy cream bandaging. Hands still, fingers a little curled, breathing slow and even. All she could do was wait and hope and silently ask forgiveness. She reached over the bed and touched his hand. Such strong fingers. So much latent power. Power enough to commit deliberate murder? *Of course he could, but he would not! He has too much honor.* Her heart whispered into the dark corners of her mind. She had never been as physically close to him as she was at that moment, as he lay helpless and under her dominance. Yet all was over between them. Must be so.

She would have withdrawn her hand from his but he moved restlessly in the high bed, his head uneasy on the pillows. So she allowed it to remain, closed warmly around his cold fingers as if to anchor him to the present. To life. Her mind drifted. Taking her back to the occasion when Lord Richard had sought out her father to ask for her hand in marriage, a formal betrothal. He had presented himself at their crowded lodgings at Westminster. Dressed to impress in green-and-black-patterned velvet, the seasoned courtier, a man who demanded simply by his presence to be noticed and respected. He had worn his sword, strapped at his waist by tooled leather. She remembered for some trivial reason the superb workmanship of the intricately patterned hilt. And the heavy cabochon ruby he had worn on his right hand. He wore no such costly rings today. Her fingers smoothed over his. No man of sense would wear such jewels to travel the roads where thieves and robbers lurked. On that distant morning he had also worn over all the heavy fur-lined cloak, sumptuous sables, against the harsh winds. And he had asked her father, with all honor and grave dignity, not imagining that he would be refused, that Sir Walter might consider a betrothal for his daughter

Her eyes now rested on his face, as still and pale as the wax of the candles. He had wanted her as his wife. And had been met with a blunt refusal. The words fell, heavy as a blacksmith's hammer.

"No, sir. You can have no claim on my daughter. Beatrice is already betrothed."

Her father's words, echoing from that distant moment, still had the power to rob her of her breath. Surely Sir Walter would rejoice in it, snatch up the chance being offered to betroth his daughter to so puissant a family. She and her mother had looked at each other, eyes wide. Lady Margery's mouth had opened to speak but no words came.

"It is so," Sir Walter had continued. "I have an understanding with regard to my daughter's marriage. It has been agreed for some years. Sir William Somerton has need of a wife."

And thus all had been decided, in that one harsh pronouncement

And Lord Richard? His eyes had sought hers. Must have read the shock, the flood of despair that had rooted her, silent, to the spot.

"Sir…" His eyes had gleamed with quick temper but he would try again. "I would ask that you at least consider the wishes of your daughter in this affair. As well as the advantages you would gain if you agreed to my proposal." He had paused, then added, for the first time, with masterly understatement. "My family is not without power and influence."

And Beatrice had been spurred into speech. "Father… If you would but consider." She had raised her hands in a desperate plea. "Not William Somerton, I beg of you."

But Sir Walter turned away. "The agreement is made. Our alliance with Somerton is important to me. You will wed him."

And then it was over, Richard bowing with stiff formality, his face a mask, to her father and then Lady Margery. And finally to herself.

"Mistress Hatton. Forgive me if I have caused you any distress. You should know that my sentiments have undergone no change." Then quietly for her ears alone. "I will not accept this decision. I will come for you."

He had walked away from her, from the room. She had only his final words to hold on to as a talisman. She had not seen him again until the day he arrived at Great Houghton with Lord Grey. Sir Walter had packed and taken them from London so swiftly, as if he feared that Beatrice might disobey his pronouncement. She had not even been able to send a message to Lord Richard, much less see him again. He had never come for her.

Yes, he had wanted her then, without doubt. But enough to kill to claim her, three years after? Her tired mind wrestled with his own admission of knowledge of his action, with her own secret desires, allowing all the longings of the past to surge back. She might have been the obedient daughter and wed Sir William, but her heart had remained in the keeping of this man who lay so deathly still under her fingers. She withdrew her hand as Lord Richard lay quietly under her touch and sat back in the chair to watch over him as darkness fell.

Eventually, in the stillness of the room, exhaustion took its toll and she slept.

Just before dawn when the light at the window was sufficient to allow soft gray outlines, he awoke. Swimming to an uneasy consciousness, he clutched at stray wisps of memory that had a tendency to swirl as smoke in a draft and escape out of his reach. He flinched as he moved unwisely against the pillows. His head screamed with pain. His ribs—well, he did not wish to think about those after the first sharp, breathtaking twinge of agony. His shoulder, he discovered, was stiff and firmly bound. He had been dreaming. He was in pain. It must be after the battle at Northampton, where everything had fallen apart, the whole of their planning becoming unraveled at the hands of Lord Grey de Ruthin. That must be the reason for his injuries… But where was he? He did not know this room.

And then it came to him as if a shutter on a lantern had been removed. He remembered.

Slowly Richard turned his head against the pillow. Saw her sitting there, head angled away from him against the high and unforgiving back of the chair. She would be wretchedly uncomfortable in the morning, was his first thought. He could not see her face, only her dark hair, unbound on her shoulders, as the light gradually brightened. Could see her pale hands folded loosely in her lap.

His scattered thoughts cleared, brought back the events of the day. What a dreadful morass of desire and guilt trapped them. All culminating in an effective ambush by the Somerton retainers who had without doubt sought his death. Had she given the fatal orders in a need for retribution? His disordered mind could not come to terms with the possibility, just as the pain in his body was as nothing to the misery in his soul. He would have stretched a hand to touch her, to find the smallest vestige of comfort, but could not find the strength.

Against his will, his eyelids fell. He lapsed once more into deep oblivion.

When he awoke again it was broad daylight. The window had been opened to allow cool air into the room and rays of sunshine slatted across the floor almost to the bed. The thudding in his head had subsided into a consistent but manageable ache. His sore ribs would not prevent him from mounting a horse.

The seat beside him was now empty. His clothes, cleaned and put to rights were laid over a coffer by the window seat. As the sunshine glimmered on the hilt of his sword, the events of the previous day once more slid into place, became crystal clear, not least the attempt on his life. Anger began to simmer through his blood. It became imperative that he leave, before any further attempt was made. If possible, he would leave without the need to see Beatrice Somerton again.

His plan failed. When Beatrice opened the door and entered, it was to stop in amazement. It took her but a second to assimilate. Lord Richard Stafford was fully dressed—although with some difficulty. At some stage he had removed the linen from around his head, revealing the angry wound along his hairline. His sword lay at hand on the table, his cloak, gloves. Stiff and unusually awkward in his movements, he held himself carefully. Deep lines between his brows bore witness to a headache, if she was not mistaken. He should not have left his bed. He was unfit to travel.

"What are you doing?"

"Lady Beatrice." His eyes, cool and gray as river water, never left her face. "As you see, I am about to take my leave."

"You cannot. You are not well enough to ride a horse. Your ribs…"

"Are sore but will not prevent me. Nor will the blow to my head, for which I have to thank one of your doughty men-at-arms. I have imposed myself too much on your *hospitality*." She had never seen him sneer before.

Here was none of the emotion of the previous day. Only a cold control of all mind and body. Well, she could do the same. She lifted her head and ordered proud dignity to rule her reply.

"I think you should not. But you must do as you think best."

Mouth firmed into a straight line, he made to pick up the weapon. Then whipped round to face her. All the tension, all the hurt and physical pain melded into an outpouring of furious and bitter reproach.

"Did you give the order for your men to lie in wait and kill me, Beatrice?"

Beatrice blinked at the attack, her own temper stirred. "I did not. How dare you suggest so vile and unworthy an action!"

"Yet you were free with your own accusations against me, without evidence."

"Without evidence?" Her eyes flashed at the enormity of his accusation after a long night when her own conscience had pointed its relentless finger at her careless words. "You said that you would come for me, and you did not. By your own admission you killed William. What more evidence do I need?"

The bitter anger overflowed around them into a deadly pool. Lord Richard found himself speaking against all his instincts. Suddenly the terrible words were said and there was no going back.

"And do you know why I slew Somerton? Do you really want to hear the truth? He was a traitor, he betrayed the cause and changed sides in the middle of the battle. Because of that, my cousin Buckingham died."

"You lie!" Her lips were white with shock. "William was always loyal to Lancaster."

"Oh no." The contemptuous sneer again that tore at her heart with vicious claws. "Your husband turned his sword against his own king. And I killed him for it."

Richard's eyes blazed. She had never seen this man before in the suave, elegantly appareled courtier at Westminster. Furious, driven by strong emotion, with the aggressive instincts of a soldier. The air positively shimmered around him.

"Was it by your order, Beatrice? If so I should go down on bended knee to thank you for bringing me back to life instead of throwing my body to the buzzards outside your walls."

Her temper snapped. Her composure disintegrated in a breath. Later she would be horrified, disgusted at such wanton behaviour. To have so little care for an injured man. But Beatrice was goaded beyond reason. She raised her hand, swift as a lightning bolt and prepared to strike, an openhanded slap at that contemptuous face that yet had the power to heat her blood. Except that his reactions, compromised as they were through injury, were still superb and even faster. In pure instinct he retaliated, grasped her wrist in no very gentle hold and dragged her close.

"No—you will not strike me, madam, unless I allow it."

Nor did he let her go. Close, closer he drew her. Until her body touched his. Until she was aware only of the heat of his proximity, the warmth of his breath against her face, against her hair. His mouth hovered a fraction from hers. A whisper of breath away. All power and dominant fury.

She waited, unable to breathe, expecting to feel at any moment the savage imprint of his fury.

But he did not come closer. The curve of his lips held no humor as he looked down at her. "Should I kiss you a fond farewell? In memory of our dead love?" The curve faded, the scorching heat faded from his eyes as he came to himself. "If I did it would be punishment, not affection. I will not do that."

He pushed her away, sharply so that she had to find her balance.

The icy restraint had returned in force. She saw his hands tremble with the need to rein back.

"Forgive me, Lady Somerton. My manners are deplorable. I would not hurt a woman or raise a hand against her. However sharp the spur."

Beatrice found herself without words. What had she done to push him so close to the brink of control? Any common ground between them had been cut away so that they stood, isolated, wrenched apart beyond redemption.

Now Lord Richard claimed his cloak, swung it around his shoulder, ignoring the quick flash of pain that exploded through his body. It colored his words with cold vitriol.

"How fortunate, lady, that we discovered that we would not suit."

Beatrice raised her chin. She would not sink beneath the emotion tearing at her heart but would respond in kind.

"Fortunate indeed. Farewell, Richard Stafford."

He inclined his head, curt and final.

"Goodbye, Beatrice Somerton."

His choice of words struck at her, much like the slap that she would have used against him. So final. It twisted, agonizingly, the blade in the wound.

I love you. I shall always love you.

She repeated it silently as he opened the door and made his way slowly down the stairs.

She had never felt so wretched in her life.

Neither had he.

Chapter Five

Once more Beatrice stood on her battlement walk to watch him ride down the road across the Great Houghton estate.

I have spent my whole life watching Richard Stafford ride from me.

As on the previous occasion, he did not look back. So finally Beatrice would have left her vantage point, lifting her hands in a little gesture of despair, but then saw an approaching rider on the road. And knew it for her brother. As the two men drew abreast they stopped. Talked for a brief moment. She saw Richard look back, saw Ned raise his arm and gesture widely. Then with a clasp of hands they parted. Richard spurred his horse on and disappeared through the thick summer foliage of a small copse. Ned came on at a slower pace to the manor.

"I saw Richard Stafford on my way here." Ned flung himself onto a bench in the Great Hall, stretched out his legs and fended off one of the hounds that came to sniff at his boots. "He greeted me with reserve—looked decidedly the worse for wear and chose to be noncommittal. Nor was he disposed to linger. He looked like a man with trouble on his mind." Ned slid a keen glance her way. "His head wound appeared to be recent. More recent than the battle, I would say."

"Yes." Beatrice could not look at her brother. "There was a…an incident here. Lord Richard was injured. But is well enough now to ride."

"Ah…" Ned now swung round and faced her directly as she brought him a cup of ale. He took it from her. "So what was he doing here? And what was the *incident* you so artfully concealed? The truth now, Beatrice."

Beatrice put down the ale flagon. "I…" What could she say? "He came to offer his condolences…for William's death. He… Lord Richard…" And then she could disguise the misery no longer. Covering her face with her hands she struggled for composure.

"Beatrice. What is it?" Shocked into action, Ned stood to fold his arms around her, even more concerned when she refused to rest there. "Tell me what happened." But he thought that he knew.

She pushed herself to stand alone, allowing her hands to fall. Her eyes were wide and dark with distress. "I love him, Ned. I love him so much. And I know that he loves me—or he did before I made it impossible. But he killed William. And perhaps he did so because he wanted to remove the one barrier between us. Which would have been my dearest wish. And that would make me as guilty as Richard. William's death would have been murder, committed by Richard and condoned by me! I will always love him but how can I be with him if that is so? Also, he said…he said…" She ran her tongue over dry lips. "He said that William was a traitor. And I told him it was a lie."

So that was it, as he had feared. "Oh, Beatrice…" Ned drew her to the settle, sat beside her and handed her his own cup of ale. It had become necessary after all to tell her the truth.

"Beatrice—it is true. Somerton turned against the king."

"No…"

"This is partly my fault—that I did not tell you all I knew of the battle—but listen now." His face was solemn. "It was a rout as I told you. We were betrayed. Our position was superbly defensive. We should never have been defeated…" Ned swore long and fluently, his hands gripping the cup that he took back from Beatrice and drained. "We were betrayed to the Yorkists," he repeated. "By Lord Grey de Ruthin, God rot his black soul! He had it all arranged. No sooner had the Earl of Warwick begun the advance against our army than Grey ordered his men to lay down their arms and allow Warwick's troops to simply drive through, without resistance, to our camp where King Henry waited the outcome of the battle." He shook his head in disbelief. "So Warwick simply marched up and took Henry captive. It was desperate—within thirty minutes it was all over."

"And William?"

Ned frowned at his sister's tightly clenched fingers, skin white over the knuckles. It was not possible to put it gently. So, baldly: "Somerton changed sides. He joined de Ruthin in his treason and went over to the Yorkists."

Beatrice could not take in the words. Richard had spoken the truth. He had not lied to her. She had accused him of a deliberate falsehood and trampled his honor in the dust. She had branded him a liar. Her heart wept silently for him and for her cruel words.

"I saw it happen," Ned continued. "I saw Somerton take his stand with de Ruthin's men under the banner of the black ragged staff. I saw him lift his sword against Lancastrians who rushed to protect the king. I saw him join the attack on Buckingham when our Commander himself came to his Majesty's defence."

"Oh, Ned." As her brother's words sank in, the tale of Grey's treachery, and of William's, she was cold to her heart, frozen with dread, cold as winter ice.

"And I saw Stafford strike Somerton down in his own attempt to save the king and his cousin Buckingham. He failed and barely escaped with his own life. You should know that the Duke of Buckingham was hacked to death,"

Beatrice sat in silence, eyes wide with the enormity of what she had done.

Then: "Why did you not tell me before?"

"To save you from the taint of treason."

A little line engraved itself between her brows. "Ned—why would William commit so foul a deed?"

Ned shrugged. "Somerton owed allegiance to de Ruthin's overlordship for some of his manors. De Ruthin would demand his feudal service. It would not do to make an enemy of such a one—de Ruthin is not the man to have against you. Perhaps de Ruthin promised him rich rewards if the plan worked. I doubt we shall ever know the truth."

Beatrice nodded. It fit perfectly with what she knew.

"Somerton was guilty of treachery," Ned continued, determined to leave no room for doubt in his sister's mind. "Stafford slew William out of no more than duty and necessity, Beatrice." He hesitated for one heartbeat then drove the nail home. "Stafford did not betray you. It was William who betrayed you. Betrayed all of us."

"Oh, Ned!" She turned her face away so that her brother would not read her shame. "And I accused Richard of killing William deliberately, for dishonorable motives. Worse than that, my own men brought him close to death." Beatrice's breath caught in her throat, tight with emotion. "He was innocent of all dishonor yet I sent him away." The horror of it stunned her. "Do you know what I did? I struck out at him! Even though he was injured and in pain. How could I have done something so ignoble?"

Ned watched her, uncomfortable with the depth of her distress, then drew her close against him. "There now—don't cry. It is done but perhaps it can all be undone."

"I don't see how. He will hate me forever. Nor can I blame him. I said such dreadful things to him, Ned. How could he retain any regard for me? I have destroyed his love and caused him such anguish."

Ned eyed his sister's pale cheeks, the firming of her lips as she sought to regain control. What his father had been about, to consign his daughter to such a loveless and unequal match! But Somerton's local influence had swayed the issue and Beatrice had paid the ultimate price. And Sir Walter had lived hardly more than a year to enjoy the benefit! Ned squeezed his sister's hand once more in quick sympathy then rose to his feet, drawing her with him.

"I must go, Beatrice. Will you be well, alone here?"

She took a deep breath and raised her head. The fault was hers and she must accept and live with it. At least she was now in possession of the truth. Of the dishonor inflicted on her family by William's decision to break faith. And more importantly of Richard's shining innocence and integrity.

"One thing, Ned, before you go... When I was sent to stay with my aunt in Lincoln before my marriage—did Lord Richard come to Mears Ashby?"

Ned was a touch shamefaced. "Yes, he did."

"What happened?"

"He demanded to see you. Demanded that our father reconsider."

"And?"

"Father told him that the agreements were signed and you were already living at Great Houghton. That you would be married within a matter of weeks."

"I see. And I was not told."

Ned slid a guilt-ridden glance at his sister, expecting a hint of temper. Could detect none. "What would have been the point?"

"None, I suppose." But her voice was strained.

"Is it important?"

"No." She shook her head. "Not any longer." It was just one more wound she had inflicted on him.

"Don't blame yourself too much." Ned made his way to the door. "But I think you should put it right with Stafford."

"I know it." She managed a semblance of a smile but it was a bleak affair. "I will not leave it like this. I think I have too much pride and the shame rides me hard—both my own and William's dishonor. I must make amends, one way or another."

What could she do to put things right?

Only one thought came to her mind. Once the decision was made, it seemed to be an easy matter to accomplish—but the outcome could not be determined. The pain in her heart was so intense as to be almost physical.

Beatrice opened the chest in her chamber, and took out a carved cedarwood box. There inside lay the ivory swan. She stroked its poor damaged foot, marveling at the strength of so fragile a jewel that it could come through the conflict with so little harm. Then wrapped the jewel securely in soft cloth, then leather, finally securing it with strong hempen twine. If the swan could survive a battle, it could survive a journey in the careful handling of a messenger. The roads seemed quiet enough. She would send it by one of her men to Elton's Marsh, Lord Richard's home in East Anglia.

Then she took a sheet of fine parchment. A goose quill pen that she sharpened. And sat at the little table in her chamber where the light from the window would fall on her efforts. But here was the problem. What could she say that he would even wish to read?

Tell him what is in your heart. Ask his forgiveness. Open yourself to his judgment. Honesty is the best path here, the only path.

So she would lay it all before him and leave the final choice to him. She rubbed her hand between her breasts as if it might ease the ache of loneliness and desolation, then dipped the pen and began. The words came slowly, were difficult and stilted, but it was all she could do.

My dearest Richard,

    I now know the truth. Too late, as I am aware, but I need to put things right with you as far as I am able. My brother, Ned, has told me of Lord Grey's perfidy, his treacherous betrayal of His Majesty in the battle which brought about the massacre of so many loyal men. And also of William's wicked decision to stand by de Ruthin, to join him in his contemptible act. And how you were driven to challenge him and to take his life in a futile attempt to keep His Majesty from capture. As well as to protect the life of your cousin, the Duke of Buckingham. My dear Richard, can you ever forgive me—that I should accuse you of putting your own personal desires before your loyalty to the Crown? I know you to be a man of the highest honor and conscience. Which William was not.

Ned also told me that you came to Mears Ashby for me. I was in Lincoln. My father lied to you—and to me.

The guilt is all mine. I know there is no excuse for what I have said. Nor for my role in the attack against you, for which my ill-considered words were responsible. I allowed my mind to accuse you of murder even when my heart denied it. You could have died at the hands of my people, acting in my name. How can I ever forgive myself for that?

All I can do is ask your pardon and hope that you will believe that these poor apologies are not just empty words. By now I expect that you will have opened the package. It is my dearest wish to return the swan to you. I hope that you can find it in you to accept it as a token of my penitence.

William died for his terrible crime against the Crown. Of all the pain and heartbreak I have caused you, I can write no more. You have all my love. You always did. You always will. I will understand if you no longer feel able to return the sentiment.

Oh, my darling Richard, I wish with all my soul, with every breath I take, that it had not ended like this. Beatrice…

She hesitated. Then wrote firmly.

Hatton

The letter was finished, all that was in her heart. Beatrice dashed her hands across her cheeks to prevent tears from falling to blot on the page. Then she carefully folded the document, wrapped it in another layer of leather together with the brooch and went to find her messenger with instructions for the journey. Before she could change her mind. A hopeless cause perhaps. She had slighted his honor and his integrity, and he was a man who, as he had proved in his desire to shield her from pain, held fast to the highest aspirations of chivalry.

So the package was duly delivered to Lord Richard Stafford's home at Elton's Marsh. The messenger returned to Great Houghton but with no reply. Lord Richard was not there but still with the Lancastrian army. Beatrice knew that she had done all she could. It was a chilling thought that gave her no comfort.

The months flowed inexorably through the final days of summer into autumn and on into the bitter cold of winter. Snow fell and lay on the ground, covering the scarred fields where so many had fought and been slain, as if to erase the memory of such brutal happenings between families who had once claimed friendship. Beatrice and her people at Great Houghton closed themselves in.

There was no news.

Christmas arrived with the promise of celebrations to lighten the heart. Beatrice would have remained at Great Houghton—she found that she had no taste for the festivities—but Ned insisted that she join the family at Mears Ashby. So she did, with pale complexion and haunted eyes. She dutifully smiled and clapped at the antics of the jester, the tunes and singing of the musicians. She danced. She played her part in the traditional games. It was a brave attempt but fooled no one: the pretence was painfully obvious. She was inclined to pick at her food and more often than not sat in silent contemplation of some unwanted and unbidden image from the past. As soon as was courteous, she escaped back to her own home.

Ned's wife, Alice Hatton, expressed some amazement to her lord that the lady could grieve so for Sir William Somerton.

"He treated her as though she was little more than a servant in her own home."

"True."

"You would never treat me so poorly, would you?"

"Certainly not!" Ned sought wildly for any excuse to remove himself from this conversation but failed.

"I never liked him. He had thin lips. Poor Beatrice."

"Yes. Poor Beatrice indeed."

"But now she is free of him. Why is she not happier? I thought she would find healing with the passing of time."

"So did I." Ned, with a surprising level of intuition, felt it wiser to keep his own council. It would be no help to Beatrice to hear Richard Stafford's name on Alice's inquisitive lips.

Back at Great Houghton, Beatrice found herself on numerous occasions standing on the battlement walk, swathed in a velvet cloak against the bitter air, watching the road leading to the house. Until she took herself to task and forced herself indoors.

He would not come. Time hung heavy on her heart and her hands.

Then rumors began to filter through of a great battle in the north, at Wakefield. A Lancastrian victory in which the Duke of York himself, newly returned from Ireland, was killed.

Had Richard fought in the battle? Beatrice shivered at the prospect as she sat before the fire in her chamber, knowing that he would have been in the thick of the fighting. But oh, she wished with all her heart that he had been safely at home

at Elton's Marsh. Did he still have the swan or had he con-
signed it to the bottom of a coffer and forgotten about it, as a
trinket of little moment and even less sentimental value.

Meanwhile she visited the tomb of William Somerton in
the village church of St Michael and All Angels. It was now
complete, magnificent with its alabaster monument of
William in full armor, his head resting on his helm, his feet
propped against a winged gryphon as on his coat of arms. His
hands were palm to palm on his chest in pious prayer. Beatrice
thought she had never seen him so much at peace. Or so com-
placently smug.

Because William, with all the petty spite of which he had
been capable, had sought to bind her to him in death, as
securely as she had been bound to him in life. His will, so
generous in its terms, had included the ultimate sting of a
scorpion. If she remarried, her inheritance and her home at
Great Houghton would be lost to her, reverting to the ownership of Sir William's eldest son. Beatrice would receive
instead the less than princely sum of forty pounds and household goods to the tune of ten marks. A poor settlement indeed
and not one to attract another husband. All in all, a nasty little
device. Beatrice touched William Somerton's cold face.

"How could you do that to me?"

William's effigy remained smugly silent.

Take care what you wish for. The words crept into her
mind. She had wished to be free of this marriage. But not like
this. Not on these terms. She hugged her guilt close. It was
not William's death that had cracked her heart in two.

A hopeless anger appeared from nowhere, as a storm out
of a summer sky, to torment her as she returned to the Hall.

"Why could you not reply to me, Richard?"

She spoke the words aloud to the unresponsive rooks

roosting in a majestic stand of beech trees. Even if his rejection of her petition was so final as to trample all her hopes into the mire, it would be better than not knowing. Were all men so intransigent? How dare he put her through this wretched uncertainty. But then the anger drained away to leave a hollow void that filled her soul.

For Richard Stafford the weeks and months were no better but, of necessity, hung less heavily. He had fought in the battle at Wakefield, surviving it without harm other than the normal scrapes and bruises from violent conflict. It had been a bloody affair, the Duke of York surrounded and hacked to death on the battlefield. Richard turned from it with distaste, disillusioned with the blood and the deliberate slaughter of the Yorkist nobility with neither clemency nor pardon and returned home to Elton's Marsh. With a need for healing and to collect a small item of jewellery that he would not again risk on a battlefield. An ivory swan that stood as a bright symbol of hope, a glimpse of light when blood and death crowded his dreams. Of a possibility for a future with the woman who, despite everything, still owned his heart. He ran his thumb over the ivory feathers with a little smile. Re-read Beatrice's letter, imagining her sitting writing it against the carved linenfold in her chamber. Remembered the softness of her mouth against his, the lingering perfume of her hair when he had released it to drift in heavy silk through his hands.

He had not seen her for six months, since he had ridden out of her life, his mind full of bitterness and anger at the capricious whim of blind chance that had placed Beatrice within his reach, only to snatch her away again. Since his conscience had applied the sharp spur of guilt, forcing him to doubt and question his own motives that day at Northampton. But in the months since then he had faced imminent death again in battle. When the noise and blood and outrageous violence robbed a man of every thought, every decision but the necessity of parrying the next blow, cutting down the next opponent. And he knew that faced with the deadly point of sword or dagger, the swing of a mace or the lunge of a halberd, there were no choices to be made other than survival. In the same circumstances, to save himself or Buckingham or the king he would do the same again, whether the man he fought be William Somerton or another. And, in striking down Beatrice's husband, he accepted at last that he carried no guilt.

Richard shrugged against the burden that he had finally cast off. Sometimes conscience and duty made uncomfortable bedfellows. But now Beatrice knew the truth of that dreadful day. The rift between them might be healed at last.

It was time for him to take the next step.

Chapter Six

It was spring. April had rushed in after a chilly, fretful March with days of warm winds and light showers. Blackthorn blossom bloomed in the hedgerows as did the primroses in secret corners of Beatrice's garden. Their pale yellow petals, the fragile green of their leaves, brought comfort to the lady. She still wore black gowns in formal recognition of her widow's status, but the new life around her teased her thoughts from their somber contemplation. William had been dead for more than six months.

She kept in touch with the outside world through Ned's visits and letters from her mother who had traveled to stay with her sister in London. Beatrice read Lady Margery's long diatribes about the ongoing battle for power, then folded the parchments and put them away. It worried at her conscience that the rise and fall of Lancaster and York seemed to matter so little to her. There was only one letter that she truly wished to receive.

The only piece of information to find its way to her door, through Ned's kind offices, that was of supreme importance in her life, was that Richard Stafford was alive, having survived the carnage of both Wakefield and later an even bloodier affair at Towton. The knowledge brought some comfort. If he could only find time to write to her… But after so long a silence she had given up hope of ever hearing from him again.

"You have a visitor, my lady."

Beatrice put down the iron shears beside the basket of sad dead-headings left over from the previous autumn.

"Who is it, Lawson?"

"He did not give a name, my lady." There had been no need. Her brows arched in some surprise. Lawson was usually particular to a point. "Then how should I know if I am to receive him? Is he known to me?"

Lawson worked to keep his expression grave. "The gentleman said to give you this, my lady. Then you would know if you wished to receive him." He held out a small package wrapped in black velvet.

Beatrice took it, as if she were watching herself in a dream, from some strange distance. With fingers that trembled in their haste, she unwrapped the soft material. Knowing perfectly well what she would find there. Her hand closed over the contents as she took a breath. And lifted her eyes to Lawson's.

"Where is he?"

"I took the liberty of showing him into the parlor. I thought that you would wish it." Now Lawson allowed himself to smile. "He is waiting for you." Much had been made clear to Master Lawson. Lord Richard was welcome in this house, more than welcome if he could make the sad lady smile again.

Beatrice did not linger for one second. He was here. She lifted her dark skirts and ran, abandoning all dignity. At the parlor door she did not hesitate but flung it open, back against the wall. Then, at the last, stopped on the threshold.

And saw him.

He looked just the same. Perhaps a little thinner, with new creases delineating the lean planes of his face, around his mouth and radiating from the corners of his eyes. She could see, immediately, the lighter scar of the healed sword wound along his hairline. But, against all her fears, it was the same Richard Stafford.

He had come back to her. Her heart began to pound within her silk bodice. All the words she had wanted to say. All the regrets and explanations, all the words of love that she had practiced saying to him if she would ever meet him again. She could think of none of them.

"I have dreamed of this moment." It was all she could manage.

"And what did you do in your dream?"

"I dreamed that…" She gave a little shake of her head, could not tell him yet. Nothing was settled between them. She did not even know why he had come to her. It was impossible to read it in his face, stern and uncompromising, a little wary. "Why are you here, Richard?" Would he return the brooch because he had no use for it and simply walk away?

"I came, Beatrice, because I could not stay away." His voice was as grave as his expression but a bright flame of hope leaped into life deep within her.

"I once said we would not suit. I regret it."

"I remember." The occasion still shamed her. Her eyes fell before his. "I regret my intransigence."

"Tell me one thing. Despite all that has happened, all that has separated us, does your love for me still hold true?"

The hope now began to burn more fiercely. Beatrice felt her cheeks flush with the power of it. Looked up. "Yes." She held her breath.

"Thank God." Richard sighed as if a weight almost too great to bear had been lifted from his soul. "So tell me, lady, what did you do in your dream?" His mouth finally relaxed in a half smile, seeing her there in the doorway, her undeniable beauty, despite her deep mourning, framed by the dark paneling. All his doubts that she would close the door against him again lifted as mist in the heat of the sun. Amongst the emotions that tripped across her lovely face, rejection was not one of them. Rather hope and a tentative joy. "What did you do, Beatrice?" he persisted. He would have gone to her, made that move forward, but rather waited to allow her that freedom.

"Ah, Richard. In my dream I did this…"

At last Beatrice took the step. And then another. Until she was running the short distance across the room. His arms opened. And closed around her. And held her tightly against him with all the dust of travel enveloping them both. It was of no consequence. She was here in his arms and the Hatton swan, clasped tightly in her hand, was crushed against his heart.

"I hurt you. Your face is scarred and it was all my doing." Her voice was muffled as she pressed her face against the curve of his neck.

"It is past. It is of no account now."

"I thought you had abandoned me, forgotten me." Her voice trembled a little as she remembered the stark desolation of the winter months. "As I deserved."

"I had never forgotten you. How could that be?" His fingers stroked her hair where it curled from beneath her veil against her temple, inhaling its lavender fragrance, as he marveled that it had happened at last. His own dream, that she should willingly step into his embrace, also had come to fulfillment.

"Don't leave me, Richard. Never again." Now, eyes bright with unshed tears, she looked up, lifted a hand to touch his face as if she still could not believe that it was not all some terrible repetitive nightmare, that he would be snatched away from her at the moment that she opened her eyes to the morning sun, to a desolate solitary awakening.

"I will not." Framing her face with his hands, he wiped away the suspicion of moisture on her cheeks. "I will never again give you cause to weep. And I will seal that vow."

He lowered his head, his kiss warm and capturing her breath. He poured into that meeting of mouth against mouth all the love and longing of the months of separation. All the regret for the pain and hurt. Until the exquisite tenderness became overwhelmed by a fire that raced through his blood, to ignite a more primitive urge to own and possess. Until kissing her was not enough and desire beat hard.

"I have wanted to kiss you, hold you, for so long." Releasing her lips, he feathered caresses over her forehead, eyelids, the soft skin at her temple, to the softer skin beneath her jaw. As her fingers dug into his forearms to hold him close, closer yet.

"I have dreamed of that, too." She turned her head to return his kisses. "Both waking and sleeping."

Now he held her a little away from him, aware that her heart beat as forcefully as his. She was as involved as he. And of one thing he was sure. That he wanted this woman more than he had ever wanted anything or anyone in his life before. And he knew, he prayed that she would want him. His eyes held hers, refusing to release her as time spun out between them, holding them in a soft net of care, of gentleness, one for the other, but with the promise of the sharp and delicious edge of passion that awaited them. Words were no longer necessary between them. He saw the delicate wash of color rise in her cheeks as she read his intent. So he would take the risk and give her the power to refuse.

"My love. I would do more than kiss you."

She understood. Gloried in his willingness to allow her the choice. So she would choose and seize what was in her heart.

"I have wanted that, too. Come then." Taking his hand she led him from the parlor to the foot of the stairs.

As Lawson, ever watchful for his lady's well-being, emerged from the shadows. "Do you have need of anything, my lady?"

"No, Lawson. We shall require nothing." Lady Beatrice Somerton smiled and shook her head. "Now I have all I need." Neither knowing nor caring what the servants would make of her willful behavior in their gossip over the midday meal. To retire to her chamber with Lord Richard Stafford in the full light of day. Not realizing that they would wish her well.

Stepping inside the room after her, he closed the door. Waited until she turned to face him. The delight and anticipation in her face left him with no doubts as he held out his hand to her. Both command and invitation.

"Nothing can come between us here. Nor will I allow it ever again."

"That is my wish. Richard—I did not trust you enough. How wicked a sin is that? And William. How could William have betrayed all he had lived by? I know that it forced you to make an impossible choice."

"Do you trust me now?"

"Yes. Oh, yes."

He kept the fingers that he lifted to her cheek almost steady. Smoothed the satin of her skin, then held her still before him. His words were perhaps severe, a painful depth of honesty. "I made that choice, Beatrice. I know that I would choose the same again, and I feel no guilt for it. The terrible cost of war is not only apparent on the battlefield. It touches everyone. It creates impossible obstacles, excavates bottomless crevasses to tear apart and divide. Betrayal and bloodshed can never be lightly overlooked, nor should they be." Then the austere lines of his face softened a little into a smile. "But for whatever reason, fate has chosen to smile on us, to give us a second chance to be together." The hand that still held hers tightened, Richard's fingers interlocking with hers in an unbreakable bond. "Somerton's treachery will not stand between us. Let your heart be at peace, my loved one."

"Can we heal the wounds?" Her regard was steady.

"I am certain of it. We can heal each other now."

Her love could have said nothing better, nothing more direct or more soothing to her troubled heart. She turned her face to press a kiss against his wrist where the blood pulsed heavily through his veins.

"I love you, Richard Stafford. My heart is yours if you will have it."

His arms came round her. "As I love you. You are my life and my soul. I will gladly take your heart into my keeping. For you most assuredly have mine." Richard turned his face into the smooth curve of her throat as the fears, which had been almost too great to withstand, finally dissipated . "It was always meant to be that we should be together."

They had waited long for this moment, believing that it would never be within their experience. Not merely the wretched months since their last parting, but through the years since their hands had first touched, their lips had first clung and parted in urgent demand. When their desires had been so thoroughly thwarted by the ambitions of a greedy, single-minded parent. Now the moment was theirs and the door of Beatrice's bedchamber was closed against the rest of the world. Locked to bar all entry. Nothing would now prevent their coming together.

She placed the swan on the coffer in the window embra-sure for safe keeping. Then turned to him with confidence that he would take care of her.

With formal grace he loosed her embroidered girdle to allow the fullness to flow to the floor. And then proved himself adept at managing the laces and ties at waist and neck until the garment slid down her body to leave her clad in a simple linen shift. And marveled. How much the fashion of the day succeeded to hide and disguise the most glorious aspects of womanhood. The soft curves and hollows of breast and waist and hip. He allowed one hand to stroke luxuriously downward from her shoulder in one long smooth caress. Then lifted her soft veil with careful fingers, removed the simple headdress. At last, as he had imagined doing so many times since that distant afternoon in the shadows of the drafty corridor in the palace of Westminster, he unpinned her hair. As glorious as he remembered, as thick and lustrous.

He had no choice but to clench his fists in it, draw her close to bury his face within its fragrant depths.

"Beatrice. Are you mine at last?"

"I am."

She, too, it transpired, was perfectly capable of disrobing a man. To push off his coat from his shoulders. To unbuckle his sword belt and lift away the heavy sword. To unlace the ties of his shirt. But her fingers trembled, surprisingly clumsy. He stilled them against his chest with his own hands.

"I think I shall be faster." Because suddenly speed was of the essence.

So she stood, took his shirt from him, his boots as he removed them. Then, her eyes on his face, she put out a hand to stop him.

"Richard…"

He looked up, saw the fleeting concern there. With sensitive understanding he led her to sit on the bed. Sat beside her.

"Do you not wish for this? Forgive me if I am impatient." His smile was rueful.

She shook her head in an unaccustomed attack of shyness. "I would have you know… I have so little experience of this. William did not come to my bed except on the night of our marriage. He had no need of an heir, you see. He preferred to take his pleasure elsewhere."

"Ah, Beatrice…" His heart bled for her rejection. All he could do was enclose her hands securely in his.

"My only experience is of…of discomfort and a cold bed," she continued. "Even on that one night he did not stay longer than…than the necessity demanded of the deed."

"It is of no importance to me, Beatrice."

"It is just that you might prefer…a bedmate with some knowledge."

So much uncertainty from so confident a lady.

"I prefer you to be yourself. Between us we have all the experience we need. It will please me to bring you both knowledge and pleasure."

The sun slanted through the window, painting the bed with golden bars as he pushed the shift from her shoulders. The linen fell to be held in check on her forearms.

"How could he resist you?" Richard murmured. "For I cannot."

Slender she might be but supremely feminine, her high breasts firm and to his mind perfect. Her shoulders begged to be kissed and so he did, and the soft joining between jaw and throat, the hollow where her pulse beat. It was intoxicating. Her skin warmed and flushed under the caress of his lips and tongue.

"Let me touch you."

The flat of her palms smoothed over his skin. Warm from the sun that now engulfed them in its brightness. Firm from exercise and the activity of warfare. She shivered as she explored, molded, as her fingertips drifted over old scars. Shivered again as did he.

It was time. With quick dexterity he pulled back the linen covers of her bed and lifted her back against the pillows. And as she waited for him there he stripped off his remaining clothes to join her.

"Now I may look at you. You are so beautiful." The long muscled lines of hip and thigh, the wide shoulders tapering oh so smoothly to a narrow waist. The curl of dark hair at chest and groin. His strong arousal, evidence of his need for her. For the briefest moment Beatrice remembered William's aging body. Then closed her mind to it. No more. No need to think of that ever again. She was here now with Richard.

And she turned to him as he stretched beside her. Lifted her arms to enclose him and draw him close as he drew her. All the doubts and fears, all the guilt of the past, were washed away as his mouth traveled over brow and closed eyes and delicately flushed cheeks. The happiness that surged from her heart was peerless in its intensity.

"You are mine, with or without the sanction of the law and the church. With or without the consent of your family. I would make it true." He murmured the words against the silken skin of her shoulder.

"As would I."

Richard had concern for her nervousness but there was no need. She would give herself to him with all the spontaneity and joy that was inherent in her character. She would learn from him with delight. He knew it as she returned his kisses, the softness of her lips an invitation and a surrender as his tongue claimed and possessed. So began a gentle campaign to seduce and awaken. Long slow caresses, the glide of smooth flesh against even smoother flesh. Nothing to hurry or concern as the hours of the day moved on. The time, the moment was their own to savor and enjoy. His breath caught at the hum of pleasure deep in her throat.

But it was not in either temperament to remain calm and unhurried in their mutual delight. Nor did their enforced separation with all its pain and uncertainty dictate a slow loving. Their mutual desire was lit by the long drugging kisses and stroke of clever fingers. It smoldered, then burned, a leaping flame, until it exploded into outrageous need to own and prove their love in spite of all that had conspired to destroy and deny this desire that consumed them both. Now they were unaware of the comfort of their surroundings, the shimmering fall of dust motes in the bright air. Ignorant of the singing of the blackbird in the apple tree outside the window. Oblivious to the whole world that could distract them from what they might discover in each other. The purest celebration of life that they were at last together.

Nothing would part them again. They held on to that one fact as Beatrice found herself standing on the very edge of sensation that threatened to overpower and send her headlong into some dark unknown territory. It leaped through her veins. It blossomed in her loins, unfurling tight petals. The intensity of it hovered between pleasure and delicious pain, a searing heat. It took away her control and her power to think.

"No!" Her nails scored the skin of his shoulders. "I cannot."

"But, yes!" Her lover had no mercy. Captured her hands, which would have pushed against him. Continued to assault every pulse and nerve-ending in her body with mouth and skillful touch. The shocking slide of teeth and tongue. Bringing every inch of finesse into play. Until his fingers slid inside her. She would have cried out but his mouth took hers, swallowing her stunned response. Then the flames engulfed her and Beatrice had no choice but to relinquish her control and step out into that unknown. And found it exquisite beyond bearing.

And also found that she was not alone. For Richard held her as she shuddered uncontrollably against him. Held her until the tremors died away and she buried her face against his chest.

The room fell into silent stillness around them. Even the blackbird had sung its fill.

"I have known nothing like that," she whispered against his throat in astonished delight, finding a need to hide her face from him. "How should I have ever known that?"

"Did it please you?" Undoubtedly he knew her answer.

"Yes."

But it did not end there. His mouth was now heated, an exciting brand against her skin, hands more demanding, their bodies slick with arousal His tongue possessed her mouth more forcefully, then left a burning trail along the elegant curve of her throat, down the soft valley between her breasts, and lower as his fingers sought and owned all her undiscovered secrets. Until she gasped and cried out again as the heat built once more, spearing her belly with the sharp demands of passion.

Until he could hold back no longer.

With swift agility he lifted his weight and held her as he wound his hands into her hair, all the dark cloud of it. Her reaction was immediate, an irresistible invitation. His weight was a delight to her. So her hips arched in timeless response, her thighs parted to hold him close. She felt his arousal hard and smooth against her and longed to know the thick heat within her.

He thrust, unable to hold back any longer. Hard and powerful. Again and again. Beatrice knowing instinctively how to mirror his movements. He stilled for a last moment as control became a matter of knife-edged urgency. Took his weight on his arms, framed her face with his hands and kissed her mouth with such tenderness, at odds with his dominant position, causing her to shiver at the glory of it.

"Beatrice..." He sighed against her mouth as he fought to prolong the experience for her.

"Richard." Her eyes, wide and the deepest of blue, locked on his and held there. It was, he thought, as if she allowed him to see into her soul, as she had taken him within the slippery heat of her body.

"You destroy me." It was a groan, his voice harsh with need.

"Is that good?"

"Oh yes." He moved against her. "It is more than good." And drove on to his own release from the unspeakable demands that raced through his whole body, because he had no other choice, watching her eyes as she, too, shook in his arms.

"Well, lady?" His breathing had settled, the thunder of his blood slowed in his veins. He had lifted his weight from her, to draw her close. He would not let her go.

"I think it was a miracle."

"Better than you anticipated?"

"It brought me no memories of William!"

"God rest his miserable soul!"

"Amen."

"I did not realise… It was… I cannot think." Planting quick kisses along his jaw, she curled into his side with all the contentment of a cat in a sunbeam. "My mind seems not to be my own."

"It can be even better."

He bent his head, his lips discovering anew her breast, the hardened peak. His tongue sent ripples along her skin. His teeth scraped sharp darts of desire.

"Oh!"

"It can be," he murmured, his breath warm, his mouth hot, his fingers insistent, "beyond belief."

"I do not see how—but you could show me." He heard the smile in her voice. Felt her hand move seductively along the length of his spine, her nails scoring. Renewed need ignited in him as she stretched against him in blatant invitation.

"Look at me." He waited until her lashes lifted, her eyes dark and full of secrets. "This time look at me when I take you. Know that you are mine."

Her smile illuminated her whole face. Forcing him to draw a breath at the beauty of the woman who lay so trustingly in his arms.

Beatrice could see the hunger in his eyes, feel it in his body as he moved over her, into her. "I know you, Richard Stafford."

"As I know you, Beatrice Hatton. I love you. I adore you. I will willingly spend my whole life showing you."

And he set himself to the task.

Epilogue

As the short April day faded she lay with her head on his shoulder, his arms holding her secure. The shadows deepened companionably around them, enhanced by the enclosing walls of linenfold paneling, the heavy damask curtains of the bed. The blackbird returned for an evening song. Richard and Beatrice absorbed all without comment. There was no need for speech, the long loving after their first dramatic coming together speaking more loudly than mere words ever could. Her blood cooled, her heartbeat steadied, as she knew Richard's did, to be replaced with utter contentment. A happiness that wrapped them around as in satin sheets.

"Beatrice? You are very quiet." She could feel his mouth smile against her hair. "I think that you are not always quiet." One hand swept in a long silken glide from shoulder to wrist. He felt her shiver against him from the same aftermath of desire that still rippled through his veins.

"No." Beatrice hid her face against the hard muscle of his shoulder as a lingering doubt touched her mind. When she was silent for a little while, he pressed his mouth against her temple.

"What troubles you?"

"Richard—I would know one thing." She pushed herself to sit up beside him but their fingers remained entwined and she gave not a thought to the linen sheet that fell interestingly to her waist.

"Well?" It was difficult to repress a smile. Or the immediate leap of response in his body. He was not done with her yet.

"Why did you wait so long to return? Why did you not write to me?" Then she saw the grief, brief but vicious, touch his face with cruel fingers, sensed the depth of his suffering and loss in the weeks of warfare, and tightened her clasp as if the warmth of her hands might heal the wounds. "I thought you might be dead. I did not know—and I worried so. There was no one who could tell me."

"Then I must ask your indulgence." He raised their joined right hands to kiss her fingers, one by one, a most delicate maneuver, which caused her belly to flutter anew. "For I deliberately did not come until now."

"Did you think I would change my mind and fall out of love as quickly as I fell into it? I am no child to do so on a whim!" The gleam in her eye, the angle of her raised chin left him in no doubt of the inner fire and quick temper. He loved her for it.

"Ah. The fickleness of women." The challenge in her delighted him. What a splendid future he would have with this quicksilver woman. He pushed himself up against the pillows, stretched to smooth her lips with the pad of his thumb. "No. That was never my fear. If you were willing to send the swan across half the country when every brigand and robber was afoot, with law and order stretched to near destruction, I knew that you must still be of the same heart and mind. My lovely Beatrice…"

Now his fingers slid around her nape to draw her closer. She did not resist the seduction of his words but leaned in to kiss him, her lips as soft and inviting as he had ever remembered them. So he kissed her again, increasing the pressure, increasing the heat. "I waited more than six months. I had to be sure in my own mind that I could come to you without guilt. And if there was to be any objection to my formal request, six months of your wearing widow's garb was an acceptable time for your family." Watching her, taking in every detail of her face, he asked the question that had been in his mind since the brooch and letter had been delivered. "Will you wed me, Beatrice? I think your brother will not oppose it."

The sudden glow in her eyes was unmistakable but her answer was solemn and typically Beatrice. "No. He will not. Ned will wish us happy. But you should know—if it had been your wish to take a wealthy widow as your bride." She watched him from beneath dark lashes.

Richard smiled at her concern. "What is it that I should know? Will you be penniless? If so, I must most assuredly cast you off."

But there was no humor in her reply. "William's influence carries far beyond the grave. He left me a rich widow. But if I remarry, my legacy becomes no more than a bed, a table and the paltry sum of forty pounds!"

"So wily Somerton would tie you to widowhood with money, just as he acquired you as his wife!"

"Yes. Richard—dear Richard—would you want a poor bride?" He saw anxiety there. And a strange insecurity. It surprised him and touched his heart.

"I did not come here to negotiate money with you, Beatrice," he replied simply. "I came to claim you as my wife."

"I shall lose this house."

"Then, of course, you will live with me at Elton's Marsh." He had no intention of allowing any other situation. He cared not for the ownership of Great Houghton as long as he had Beatrice Hatton.

"I shall lose the estate and its income."

"Then *I* must pay for your jewels and extravagant clothes, lady."

"I can be very extravagant." Beatrice laughed, a suddenly lighthearted, joyous sound in the quiet room.

"Beatrice?" Now all that was needed was the formality of the thing, Richard pushed her a little away so that he might look at her, watch her response as he spoke and she answered. "Listen to me." His fingers closed harder because her reply meant more to him than he would ever have believed. "I want you, Beatrice Hatton. With or without an inheritance. Will you grant me your hand in marriage? Will you come and live with me at Elton's Marsh where I might love you? Will you carry my heirs and live with me until death?"

For a long moment she looked at him, at the much beloved features, acknowledged the splendor of his generous soul, marveling that he was now hers. William's hold over them was finally loosened, the wounds of the past cleansed and healed.

"Well, Beatrice?" There was an edge to his patience. But there was no need to fear.

"Yes, Richard Stafford." She reached to touch her fingers to his lips. "Yes. I will do all of those things. With my whole heart."

**Four sisters.
A family legacy.
And someone is out to destroy it.**

A captivating new limited continuity, launching June 2006

The most beautiful hotel in New Orleans,
and someone is out to destroy it. But mystery,
danger and some surprising family revelations
and discoveries won't stop the Marchand sisters
from protecting their birthright…
and finding love along the way.

This riveting new saga begins with

In the Dark

by national bestselling author

JUDITH ARNOLD

The party at Hotel Marchand is in full swing when the lights suddenly go out. What does head of security Mac Jensen do first? He's torn between two jobs—protecting the guests at the hotel and keeping the woman he loves safe.

A woman to protect. A hotel to secure. And no idea who's determined to harm them.

On Sale June 2006

**Hidden in the secrets of antiquity,
lies the unimagined truth...**

Introducing

ROGUE Angel™

a brand-new line filled with mystery
and suspense, action and adventure,
and a fascinating look into history.

And it all begins with DESTINY.

In a sealed crypt in
France, where the
terrifying legend of
the beast of Gevaudan
begins to unravel,
Annja Creed discovers
a stunning artifact
that will seal her destiny.

*Available every other
month starting
July 2006, wherever
you buy books.*

GRA1

Baseball. The crack of the bat,
the roar of the crowd…and the view
of mouthwatering men in tight uniforms!
A sport in which the men are men…
and the women are drooling.

Join three Blaze bestselling authors in
celebrating the men who indulge in this
all-American pastime—and the women
who help them indulge in other things….

Boys of Summer

*A Hot (and Sweaty!)
Summer Collection*

*One book,
three great
stories!*

FEVER PITCH
by Julie Elizabeth Leto

THE SWEET SPOT by Kimberly Raye

SLIDING HOME by Leslie Kelly

On sale this July
Feel the heat. Get your copy today!

www.eHarlequin.com   HBBOSJUL